Any Woman's Blues

Stories by
Contemporary Black Women Writers

Any Woman's Blues

Stories by Contemporary
Black Women Writers

Edited and with an Introduction by
Mary Helen Washington

Published by VIRAGO PRESS Limited
Ely House, 37 Dover Street, London W1X 4HS

First published by Anchor Books, New York, 1980
under the title *Midnight Birds*

Printed in Great Britain by litho
at The Anchor Press, Tiptree, Essex

British Library Cataloguing in Publication Data

Any woman's blues.
  1. Short stories, American
  I. Washington, Mary Helen
  II. Midnight birds
  813'.01'08 (ES) PS648.S5

ISBN 0-86068-204-8

ACKNOWLEDGEMENTS

Grateful acknowledgment is made to the following contributors for permission to reprint the material contained within this anthology:

Toni Morrison for "Eva Peace" from *Sula*, reprinted by permission of Alfred A. Knopf, Inc., New York, © 1974 and Chatto & Windus Ltd, London ©, 1980.

Ntozake Shange for "comin' to terms" by permission of the author and "aw babee, you so pretty" in *Essence*, April 1979.

Toni Cade Bambara for "Medley" and "Witchbird" from *The Sea Birds Are Still Alive*, Random House, New York, © 1977.

Frenchy Hodges for "Requiem for Willie Lee" in *Ms.*, October, © 1979. By permission of the author.

Sherley Anne Williams for "Meditations on History" by permission of author.

Alice Walker for "Advancing Luna—and Ida B. Wells" in *Ms.*, July © 1977. "Laurel" in *Ms.*, November © 1978.

Alexis DeVeaux for "Remember Him a Outlaw" in *Black Creation*, Fall © 1972, and "The Riddles of Egypt Brownstone" © 1977, by permission of author.

Gayl Jones for "Asylum" and "Jevata" in *White Rat*, Random House, New York, © 1977.

Paulette Childress White for "The Bird Cage" in *Redbook*, June © 1978, and "Alice" in *Essence*, January © 1977.

"We was girls together" from Toni Morrison's *Sula*, Bantam Books, © 1975, p. 149.

"Seduced and betrayed" suggested by the title of Elizabeth Hardwick's book *Seduction and Betrayal*, Vintage Books, New York, © 1975.

"A thinking woman sleeps with monsters" from Adrienne Rich's poem "Snapshots of a Daughter-in-law" in *No More Masks*, ed. by Florence Howe and Ellen Bass, Doubleday Anchor, New York, © 1973.

"i am not movin" and "the suspect is black & always in his early 20's" from Ntozake Shange's *nappy edges*, St. Martin's Press, © 1978.

This book is for Ponchita.

CONTENTS

a few soft words have sent many a woman to her back
with her thighs flung open & eager/a few more/will find
us standin up & speakin in our own tongue to whom-
ever we goddam please

nappy edges,
ntozake shange

These the old blues
and I sing em, sing em, sing em. Just like
any woman do.
My life ain't done yet
Naw . . . My song ain't through.

Any Woman's Blues,
Sherley Anne Williams

Then we hungry midnight birds will have our chance to
swoop at a morning sky.

The Bird Cage,
Paulette Childress White

In pursuit of our own history

Any Woman's Blues comes exactly four years and six months after the publication of *Black-Eyed Susans* (1975), an anthology which the Los Angeles *Times* described as "just the briefest glimpse of what lies in store as black women fiction writers come into their own." It is a book that began with the consciousness of both pain and power. When black women told the stories about their real lives and actual experiences, they proved the power of art to demolish stereotypes; and if power (at least the beginning of it) is the ability to name one's own experience, *Susans* was a first step toward power, for it celebrated the legends of black women, weaved dreams into myths that allowed us to recover and name our own past.

It is instructive to recall as a kind of footnote that white men have always held this power, a power in evidence everywhere in the world. In all the great capitals—I am thinking particularly of Washington and London—there are hundreds of monuments to them, bronzed busts of immense proportions, statues of figures in ceremonial robes, documents and signatures on display in museums, all witnessing the historic power of men to mythologize themselves, to remake history, and to cast themselves eternally in heroic form. There is hardly a trace of women's lives. We have been erased from history.

Black-Eyed Susans placed black women squarely in the center of their own historical experience, made them the dynamic interpreters of their own lives. It began the task that critic Hortense Spillers has demanded we undertake: "women must seek to become their own historical subject in pursuit of its proper object, its proper and specific expression in time."[1] What Spillers proposes and *Susans* intended was nothing less than the revision of history, the reclaiming not only of the past but of a central place in that past. With the written word we would sculpt the heroic molds for our own ceremonies. The women whose image had been controlled and distorted by almost everyone who had taken up the pen, women once described as the "mules of the world," chose for themselves some brand-new imagery: the hardiness and resilience of black-eyed susans, the yearning and impatience of the mysterious midnight birds.

Black-Eyed Susans also began with pain. The lives of the women in *Susans* were marked by isolation, loss, vulnerability, and victimization, and we needed to finger the grooves of our scars until we knew the designs by heart: black girls dreaming of being transformed into light-skinned, long-haired beauties: a child crushed by the southern sharecropping system: black women devalued in comparison to privileged white women, protecting themselves behind powerful masks; images of the domestic living out her life sleeping in at other people's houses, black migrant women heading North to have their romantic illusions destroyed. One of the most enduring images from *Susans* is Toni Morrison's character Pauline Breedlove, dark and poor, with a front tooth missing, trying to fix up her hair so she will look like Jean Harlow.

The anger in *Susans* is muted, at times turned inward, and there are no shrill, loud-mouthed, bad-talking women to express it openly. The steps toward self-definition are tentative. Without the benefit of a strong feminist perspective (most of the stories in *Susans* were written in the early 1960s or before), there is little sense of the possibility of powerful bonds between women. There are only two stories of women reaching out in solidarity to other women; and the theme of reconciliation, when it occurs, is between women and men.

"This above all, to refuse to be a victim." [2]

If *Black-Eyed Susans* was a brief glimpse of black women, then *Any Woman's Blues* is a wide-angled lens, opening up the picture of black women's lives in every direction. It is a sturdier collection, more open to adventure, prouder, more strong-minded, more defiant. There is open revolt against the ideologies and attitudes that impress women into servitude. The hostility between black women and white women is out of the shadows, being examined full face. There are heroic women pursuing courageous ideals with the expectation of triumph. There are artists, single-mindedly plying their craft, refusing to be denied the right to paints, chisel, and pen. And there *are* some loud-mouthed women, talking about not moving until some things get changed. The narrator in Paulette Childress White's story "The Bird Cage" expresses the aim of this collection: "I would paint. I would paint myself. On huge canvases I would paint my soul's songs, search out my own truths."

Any Woman's Blues is carrying on a tradition, for, as we saw in *Black-Eyed Susans*, there are distinct and unique patterns in the fiction of black women. It is unique that black women have consistently given us a heroic image of the black woman. Not the conquering hero of daring exploits but women like Zora Hurston's Janie Crawford, Nella Larsen's Helga Crane, Ann Petry's Lutie Johnson, Gwendolyn Brooks' Maud Martha, Paule Marshall's Reena, Alice Walker's Meridian, Toni Morrison's Sula. These are women who struggled to forge an identity larger than the one society would force upon them. They are aware and conscious, and that very consciousness is potent. In searching out their own truths, they are rebellious and risk-taking, and they are not defined by men.

No other writers have allowed black women this kind of heroic stature. In the writing of black men, women are almost always subordinate to men. They are often relegated to domestic roles, while the men are involved in the "larger" issues of life. The quest of the black man to achieve manhood has always inspired the highest respect, but the equivalent struggle of the black woman has hardly been acknowledged—except by black women writers. Critic Robert Stepto is absolutely right that "the rise of a feminine voice in contemporary Afro-American fiction may be directly related to the narrow and confining portraits of black women in earlier modern fiction."[3]

As evidenced by *Any Woman's Blues*, black women are searching for a specific language, specific symbols, specific images with which to record their lives, and, even though they can claim a rightful place in the Afro-American tradition and in the feminist tradition of women writers, it is also clear that, for purposes of liberation, black women writers will first insist on their own name, their own space.

"We was girls together"

Any Woman's Blues begins with "Alice," the story of a woman reaching out to another woman. That story announces one of the important themes in women's literature: women's reconciliation with one another. The housewife in "Alice" returns to her old friend when she realizes that her own womanhood has been nurtured by Alice's fierce strength, warm laughter, and "bad-woman" talk. For the same reason, the young housewife-narrator in Paulette White's second story, "The Bird Cage," joins the circle of black women as they ritualize the experience of womanhood, initiating her into its secrets and terrors.

This need for women to re-establish connections with one another is powerfully rendered in Toni Morrison's *Sula*. Sula leaves home for a life of independence and adventure while her friend Nel chooses the more conventional domestic life. Eventually they are reunited, renewing a friendship so close that they were "two throats and one eye and we had no price." Commenting on her effort to explore a relationship between two women, Morrison says,

> We read about Ajax and Achilles willing to die for each other, but very little about the friendship of women, and them having respect for each other, like it's something new. But Black women have always had that, they have always been emotional life supports for each other.
> That's what I was trying to say in *Sula*, when Nel discovered that it was not her husband that she had missed all

those years, but her friend Sula. Because when you don't have a
woman to talk to, really talk to, whether it be an aunt or a
sister or a friend, that is the real loneliness. That is
devastating. And it is the same with men needing the company
of other men.[4]

The most celebrated and controversial example of black
women seeking reconciliation with one another is the final
act of Ntozake Shange's choreopoem "for colored girls who
have considered suicide." In the scene called "the laying on
of hands," the seven women come together, arms around
one another, singing softly over and over, "i found god in
myself & i loved her fiercely." In Shange's play, reconciliation is finally and completely a feminine and a feminist act.[5]

A truly uncomplicated and unaffected treatment of
women's solidarity with other women is found in the stories
of Toni Cade Bambara. Bambara is almost casual in the
inclusion of scenes which show an easy camaraderie among
women. In "The Johnson Girls," a story in her earlier
collection, *Gorilla My Love,* four young women size up the
relative merits of the men they know, trading the secrets of
their exploits with so much authority over their sexual lives
that the notion of female passivity is almost invalidated. It is
a cool and level-headed self-confidence they pass on to the
youngest girl so that she won't have "all this torture and
crap" to go through when she jumps into her woman stride.
In "Medley" and "Witchbird," the two stories in this
anthology, Bambara presents the same kind of woman-to-
woman nurturing as a traditional aspect of black women's
relationships. Bambara credits the women who were part of
this communal network in her own life, giving her advice
about men and "beautification," as important influences on
her art and her life:

the beauty parlors in those days were perhaps the only
womanhood institutes we had— it was there in the beauty
parlors that young girls came of age and developed some sense
of what it means to be a woman growing up—it was those
women who had the most influence on the writing.[6]

Reconciliation commonly suggests a restoration of harmony with others, but on a deeper level it can mean
becoming consistent or congruous with oneself. To establish
consistency with oneself is to reclaim the real self underneath the layers of imposed restrictions; it is to recognize
how much like other women we are, how much we needed
them to grow on, and how good it is to appreciate these
connections. This act of reconciliation admits respect for the
common world we have shared; it is that essential ingre-
dient of a tradition: "a dialogue with brave and imaginative
women who came before us."[7]

"A thinking woman sleeps with monsters"

The love stories in this anthology pose more questions
than they answer; but the nature of the questions suggests
that love as written about by black women will not be based
on the surrender of the woman's power as it often is in the
fiction of men. These are the inquiries, and they are
challenges to the old ways women have been involved with
men: Can women be honored for their real powers—their
integrity, their humor, their intelligence? Or have the old
male rituals— the slick rap, the assertion of physical power,
the sense of women as a man's property (his *lady* or his *piece*
as black teenagers say)—hardened into immutable patterns? Must a woman who achieves some triumph as artist,
some heroic or extraordinary stance, or one who is passionately devoted to her craft always end up without a man?
(As poet Carolyn Kizer puts it, will you always be "Up a
creek alone with your talent"?) Can any man ever love a
really free women, or does the woman who casts too bold a
shadow create irreconcilable antagonisms in a love relationship?

Five stories in *Any Woman's Blues* are primarily concerned
with love between men and women. With the exception of
one ("Jevata") they maintain clearly that if love is predi-
cated on the surrender of the woman's power, if it com-

promises her authority over her own life, *it is not acceptable*. In Bambara's story "Medley," the woman, Sweet Pea, leaves her man because he "wasn't ready to deal with no woman full grown." The woman in Ntozake Shange's story is cautioned to resist the fake male flattery of "aw, babee, you so pretty" as an age-old rip-off which the "world wide un-beloved black woman" has been subjected to. Mandy, in Shange's story "comin to terms," values her independence at least as much as her love for Ezra, and grows to cherish "hearing her own noises in the night, waking up a solitary figure in her world."

Neither the love stories by black women nor the dilemmas inherent in them should be considered a forecast of doom or despair. In the majority of these stories, men and women find ways of loving and staying together, though they are imperfect and fraught with difficulties and certainly not any Hollywood, happy-ever-after fantasies. What is more significant than the problems of heterosexual love arraigned here is that in ten out of fifteen stories, romantic love is not the central issue at all: *Being loved is not regarded as the urgent business in the quest for identity*. In Spillers' words, "male absence or mutability in intimate relationship is not the leading proposition of a woman's life, but a single aspect of an interlocking arrangement of life issues."[8] These women are not stalking lovers. They are laying claim to the freedom and triumph that were forbidden little black girls in this century,[9] and, in the process, springing from their own heads, fullgrown.[10]

"Secrets and silences": black women and white women

Laying claim to freedom requires black women to confront the racism of white women as well as patriarchy. Unquestionably the areas of commonality among black and white women are as deep as sexual oppression. We are enmeshed in the same sexual webs, compelled by the same themes, as though an involuntary equality were ordained in our psychic worlds. The search for a real self that often takes a woman back to her girlhood, the need for solitariness, a space and time for oneself, the fear of male domination, the need to be the Angel in the House at the cost of one's own creativity—these are the themes dominating the fiction of black and white women.

Despite these shared concerns, the black woman is defined as, experienced as, treated as the "Other" by most white women writers.[11] Anthologies and literary texts either exclude black women or include them as a kind of afterthought. The attitude prevails that white women are the standard, the norm, the originators of feminist thought, the major voices in women's literature. It is rare to find black writers or thinkers quoted as authorities in the writings of white women. With characteristic honesty, Adrienne Rich asks this accusing question of white women scholars: "Why should we feel more alien to the literature and lives of black women than to centuries of the literature and history of white men?"[12] And yet, wrongs acknowledged and challenged, silence broken, signal a distinct change for the relationship between black and white women. Perhaps we are, as Gloria Steinem predicted, entering into the second stage of feminist understanding, which is a time for "measuring the diversity, and understanding what chasms there are to bridge."

Certainly the story about the friendship between a black woman and a white woman in this anthology, Alice Walker's "Advancing Luna and Ida B. Wells," does not have the mute, painful, and bewildered quality of the confrontations in the stories in *Black-Eyed Susans*. There is no reconciliation between black women and white women in "Luna," but at least the women are real to each other, not some bloodless fantasies haunting each other from the past. They square off and look each other in the face and do not settle for either silence or stereotype. This story contains images and symbols that reveal the problematic nature of any relationship which crosses racial lines. After Luna tells her friend, a young black woman, that she was raped by a black man in the South and did not report it for fear he would be lynched, the rape becomes a third presence in the story, a blood-knot, uniting the two women in an uneasy and unwilling sisterhood. But the rape is also a bond between black women and black men because it has historically been used as a savage measure of intimidation against black men.

Walker calls on the memory of Ida B. Wells, conductor of a one-woman crusade against lynching, to symbolize the profound sense of identification black women have toward all oppressed people—including men—and to show the black woman's unresolved conflict. Even though these two women have shared their lives, the power and privilege of the white world cannot be ignored.

At the end of the story, the black woman summons all her knowledge of politics and history to attempt some kind of final reconciliation. There is none. The story ends without resolution. But with the loss of innocence, with the wisdom derived from suffering and disillusionment, they both may have achieved a new power and the courage to negotiate the chasm.

What my name is

The old slave woman in Ellison's *Invisible Man* says that freedom ain't nothing but knowing how to say what's up in your head. But to say what's in your own head, to speak your own truth, requires a new language and new myths. Such a transformation is evident in the blues imagery and blues sensibility of Gayl Jones; in the improvisational, jazz-based techniques of Toni Cade Bambara; in the hip, dislocated, elliptical style of Alexis DeVeaux; in the mixture of fiction and journalism of Alice Walker; in Paulette White's merging of prose and poetry; in Ntozake Shange's attempts to capture the peculiar colloquial style of black women; and in Toni Morrison's evocation of the tone and timbre of Black Bottom, where a neighbor woman might call out the slow, familiar greeting, "Hey girl. What you know good?"

There are memories stored away in our heads we never

suspected were materials for literature. These stories made me call up some almost forgotten fragments from my own black and female past: memories of women who "did hair" in their basements, girls holding their ears so the hot comb wouldn't burn them; women in their forties and fifties who had "boyfriends"; dayworkers waiting for the Rapid Transit in Shaker Heights (they live there now), carrying their uniforms in paper bags; churchwomen who kept the South alive in the middle of an urban ghetto, growing roses, canning peaches, baking biscuits, singing in churches on Sunday in crisp white nurse's outfits; women preachers with their own storefront churches; the utter reverence our mothers showed for black women of achievement, knowing by heart the names of the first black woman Ph.D., the first black woman school principal, the first doctor. We didn't suspect then that these experiences, these memories, were important enough to write books about, and yet these were our lives, the black woman's unspoken truths, kept silent in our hearts and minds, tarrying for the evangels with the power to reveal their true significance.

One story in *Any Woman's Blues*, "Meditations on History" by Sherley Williams, reaches far back into the black woman's history as slave for patterns and symbols to rename her experience. Under slavery, black women achieved an ironic equality. As early American feminists, they worked like men, were autonomous within the slave community, and helped to subvert the racist power of their owners.[13] Williams draws on this aspect—the subversive power—of the slave system to create the main character of "Meditations." Odessa is an activist in a slave insurrection; under the laws of slavery, a criminal. The white historian interviewing her calls her "she-devil" and "savage." As defined by this white man, she is foreign, different, inferior, non-white, and non-male. We finish this story, however, convinced of *her* power, not his. She learns enough about his psychology to engineer his defeat, and though she cannot speak the language as he can, her words are as clean and swift as a double-edged razor: "I kill that white man cause the same reason Mas' kill Kaine. Cause I can." Next to her man Kaine she is an equally heroic character.

It means something that black women trace their line back to such women as Odessa. From them we inherited the natural instincts of the feminist—the resistance to the status quo, rage at our treatment, and a deep conviction that the authority of the patriarchy is illegitimate.

Several writers—among them Sherley Williams and Toni Cade Bambara—have also used the early blues singers to express something of the uniqueness of black women's lives. Women like Ma Rainey, Bessie Smith, Billie Holiday were personal charismatics in the black community. Beneath sequined dresses, ostrich plumes, and bittersweet smiles, they concealed the heartaches and violence of their lives; but they had some powerful vitality that also broke through. They were given titles: "Empress," "Queen," and "Lady Day." For years they were the only black women allowed to express themselves as artists. Bambara and Williams have used these singers to symbolize both the creativity and captivity of the black woman artist. In Bambara's terms, these blues women are like her character Honey—hostages waiting to be released from all the fictions that have locked up their lives. When Honey is free to sing and act without being thrust into the "bronze Barbie doll" or "Aunt Jemima" stereotypes, she will use her art and her pent-up rage to free all those unheard voices of black women calling to her from history.

The full significance of the black woman as mythmaker is yet to be known. But, if the difficulties of sustaining the gift of creation are great for any artist, then we know the odds against the survival of black women artists. Consider what they need to be productive: "Predecessors, ancestors, a body of literature, an acceptance of the right to write."[14] Certainly for the imagination to flourish, they need a supportive community, i.e. someone to publish what they write, someone to read their books, someone to provide adequate, honest critical attention. They need connectedness with other writers.

Even more than these requirements, they need to see the full effect of their work made visible in the lives of black women. That is essential, not only for the writers, but for the rest of us. Black women cannot fully comprehend their lives without these writers, for they celebrate and rename our experiences in powerful ways. In the legends and deeds of black women, there is a new Eve awaiting creation; she will enlarge the world for black women and ultimately enrich the lives of all.

Mary Helen Washington
Cambridge, Massachusetts
October 17, 1979

Notes

1. "The Politics of Intimacy," in *Sturdy Black Bridges*, ed. Roseann P. Bell, Bettye J. Parker, and Beverly Guy-Sheftall, Doubleday Anchor, 1979, p. 105.

2. Margaret Atwood, *Surfacing*, Virago Press, 1979, p. 191.

3. "I Thought I Knew These People: Richard Wright and the Afro-American Literary Tradition," in *Massachusetts Review*, XVIII (Autumn 1977), p. 539.

4. In "The Triumphant Song of Toni Morrison" by Paula Giddings, in *Encore*, December 12, 1977, p. 30.

5. "In a review of Shange's choreopoem, critic Jean Carey Bond objects to the play's finale as a futile and narcissistic gesture, an exercise in self love and a last resort substitute for the elusive love of men." *The Easy Guide to Black Arts*, September 1, 1976, p. 12. Others, including myself, have pointed out that the emphasis in the finale is on communality and collectivity among women.

6. "Commitment: Toni Cade Bambara Speaks" by Beverly Guy-Sheftall, in *Sturdy Black Bridges*, op. cit., p. 234.

7. Adrienne Rich, "Conditions for Work: The Common World of Women (1976)," in *On Lies, Secrets, and Silence: Selected Prose 1966-1978*, Virago Press, 1980, p. 205.

8. "The Politics of Intimacy," p. 105. In this article Hortense Spillers indicts James Baldwin's conception of women in his novel *If Beale Street Could Talk* for making the woman (Tish) a pawn in Baldwin's romantic love myth. The male (Fonny) is a figure of power while Tish merely exists for him, an extension of his need but without chisel and stone and work of her own. Spillers' insistence that romantic love is only a single issue in women's lives is, of course, clearly supported in the fiction written by women.

9. "Because each had discovered years before that they were neither white nor male, and that all triumph was forbidden to them, they had set about creating something else to be." *Sula* by Toni Morrison, Bantam Books, 1975, p. 44.

10. This line from Carolyn Kizer's poem "Pro Femina" is suggested by the myth of Athena, goddess of wisdom and the arts and sciences, who sprang full-armored from the head of Zeus.

11. Much of my thinking over the past few months about the relationship between black and white feminists has been challenged and shaped by Barbara Smith's essay "Toward a Black Feminist Criticism" in *Conditions: Two 1* (October 1977), pp. 25-44, and Adrienne Rich's insightful and probing article, "Disloyal to Civilization: Feminism, Racism, Gynephobia," in *On Lies, Secrets, and Silence: Selected Prose 1966-1978*, op. cit., pp. 275-310. Alice Walker also challenges the racism inherent in white women's scholarship in her essay "One Child of One's Own," in *Ms.* (August 1979); see my essay on Alice Walker in this anthology.

12. "Disloyal to Civilization," p. 307.

13. The argument for the centrality of the black woman in the slave community is powerfully articulated by Angela Davis in her essay "Reflection on the Black Woman's Role in the Community of Slaves," *The Black Scholar*, 3 (December 1971), pp. 3-15.

14. Tillie Olsen, "One Out of Twelve: Writers Who Are Women in Our Century," in *Silences*, Virago Press, 1980, p. 23.

"We was girls together"

PAULETTE CHILDRESS WHITE

When I am asked to speak about myself, this necessarily comes first; I am married and the mother of five sons. I cannot imagine an occupation more in conflict with writing than homemaking. I am usually asked where I find the time to write and I usually answer, just as logically, that I don't know. I do as I can.

I was born and have lived all my life in Detroit. At thirty, I am still just becoming a writer. Growing up, I had this dream of being an artist. I did attend art school during the year following my graduation from high school but for a variety of reasons (not the least of which was financial), I didn't last long. I was living and helping out at home and my clerk-typist salary simply didn't cover tuition on a dream.

I married an artist. For a while I was content to watch him paint. I dabbled a bit and had babies and meanwhile began to write these stories that were poems and poems that were stories. While it's true that I'd never been serious about writing, it had always come easily to me. In fact, the one incident that might have turned me on to writing was as negative as it was positive.

My junior year in high school, I had English comp with a fiftyish, white, male teacher whose love of literature was legendary in the school. Often, he'd spend the entire class hour reading, interpreting, explaining, defining and confusing us about every dead or distant writer there was. Even the brilliant student, Karl Kruger, to whom the teacher's zeal was usually directed, listened dully and commented sparsely while I, unnoticed in my brown and female skin, was rapt. We were required to do two-page theme papers twice weekly and even my best efforts never earned me more than a "B." Then came the day teacher returned my paper, clucking disappointedly, as he gave me a paper marked with the largest, reddest "E" I'd ever seen. I flipped to the back page for an explanation and there he scrawled, "Where did you copy this?"

I was innocent, of course, but my protests fell on deaf ears. I took the matter to the principal (who was also fifty, white and male), and accepted his reluctant promise to look into the matter. Next day, the class was assigned an impromptu theme to be completed within the class period. We were given a choice of five topics listed on the blackboard. I chose "No Man Is an Island," gathered paper, pen and my powers about me and wrote. I suppose I really told him why no man is an island; the following day in class he stood before us and read my paper. When he finished I'd have sworn there were tears reddening his eyes.

Coincidentally, a young Black woman who had graduated a few years previously and was then attending college had chosen this day to pay the old school a visit and was sitting at the back of the class. I remembered her vaguely as one of the colored elite. Teacher called on her for a comment and she stood and very neatly observed that my theme might well have been composed by a sophomore such as herself. I remember thinking that perhaps she too had sat in this class, absorbed in the magic words, given her best for "B's"—in a brown and female skin, sat unseen. Perhaps she had come to slay the dragon, and on that day, we did.

I was returned "No Man Is an Island" with the reddest, largest "A" I'd ever seen. As for the paper that created the stir, it was returned a few days later with one or two corrections of punctuation and my usual "B." And no apologies.

From that point on, I felt a sense of freedom through language that was much the same as I'd always had in my art. As I said, after I married I began to write. I bought myself a desk, a typewriter and a thesaurus and soon I had drawers full of would-be poems. These, I recited to my husband and whoever else was close and kind enough to listen. My husband was encouraging and prompted me *to do a few public readings as occasions arose, but for the most part I hid them away, waiting for the magic that would someday make me "ready."*

I figured to haul a stack of poems over to Dudley Randall at Broadside Press and be discovered. What I did do, finally, was attend a writers' workshop where poet Naomi Long Madgett was conducting a session on poetry. Ms. Madgett went through the pile of submissions, selected two of my poems, read them to the group and asked me to stay after. In 1975, with Naomi's help (she taught me what a poem really is), I published a collection of my poems out of Lotus Press in Detroit.

Soon after, I was invited to join a small group of talented and dedicated Black women writers in an informal monthly workshop. We'd meet, share our writing, exchange criticism, talk about our lives and give positive support to one another. In 1977, I published my first short story in Essence *magazine. In 1978, I sold my second to* Redbook *magazine. My after-hour sessions on the typewriter and the creative support of the workshop members—Mary Helen Washington, in particular—were making fantastic changes in my life. So now, the second thing I say about myself is that I am a writer.*

The work of Paulette Childress White suggests the Impressionist artist who painted hundreds of scenes in his thirty-year career, all within a twenty-five-mile radius of his home, which he never left. Born and raised in Detroit, White uses that city as the setting of her poetry and short stories. In her first book of poetry, *Love Poem to a Black Junkie* (Lotus Press, 1975), White is searching through a variety of approaches to find her own voice. Though her poetry is never clichéd, there is a strong sense in that early poetry of the black nationalism that was typical of black poetry in the sixties. There are images of the black woman as a bronze queen of Benin, an ebony African face, a body swollen with life like Mother of the Earth. Even in this embryonic period, the poet's deep-rootedness in the black side of the city emerges. In this way she is much like that poet of the unheroic, Gwendolyn Brooks, who has immortalized the black street corners of Chicago in her poems. White paints vivid portraits of an old black janitor, innocent, deathly boy-junkies, paint peeling on the city's Wall of Respect, old black churchwomen. What is striking in a poet of only twenty-four years (as she was in 1975) is her ability to record with total empathy and real sorrow the lives of the least visible people in this society.

In 1977, Paulette White published her first short story, "Alice," in *Essence* magazine. As her poetry had told stories, this first story was much like a long poem, with rhythms and cadences meant to be spoken aloud, poetry and prose merging in an extended reverie:

> *Alice. Drunk Alice. Alice of the streets. Of the party. Of the house of dark places . . . Alice, tall like a man, with soft wooly hair spread out in tangles like a feathered hat.*

"Alice" is a story about the reconciliation and rebirth that must take place among women, a theme suggested by White in both of her stories and a common theme in women's writing. Women write often of the need to return to their past, to the women who were part of that past, to girlhood when a self existed that was individual and singular, defined neither by men, nor children, nor home, almost as though with the layers of roles and responsibilities they have covered over a real person and must now peel back those layers and reclaim the self that was just emerging in adolescence. Isn't the reason for the narrator's rejection of Alice simply the disdain and abhorrence all women have for the stunted, dreamless lives they are forced to live? Her smart, clean government job is the way of escape, but it does not work; the pull of domesticity and compliance is strong, and she does not resist for long. In "The Bird Cage" the young wife/mother recognizes that she was "eager prey" anxious to make the offering of herself in return for marriage and babies, such a clear and easy resignation. But her fantasies, where she nurtures an inner life, are cast in the imagery of re-creation: there she has one of everything, she has an adolescently thin body, and she paints herself anew on huge canvases.

Much of Paulette White's fiction and poetry is strongly autobiographical, and from that fact flows the irresistible power in her work. This willful, discontent woman, self-described as a "closet feminist" talking of independence, personhood and freedom (a far cry from those earlier African queens and Earth Mothers), has used her own life with unflinching honesty to probe for answers to the question of keeping creativity alive, specifically the creativity of the black woman whose life is an amalgam of bitter city tensions, work-burdened days, cancelled dreams, and a hunger for freedom. With these materials for paint and easel, and her own unique sensibility, White is beginning work on a canvas from which will someday come a profound picture of the black woman's reality.

Alice

BY PAULETTE CHILDRESS WHITE

Alice. Drunk Alice. Alice of the streets. Of the party. Of
the house of dark places. From whom without knowing I
hid love all my life behind remembrances of her house
where I went with Momma in the daytime to borrow
things, and we found her lounging in the front yard on a
dirty plastic lawn chair drinking warm beer from the can
in a little brown bag where the flies buzzed in and out of
the always-open door of the house as we followed her into
the cool, dim rank-smelling rooms for what it was we'd
come. And I fought frowns as my feet caught on the
sticky gray wooden floor but looked up to smile back at
her smile as she gave the dollar or the sugar or the coffee
to Momma who never seemed to notice the floor or the
smell or Alice.

Alice, tall like a man, with soft wooly hair spread out in
tangles like a feathered hat and her face oily and her legs
ashy, whose beauty I never quite believed because she
valued it so little but was real. Real like wild flowers and
uncut grass, real like the knotty sky-reach of a dead tree.
Beauty of warm brown eyes in a round dark face and of
teeth somehow always white and clean and of lips moist
and open, out of which rolled the voice and the laughter,
deep and breathless, rolling out the strong and secret
beauty of her soul.

Alice of the streets. Gentle walking on long legs.
Close-kneed. Careful. Stopping sometimes at our house on
her way to unknown places and other people. She came
wearing loose, flowered dresses and she sat in our chairs
rubbing the too-big knees that sometimes hurt, and we

gathered, Momma, my sisters and I, to hear the beautiful
bad-woman talk and feel the rolling laughter, always sure
that she left more than she came for. I accepted the ten-
der touch of her hands on my hair or my face or my arms
like favors I never returned. I clung to the sounds of her
words and the light of her smiles like stolen fruit.

Alice, mother in a house of dark places. Of boys who
fought each other and ran cursing through the wild back
rooms where I did not go alone but sometimes with Alice
when she caught them up and knuckled their heads and
made them cry or hugged them close to her saying funny
things to tease them into laughter. And of the oldest son,
named for his father, who sat twisted into a wheelchair by
sunny windows in the front where she stayed with him for
hours giving him her love, filling him with her laughter
and he sat there—his words strained, difficult but soft and
warm like the sun from the windows.

Alice of the party. When there was not one elsewhere
she could make one of the evenings when her husband
was not storming the dim rooms in drunken fits or lying
somewhere in darkness filling the house with angry grunts
and snores before the days he would go to work. He sat
near her drinking beer with what company was there—was
always sure to come—greedy for Alice and her husband,
who leaned into and out of each other, talking hard and
laughing loud and telling lies and being real. And there
were rare and wondrously wicked times when I was
caught there with Daddy who was one of the greedy ones
and could not leave until the joy-shouting, table-slapping
arguments about God and Negroes, the jumping up and
down, the bellowing "what about the time" talks, the
boasting and reeling of people drunk with beer and laughter and the ache of each other was over and the last ones
sat talking sad and low, sick with themselves and too
much beer. I watched Alice growing tired and ill and
thought about the boys who had eaten dinners of cake
and soda pop from the corner store, and I struggled to de-
spise her for it against the memory of how, smiling they'd
crept off to their rooms and slept in peace. And later at

home I, too, slept strangely safe and happy, hugging the feel of that sweet fury in her house and in Alice of the party.

Alice, who grew older as I grew up but stayed the same while I grew beyond her, away from her. So far away that once, on a clear early morning in the spring, when I was eighteen and smart and clean on my way to work downtown in the high-up office of my government job, with eyes that would not see I cut off her smile and the sound of her voice calling my name. When she surprised me on a clear spring morning, on her way somewhere or from somewhere in the streets and I could not see her beauty, only the limp flowered dress and the tangled hair and the face puffy from too much drinking and no sleep, I cut off her smile. I let my eyes slide away to say without speaking that I had grown beyond her. Alice, who had no place to grow in but was deep in the soil that fed me.

It was eight years before I saw Alice again and in those eight years Alice had buried her husband and one of her boys and lost the oldest son to the county hospital where she traveled for miles to take him the sun and her smiles. And she had become a grandmother and a member of the church and cleaned out her house and closed the doors. And in those eight years I had married and become the mother of sons and did not always keep my floors clean or my hair combed or my legs oiled and I learned to like the taste of beer and how to talk bad-woman talk. In those eight years life had led me to the secret laughter.

Alice, when I saw her again, was in black, after the funeral of my brother, sitting alone in an upstairs bedroom of my mother's house, her face dusted with brown powder and her gray-streaked hair brushed back into a neat ball and her wrinkled hands rubbing the tight-stockinged, tumor-filled knees and her eyes quiet and sober when she looked at me where I stood at the top of the stairs. I had run upstairs to be away from the smell of food and the crowd of comforters come to help bury our dead when I found Alice sitting alone in black and was afraid to smile remembering how I'd cut off her smile when I thought I had grown beyond her and was afraid to speak because there was too much I wanted to say.

Then Alice smiled her same smile and spoke my name in her same voice and rising slowly from the tumored knees said, "Come on in and sit with me." And for the very first time I did.

ALEXIS DeVEAUX

WHERE DID YOU GROW UP/WHERE BORN/HOW
DID YOU GET TO THE PLACE YOU ARE NOW

*Grew up in Harlem and the South Bronx in New York
City. Born in New York City.*

*Wrote no matter what else I had to do, no matter what
kinds of non-writing jobs I had to take to support myself.
Have stuck to developing the sacred gift I've been en-
trusted with. And I have not allowed myself to misuse or
abuse that gift. Every step I have made, every word or
piece I have written has led me to this particular point in
time. It has been both magic and hard, often lonely work.
Though I would not say that I have "arrived," I would
say that I am successfully alive, in good health, and creative, for it is not my desire to "make it." It is only my
desire to live and evolve as a human being.*

IS YOUR RELATIONSHIP TO YOUR MOTHER AN
IMPORTANT INFLUENCE

*Yes. The more I unravel my life, the better I understand
hers, and the better I am able to communicate with her
and to her about our life. My mother's mother died when
my own mother was very young, so my mother never really had the benefit of a mother-daughter relationship or
the dynamics of that kind of communication. Because of
that, she was unable to communicate to my brothers and
sisters and me. Wanting to communicate on an intimate
level with her was, I believe, part of the reason I started
writing.*

IMPORTANT EXPERIENCES THAT HAVE HELPED SHAPE ME AS A WRITER

I have always been attached to books, words. Ever since elementary school. I was an overzealous Book Report-writer, and thoroughly meticulous about compositions, my handwriting, anything that had to do with books. In the street/at home, I eavesdropped on other people's conversations. Being just plain nosy, but not terribly communicative, shy. I would write poems a lot then. And I always had teachers who encouraged me to write. Writing became a way of talking . . . The Literary Renaissance of the 60s and the whole re-examination of the Harlem Renaissance of the 20s were important influences on me as far as developing a socio-political consciousness with respect to writing. Without that movement, and its liberating thrust, my writing would not have had the strength, and the connection to my "root/source," the neo-Africanist point of view it has now. The literary movement and the movement for freedom which engulfs us provides me with the knowledge of a vitally rich, ancient continuum.

IMPORTANCE OF FORMAL EDUCATION IN DEVELOPMENT OF MY WRITING

It wasn't. I never studied writing or how to write while in school. School kept alive my interest in books, but the actual craft of writing was something I studied and sought out on my own, outside the traditional educational environment. I found workshops and programs where creative writing was stressed. I became active in a couple of community organizations where writers' workshops were offered. That's how I got to meet other writers, known and unknown, to hear what they were doing, saying, feeling, striving for. By the time I got a B.A. through an independent study program (and several aborted attempts to finish college in all the wrong, but socially acceptable majors including psych and sociology), I was fully entrenched in writing, not only as a career, but as a way of life.

OTHER IMPORTANT INFLUENCES THAT HAVE SHAPED ME AS A WRITER

The emergence of Lorraine Hansberry (in 1959) as a gifted, spirited, visionistic woman. And the power behind her work. The fact that she was writing for the theatre made no difference since I did not see any boundaries between what was on the stage and what was on the page (and I still don't; often combine techniques of one form with those of another). The image of a Black woman as artist and writer living in the world at the same time I was, was a powerfully mesmerizing image for me. Also, meeting such writers as James Baldwin, Toni Morrison, Paule Marshall, J. E. Franklin (of Black Girl) Adrienne Kennedy, etc. made the possibility of becoming a writer, and surviving at it, a viable one; meeting and seeing them in the flesh made the reality of a life-style/career in writing all the more plausible and exciting.

CONNECTIONS BETWEEN MY PERSONAL LIFE AND THE IDEAS/IMAGES ETC. I WRITE ABOUT

There is an inseparable connection between who I am and what I realize I must write about, be it a poem, short story, book, or play. Writing helps me unravel the images and forces at work in my own life, and therefore, by extension, in the lives of Black women and Black people around me. I hope to communicate something not just about my life, but about our life. It's all one life—isn't it? And I'm very concerned about the images of Black women in literature because whatever is written down becomes the word, and the word is permanent, and stays, long after the writer and the people are gone. I want to say something about the Black woman as three-dimensional human being. So often we've seen her depicted as white-man-concubine, mammy, tragic mulatto, maid, prostitute, destitute, one stereotype after another: ugly and useless. I want to change that. In the most radical and revolutionary ways possible. I want to explore her questions, strengths, concerns, madnesses, love, evils, weaknesses, lack of love, pain, and growth. Her perversities and her moralities. I draw on my own feelings as a source of material, and then I try to flesh out these feelings in characters who may or may not have had my particular experiences but who certainly reflect my own concerns, politics, philosophies, etc. I said earlier that as a young person, I was shy. I think that shyness came out of smothered feelings, and a sense of inferiority, an ugliness (anything Black is ugly) vis-à-vis White society. Writing is a way of conquering those feelings of inferior beauty, inferior life, and giving vent to an extremely active imagination. When I am creating characters and the threads of their stories, I am able to free myself, cleanse myself, of old feelings/old scars, psychic imagery, desires, etc. Writing is a healing art/experience; it is a form of meditation.

WHAT TURNING POINTS IN YOUR CAREER/LIFE HAVE BEEN TRANSFORMING

1) *Winning the Black Creation Literary Contest in the fall of '72*
2) *Having my first play produced (CIRCLES) in '73*
3) *Getting my first book published (SPIRITS IN THE STREET) in '73*
4) *Witnessing the immensity of poverty in Haiti in the summer of '75*
5) *Going to Milan, Italy, in March of '78*
6) *Turning 30*
7) *Giving up all meats, cigarettes, and drugs in '77*

CHILDREN AND MARITAL STATUS

At present I have no children and my marital status doesn't make a difference to my career. I write whether I am single or married.

Poet, playwright, novelist, and free-lance writer, Alexis DeVeaux was born and raised in New York City, specifically Harlem and the South Bronx, which are the settings of most of her stories. In "The Riddles of Egypt Brownstone", the menacing Harlem streets are the landscape for Egypt's discovery of womanhood. The name *Egypt*, the tribal markings on her mother's face, the Fanti charm doll are the ancient icons of Egypt's heritage, an ironic contrast to the slum projects her family inhabits and the indignities she encounters in the street. The riddle of Egypt's life is this: if, in the twentieth-century a child is designated illegitimate, female, Negro, Egypt, who is she, what can she become, by what name and deeds will she be known? And are all the answers pre-ordained?

The unconventional style DeVeaux uses—hipster language, no capital letters, short, staccato sentences, black urban slang, African cultural remnants—is an attempt to capture and reproduce in her writing a mostly hidden subculture and to make its much maligned ways understood. In "Remember Him A Outlaw", the conversation between Uncle Willie and the storeowner is part of a ritualistic exchange which indicates the nature of Willie's position in the community:

nigger where you been? dont put your greasy lips on me. much as you smell.

you know you like it. stop actin so funny.

your nigger must be somewhere in here. listen flossy— let me have 6 cones. yeah 6. these richie kids. whats the damage on that? put it on my bill

you aint got no bill here

long as this your store momma—i got me a bill

The "neo-Africanist point of view" which DeVeaux asserts as part of her trademark, is shown in the language of this story and in the sensibility of Uncle Willie's niece, Lexie. Lexie respects and celebrates Willie's unique aesthetic—his green silk pants, green alligator shoes, his "purple magic," his strut. And through Lexie we are made aware of the social and political forces which claim Willie's life and create his death. The non-traditional forms that DeVeaux experiments with enable us to see both Egypt Brownstone and Uncle Willie, a so-called outlaw with a new consciousness.

Ms. DeVeaux has taught creative writing and theatre workshops in New York City and Connecticut. She has published a novel, *Spirits in the Street* (Anchor Press/Doubleday), an award-winning children's book, *Na-Ni* (Harper & Row), and her work appears in *Black Creation, Encore, Sunbury 2 Poetry Magazine, Black Box,* the *New Haven Advocate, Nimrod, ESSENCE,* and recently, two of her plays were shown at the INPUT Public Television Conference in Milan, Italy. She is currently on the staff at *ESSENCE* magazine as Poetry Editor.

Productions of her plays include *Circles* and *The Tapestry* produced as teleplays by KCET-TV ("Visions") for PBS (1976); *The Tapestry* performed at the Quaigh Theatre in New York City (1977); and *A Season to Unravel* produced by the Negro Ensemble Company in New York City (1979).

The Riddles of Egypt Brownstone

ALEXIS DEVEAUX

Push sweat violent lavender blue pain sing woman
come sing one hundred ninety nine
sweat girl dance the thigh dance pain
ninety eight ninety seven ninety six
born to push grunt rip life
tear out tear through purple birth murmurings
through sterilized galaxies of nurses and doctors
sing/ninety five ninety four stompin at the savoy

Above her body outstretched on the hospital table a white metal light licked at the starched gown pulled over her stomach heaving.

Bring baby down the Nile

Esther let her knees shut Esther let her eyes buck.

Momma October 13th shoulder pads and zoot suit city
sing woman Lena Horne momma hit the number ninety three
one two buckle my shoe who? whos the father yes no maybe so
doctor/lawyer/indian chief

She screamed sweat wet and birth crazy

Rich man poor man beggar man thief

Harlem Hospital. City of New York. Attending physician Dr. Edmund Greer. October 13 1945. 6:43am. Race Negro sex girl. Name Girl Brownstone. Mother's name Esther Brownstone. Address 50 West 138. Date of Birth

April 9 1928. Occupation usher. Age 17. Previous births now living none. Place of Employment RKO Theatre 116th Street was her mother's side of the birth certificate. Her father's side was blank.

.   .   .

In search of lush black nipple the minuscule mouth beside Esther in the hospital bed made a sucking sound.

"I named her Egypt, momma."

Edith Brownstone leaned over. A tiny West Indian silver bracelet she slipped on the grandchild's wrist.

"Blackest lil girl I ever saw" Edith said.

.   .   .

She collected riddles growing up. They fascinated her. After school at the library. Reading books on silver barges through the royal night. Excursions up the Nile of ancient history. Riddle me this. Riddle me that. Time and the twentieth century: what has a mother who is a father name a child Girl Negro sex female born feet first.

"My teacher say you got to sign this free lunch paper momma."
"Who wrote this word here Egypt?"
"Miss Jackowitz did. Everybody got one."
"Hand me that god damn pencil eraser girl. Wasnt nobody illegitimate when they was on top pumpin womens in the huts of nigga quarters."

.   .   .

She had thick red hair dusty black skin at 13. One brown and one light brown eye. Grew big titties. Was shorter than any of her friends. A Fanti charm doll she considered herself deformed.

> *"E my name is Egypt. (bounce)*
> *My father's name is Esop. (bounce)*
> *We come from Ethiopia. (bounce bounce)*
> *And we sell elephants." (bounce)*

Her spalding ball sang against the sunday summer morning concrete. Bounce bounce. Black palm to pink rubber ball. Feel air and space outside. Not like upstairs was. Too hot in the bed too many people. A taste for watermelon. Black ball to pink rubber palm to Harlem sidewalk. Smell saturday night in sunday street. Cars and buildings hung over. Bounce bounce ball over short black leg up over ball over was-white sneakers. Bounce. Bored. Hit the ball against the stoop.

> "Who wanna play stoop ball?
> Who wanna be on my team?
> So what. I can play if I want to.
> Mind your own business Georgie Christmas.
> I aint no tomboy shit."

The third floor window opened abrupt. Her mother's face hung out. Squinted eyes cruised the street below. A camel cigarette stuck to her lips. Egypt liked her mother's lips. Egypt liked her mother tough but not mean. Esther spotted Egypt bent over pitching fifteen pennies at the stoop step.

> "Take that ball out your sock girl. How many times I got to tell you your name aint Henry?"

A stained white was-once a towel wrapped itself around Egypt's mother's head. Henna mud streaked rivers/red tribal markings down her butternut face.

> "Go to the grocery store. Tell Prince I say dont forget my cigarettes this time."

Paper floated from Esther's thick fist crumpled. Egypt positioned her reluctant self to catch the sailing grocery list.

> why cant somebody else go get the groceries
> sometime momma why it always gotta be me
> soon as I get grown Im cuttin out she see

The third floor window closed. Down the block Egypt peeled her left sock away letting free the rubber ball.

> *shoot she know I dont like him*
> *'s why I never say nothin when he come see her*
> *he aint my father shoot I aint eatin none a*
> *his ole nasty food*

Bounce bounce pink rubber ball to Black angry palm.
Across the street through the Taft Projects. A low income
public dream. Stack them up stack them higher. One way
in one way out. Project families versus tenement families
versus the city is everybody's landlord no matter how you
frost the cake.

•   •   •

On the edges of El Barrio graffiti poems are rainbows that
promise Debbie loves Jose forever baby I need your luvin.
Windows half open tell the secret of last night's party.
Hot thighs sweating teenage blues under skirts with no
panties and zippers open standing up/sitting down/up-
side second hand refrigerators in dark kitchens. Please
baby gimme some. I die if you dont. Please sugar oh lord
you soo good. Yeah I love you anything baby anything.
Oh jesus oh the Shirelles and do-rags conkoline and red
lights. From a record player on the tenth floor Etta James
crooned. In the center of the projects a gang of kids raced
each other to the metal swings. Egypt walked through the
artificial park to the other side of time. King Tut somer-
saulted beside her. He stroked the false beard of Egyptian
royalty. King Tut the boy was King Tut the man was
King Tut the dancing Pharaoh. She loved his dip and
glide intoxicating two step through the monkey bars.

> *"Are you ready my dear? Shall we go?"*
> *"Cant."*
> *"Oh but my dear why not? I have prepared every-*
> *thing you know."*

He dipped and glided a royal strut his robe shimmered di-
vinity.

> *"Aint solved the serious riddle" she said.*
> *"Whats a what with a who has a what born on the*
> *same day one month apart?" he said.*

And split for home through a crack in a breath Egypt inhaled.

how come all of a sudden we gotta take his food
why cant she buy food like everybody else mother
maybe he aint there maybe the stores closed

Lenox Avenue and 116th street. A red and white sign proclaimed PRINCE'S GROCERY STORE AND FRUIT STAND was open. To see how many people were inside she peeked through the pane glass window. She saw only Prince. He saw her staring. He winked her inside. The stingy brim olive green hat pushed back made his forehead jut forward. A well groomed mustache hid the true thickness of his upper lip. Stains and chicken do rusted his white butcher's apron. She thought she saw something in his face/she thought she saw his blood rise. With false boldness Egypt pushed the glass door open. Against the potato bin she leaned and wrestled Esther's grocery list from her dungaree pocket. She held it out to him.

"Hi. Momma said make sure you send her some ciga-
rettes."
"Hi yourself."

He did not take it. He kept stamping 2 for 31¢ on cans of Campbell's Chicken Noodle soup. Egypt watched. Prince watched Egypt watching Prince through the corners of watching eyes. *Do you see me/I see you?*

"What else your momma say?"
"Nothin."
"She tell you come straight back?"
"Yeah."
hurry up Prince shoot take the list gimme the gro-
ceries dont be no riddle please Prince why we gotta
play this game every week

"Wanna ice cream sandwich?"
"No thanks."
"Nice tee shirt you got."

Egypt laid the crumpled list on the counter. Prince ripped open a second box of soup cans. He watched her watching. Egypt shoved her hands in her pockets and walked around the store. She felt her face hot. She felt her stomach twist in anxious knots.

The aisles of the small Lenox Avenue grocery store were pregnant with boxes of canned vegetables crackers canned juices apple sauce jars and toilet paper. Egypt read the labels. Prince watched her wander up and down through the giant mirror at the back he kept for watching shoplifters. He saw her finger her way into a package of Oreo cookies slip several in her pocket one in her mouth and continue a nonchalant journey. He watched her in the mirror. He watched her watching him.

"Hey Tuna man. Come out here and finish these cans for me will ya?"

A good friend an old sailor he never went to sea. Smelled like fridays fish 2 pounds for a dollar. Didn't eat no tuna said they were sacred. He worked for Prince on the weekends. Visited aquariums every wednesday and monday and told fish tales. From the back of the store Tunafish came out whistling *Mona Lisa Mona Lisa* his white sailor cap and white sailor pants stiff with starch.

"Prince man why didnt you tell me your daughter was here? How you doing lil bit? Hows your momma?"
"Fine Mr. Tunafish."

She talking this way and watching that way watching Prince hand Tunafish the can stamper.

he aint my father hes my brothers father
hes her boyfriend he aint nothin to me
I dont even like eatin his food when I get home
Im a tell her that

Prince lit a Pall Mall cigarette and picked up the grocery list puffing smoke his eyes like bird slits his body like Mr.

America's only blacker than blackberry brandy jam. From behind the counter he came out not paying Egypt no mind sneaking Oreo cookies out her pocket with her face turned towards the picked over tomatoes and grapefruits spoiling in the bin near the store door. He slipped his arm around her shoulder.

"Come on girl" he said *"lets see what your momma want."*

Pushing a shopping cart in front of them he guided her up and down the aisles. His large ashy hand weighed a ton on her broad hand ball shoulders. Prince pretended to read what he knew by heart: salmon eggs white bread white grits pasteurized cheese ready made food. He let his hand fondle her bra strap tensed. She moved out of step. He brought her firmly back in.

"Here" he said *"you might as well finish what you started."*

The open package of Oreo cookies betray her like a laughing enemy. His hand tasted her breast trembling. Long fingers squeezed roughly.

"Why you always so quiet, huh girl? Hand me two cans of that salmon will ya?"

He let go long enough for her to reach the green and pink cans.

"Please Prince please cant you see Mr. Tunafish in the mirror watchin. Please Prince hes laughin he might tell."

Egypt felt Prince's hand rub and squeeze. At the back of the store he pressed closer. In front of the meat case Prince stood behind her. Prince stuck his hand inside her tee shirt.

"You think your momma want some pork chops?"

When he squeezed her hurting he pulled the blue and yel-

low tee shirt up over Egypt's tears palpitating incantations
to Ra the All Seeing Eye of Upper and Lower. Ra the
father/Lord of Kemet. Let there be light. Let there be
riddles. Amen.

 "You gonna tell your momma our secret?"

He said he wasn't going to bite her. He said they ought to
be glad he had a grocery store. He said don't ever tell
your momma you hear me?

The grocery list never changed. She never told. He always
sent something extra. It was the first secret she learned to
keep from her momma that summer until the sunday
morning the grocery list changed. Esther added: one box
Kotex and put it in the bathroom on the floor between the
toilet and the bath tub without a word but kept walking
behind Egypt smelling her odor and waiting and watching
Prince who was "her nigga" watching Egypt do the dishes
watching him watch her sideways out of one eye. So that
sunday Esther finally smelled it Egypt was standing in the
kitchen straightening her hair burning her neck in the
back when Esther frowning at the door said "aint gone be
no woman-wars in this house" and told her not to go to
Prince's store no more she had stopped shopping there.

·　　·　　·

Egypt wondered when was the last time Esther kissed
Bull. Was it that night they made her on the roof it was
too cold to take their coats off he promised? It was long
since then she knew when she heard Esther telling Prince:

 *"This aint got nothin to do with you Prince. Thats
 his kid. Every Christmas he sends her this money.
 Dont start somethin you cant finish honey. What you
 talkin bout? Bull didnt leave me. We was just too
 young my father said. This aint got nothin to do with
 you Prince."*

·　　·　　·

She had seen him her birthday every year. He waited on
the corner 127th Street and St. Nicholas. Bull David Phil-

lips was her father. She looked like him in the face a little in the eyes. He loved clothes and imported hats. Esther said he made his own suits and only wore blue suede shoes. She wanted a pair on her 18th birthday. They went to every store 125th Street looking for a pair of midnight blue suede ladies shoes.

. . .

"*Maintenant, nous étudierons la conjugaison des verbes. Mademoiselle Brownstone. Pouvez-vous traduire pour la classe s'il vous plaît?*"
"*Oui Madame. We will now study the conjugation of verbs.*"

I am sitting in a beige classroom full of right handed beige desks. I am one of twenty six students in this City College French 101 class. The instructor is a Black woman name Madame duFer. She has lived in Martinique Paris Haiti and Guadeloupe among the folk. Her shoulders are square Egyptian. Her face is moon black. She drowns me with her slanted eyes. She sees me looking at her mouth when she speaks. I doodle in my notebook: I am into thick lips (are good for sucking). She says her hair is au naturel. The world is changing. Civil rights and Black Power/it's 1963. I'm smiling at her with my frown. When she calls on me the others know I am the favorite.

"*Répétez après moi classe. J'ai un secret. Tu as un secret. Il a un secret. Elle a un secret.*"

I like those European tailored suits she wears with the skirts cut just above her calves. *E my name is Ellie. My father's name is Eclipse. We come from Eatonville. And we sell eggplants.* Madame duFer looks like a woman. Madame duFer does not look like a woman. Madame duFer looks like more than a woman or a man.

"*Ecoutez classe. Listen carefully. Je suis née à Harlem. Tu es née à Harlem. Il est né à Harlem. Elle est née à Harlem.*"

I am watching her mouth move thickly in a light French

dance to conjugate the present past future tense. April is
the month of reincarnated verbs: to spring to jazz to poet.
Tonight I am invited to her house for dinner. Suite 3c.
Eighteen Hamilton Place. The old Sugar Hill section of
Harlem.

> *"My three sisters and I share a bedroom. I do my
> homework in the bathroom."*
> *"You could live here if you like. When the semester
> is over we can be friends. You wont have to call me
> Madame duFer."*
> *"What about your husband?"*
> *"He has his life. I have mine. Are you frightened?"*
> *"Yes."*
> *"You are the most beautiful student I have ever had.
> Always coming and going. Much as myself."*
> *"I believe in riddles like my father."*
> *"Do you object to being a kept woman?"*
> *"No."*

Esther's mother Edith said Bull had been in a bar flashing
his money in the wrong woman's face when he fell out. In
the hospital a doctor said Mr. Phillips had been quite sick
more than a year with a kidney ailment that had gotten
progressively worse. Esther said Bull loved himself some
Chivas Regal said he always loved to drink a fifth of it for
lunch. The electric kitchen clock he had given her last
Christmas fell off the wall that morning while she was
having coffee and something said "a bull with one horn
cant last too long" and instead of going to work Esther
turned on the record player and played her favorite Nat
King Cole album for old times sake.

After Bull's family called Esther called Egypt and Egypt
took a cab all the way to Brooklyn. *What has a mother
who is a father and who is he 127th Street once a year?*

> *"I needed him to solve the riddle momma"*

She told Esther outside the Intensive Care Unit. Pulled up

the leg of her dungarees and took a pink rubber ball out her sock. Bounced it fiercely against the hospital wall. It pounded

> E my name is Ethiopia
> My father's name is Egypt
> We come from Esop
> And we sell Eclipses

And then it stopped pound-pounding. The doctor handed them a bag of clothes he had worn. Egypt took out her inheritance. Put them on. Stuffed the hospital report in the toes. And wore his blue suede shoes to the funeral.

Seduced and betrayed

The Bird Cage

BY PAULETTE CHILDRESS WHITE

It's Monday. Midnight. The house is quiet, my family asleep. The row of sober-faced brick homes leading from my house on the corner is silent now, and the people in them are probably asleep. As is most of Detroit by this time on a Monday night.

Except for me. I spend the hours around midnight back here in the sunroom, sipping cool drinks and looking for some light. Inner light. Inspiration, that I might, before my eyes give out, distill a line or two of poetry.

There is also this troubled flock outside on the street, beyond my green-curtained windows—a boisterous gathering of men. They're bickering again and again and I'm wondering why I ever wanted this house. I knew about the Bird Cage.

"Man, I wont my money," one says. *"Hey,"* comes the answer, *"would I stick you like that, man? For five?"* *"Aw, I don't wont to hear all that,"* one says again, and a little chorus sings, *"Yeah, just give the man his money!"*

Three, maybe four, voices—mean, melodious voices—rise and fall. A mad quartet.

These are none of the good neighbors that keep the tidy homes and lawns down our shady street. Those sensible, hard-working folk went to bed at a decent hour and would have no truck with these out here now. But in my corner house, the left side of which is exposed to Woodlin Avenue—a semicommercial thoroughfare—and its noisome night life, I have come to know them.

They are men and women. Young and old. Up and sometimes, like now, down. They talk too loudly and laugh too hard and they argue too much. They wear tight, deep-colored clothes—purple and russet and forest green. Clothes that bind their strongly shaped bodies too close, as does the fabric of their lives, so that all their songs become cries. They are bright, nocturnal birds out looking for some light, for what joy or sustenance they do not have by day. I know them. In fact, I am one of them. We all take our pleasure in the night.

But what I wanted here tonight was solitude. None of this drama. That is for Fridays or Saturdays, when I have nothing to do but do my feet or my hair. It can be entertaining then to referee their fights, mull over their philosophies, laugh at their humor, be one of them while I clip my toenails or put my hair up. But weekday nights I don't usually waste on such things.

I spent this day, as I have nearly every weekday for the last two months, in the kitchen on my hands and knees. Between changing diapers and preparing meals, I'm piecing together a floor of slate tile in mortar I mix myself.

It's nothing high-minded. I'm not doing it for any kind of creative expression or fulfillment. I'm doing it because I want a rustic country kitchen in a rustic country house and doing it myself may be as close as I get to having one. So what if it's inside a house that sits on a busy corner in the heart of the city? So what if it takes me years?

The point is, after I labor over that floor all day—not to mention the kids—I don't want to be disturbed. This sunroom is my midnight sanctuary.

"Let me make this run." "Hey . . ." "Is that all right, man?" "Give the man his money." "Man, you been in there sportin' all night." "Look, you let me make this run. I'll have your five dollars when I get back. Is that all right?" "Man, all I wont is my money."

Gracious. All I want! All I want right now is some quiet. Country quiet would be nice. In fact, I'd like to take this entire city to the country. We could have a sensitivity session. Back to nature. A workshop in life. Be about life and people, about growing things. Rolling hills and thick green fields. But, you know, some people would just drag their city ways on out to the country with them and miss the whole point.

Besides, this is home. My home. And they do say there is no place like home . . . until you move. Until you leave it.

"I wont my money."

Here is proof, I think, that you *can* get the country out of people. Because despite the rural accents, these are definitely city people out there. These people have forgotten all about the country.

But see what happens to me? I sit down to do a really moving piece. Something insightful. Heavy. Then I'm invaded by this silly business of the five dollars and it gets me sidetracked. The situation apparently demands some attention. . . .

The Bird Cage is a lounge. A bar. A squat, brown, brick-and-glass storefront bar. The only thing that keeps the Bird Cage and its variegated fowl from my side door is a four-lane street, with litter-laced curbs and two sidewalks, called Woodlin Avenue. Does "avenue" imply strolling leisurely? Quaint little neighborhood shops? Trees or flowers, even?

Not any more. All of that was before the riots of '67. Back when the neighborhood first began to change. Woodlin is like Main Street in Dodge City now, and the Bird Cage is your friendly neighborhood saloon.

Nights, like now, the bulbs of a little square marquee blink the Bird Cage's dumb, unceasing promise of "Girls! Girls!" Girls in the Bird Cage. Days like tomorrow, when I go out back to hang clothes, I'll have to turn my eyes away from the big orange bandage with purple words announcing that the Ice Cream and Cake Revue is now being featured. (Ice Cream and Cake, a duo obviously as good as its name because the bandage has been up there across the front of the Bird Cage for the entire year that we've been in this house.)

I've seen them as I've passed the Bird Cage—one Black

and the other a white blonde, making half-nude dashes around the dance floor. It's almost as if I know them.

No doubt I never will, though I have imagined that one day I might step out past my hedges in these spotted overalls, plastic thongs slapping on my feet, and smilingly introduce myself to them: "Hi. I'm the lady in the house across from the Bird Cage and aren't you Ice Cream and Cake?"

No, that wouldn't do. We're separated by a lot more than Woodlin Avenue. It's just that, like them, I know what it is to be a girl in the bird cage.

"Hey, you gon' give me my money?" "Man, I can't give you what I ain't got."

That's true. And it's also true that sometimes you take what you can get. Like the house. Sure, I'd rather have been able to buy out in Palmer Park like my cousin Sherri, whose husband is in the hauling business (he must be hauling those gold bricks out of Fort Knox) and can afford it. However, this was a deal we couldn't refuse. The man practically gave us the house.

He was the son of a Polish immigrant. The first time we looked at the house, he led us from room to room. It was big and old and in need of some repair. But there was the sunroom. I wanted the sunroom.

"This," he said, "is the sunroom. My mother kept her plants here. For the light, you see . . . all the windows."

It was off the dining room, toward the back of the house. A small, airy room with seven long windows, and through the windows a lush of ivy. Green, green ivy foaming up around the back side of the house, spilling over onto the seven windows, and the sun sifting in softly, greenly, as though the sunlit foliage would spill into the room to touch you.

I like the sunroom, I thought, old wet-eyed white man. We'll take the house of your childhood. Your mother's house. We'll fill it with our own dark dreams. And sun. And plants. Dry your eyes. It is all right to leave the piano. Yes, the old piano, though it isn't any good any more and we don't play. And yes, the attic things. What-

ever. We'll use them—or burn them, is what I thought
then, seeing the son of the Polish immigrant peer out of a
sunroom window, understanding his glance over at the
Bird Cage, hearing him think to say, "We have stayed on
as long as we could . . . things have changed, now, you
know. . . ."

Yes, I wanted the house. And he nearly gave the house
away; he was moving on to a place in the country.

"My money!"

And the garage. My husband saw the garage. He is an
artist and a keeper of things. A saver and user of things.
He is a man who needs a garage. One day the garage, facing Woodlin as it does, will make a fine studio-gallery. A
place to hang the unsold paintings and the portraits of
himself. Until then it is such a fine place to keep things.

I learned about my husband when I was fifteen, before
I ever met him. It was through my Aunt Bertha. She
would pick me up some Saturdays and take me to her
house, where I was to help her with the cleaning. She,
a busy brown squirrel of a woman, would lead, digging
through the dust and clutter, wheezing and snorting with
asthma, while I followed, confused, pleading from time
to time, "What to do . . . what to do with *this?*" And
though it would be only a faded calendar or a paper fan
or an empty, broken box, her eyes would grab at the thing
as if they were saying, "Oh, save it! I want to save that.
Yes, save it, save it." When we were done there would
be only a paper sack filled with dust to throw away and
the mountains of her life would have been merely rearranged. Aunt Bertha—even in repose her hands curled
clawlike, clutching nothing. She would not understand that
things must be let go of. That nothing is ours to keep.

My husband is like Aunt Bertha. He never lets go. He
likes the garage and the huge web of an attic and the
dank corners of the basement, for he is a man who saves
things, squeezes things, drains things. He says, "Everything I have is important to me. I value everything that's
mine. Yes, from the tiniest nail . . . to you."

"Man, I wont my money." "Run me ovah there. My man

*gonna run me ovah there. I'ma leave my car. I'ma leave
the gray goose here. Yeah, leave the gray duck here."
Laughter. "The gray goose. Well, whatevah. Go on, get
the man five dollars." Laughter. Murderous little ripples of
laughter. The sounds of a car leaving. The sharp peck of
feet and low, stultified voices crossing the street, back to
the Bird Cage.*

I have my own arguments to carry on in here. Such as,
Why am I here? I did not mean to be here. This is not
where I meant to be. By the Bird Cage. In the bird cage.
I wanted to go out somewhere in the world. I only wanted
to dip down in here on occasion.

"You got a talent, girl. Get yourself a education. So you
don't have to depend on no man for nothing. So you have
something to fall back on." And I, the little girl, would
look up from my drawings at them—Momma, Aunt Bertha
and the other mothers of my childhood. I would listen
without hearing.

As a child I was safe, safe in my imaginings of a future.
In my drawings of television ladies, magazine ladies, ladies
with red-lipped smiles and glossy pageboys and pretty,
gathered skirts. Safe I was in the vision of myself as one
of those free ladies who ruled big houses and wealthy husbands and proper children. Whose lives were orderly and
comfortable and clean.

What I got from my real-life mothers came on me as I
grew. Was deeper and more lasting. Was understanding
—accepting the fact that I was one of them and that life
was mean, work-laden, painful. That men were a necessary
evil and children a chore.

"If I had known *then* what I know *now* . . . I wouldn't
be where I am today." They would say this over a big pot
of something boiling and the sweat would make rivulets
in the dark folds of their skin and run down; or they would
be sitting on low sofas, pushing their baby-filled bellies
out for more room, and their eyes would glaze and wizen
hard; or they would be blowing over hot coffee they were
having after the husband-daddies were gone, when they
made time together, their faded dresses limp around them

like the once-bright curtains flagging at the open windows.
They would say, "I wouldn't *be* where I am today," and
suck the scalding coffee through the wreaths of their lips
while their eyes traveled slowly toward the open windows
and then dropped like stones to the floor.

I would not be where I am today. I would be in airy rooms
in a quiet place. On a green hill, in a clapboard bunga-
low with gingerbread trim, painted sun-yellow. I would
have one bed, one chair, one table and one, just one, of
anything. I would dress in too-tight jeans that hugged the
narrow bow of my hips and in loose shirts through which
the unsuckled nipples of my breasts would make interesting twin dots and I would wear a few special pieces of
jewelry—gifts that would be remembrances of some gentle
soul and that would bring a soft, bittersweet smile to my
lips.

I would paint. I would paint myself. On huge canvases
I would paint my soul's songs, search out my own truths.
I would not write these long, racking poems but make
paint talk, smile, cry, touch. My year in art school would
not have ended in defeat. In pregnancy.

Babies. In other rooms I have four sleeping babies. I
never had a pregnancy I wanted but I wanted all my babies. Sweet-skinned, newborn babies, I wanted them—how
I wanted to want them! Now that their growth is upon
me, meaningless is the memory that I had not wanted
them. Even as they sleep I sense the cling of their eyes,
hear their voices circling round me, "Momma, Momma!"
I am theirs.

"Girl, what are you trying to prove?" Women, my
friends, asking me, for my own good, "How many babies
are you going to have? Do you want? You're gonna be just
like your momma. And *you* don't have to be having all
these babies. Any more. *Do* something. The Pill . . . oh,
you're gonna be just like your momma."

Meaning, they would be meaning, You have become
heavier with each child, heavier and less happy. We see
it. Your body will be wasted. Do something. Who will

want your baby-scarred body when he has left you, or you him? What will you do when the children grow up to love someone else and then he looks at you and discovers that he, after all, is still young? Oh, what will you do? Meaning, You do not have our support. Meaning, Fool.

Until the last, I smiled. *He* wanted the babies. He *wanted* the babies. That makes a difference. And I was safe enough in the marriage. Who wanted to swallow a pill each day, every day, for forty years? Not I. I smiled through the stupor of marriage until the last birth. Then I cried to the doctor, the good man of a doctor peering down at jelly me, bloody red jelly me, "Fix it," I said. "Fix it that I don't have any more." And his eyes were flat and shocked as a rag doll's when he asked, "Are you sure?"

"Yes." It did not matter that I never gave birth to a girl. What have I to offer a girl? I have yet to give birth to myself.

It is late. Outside, feet pattern a senseless music. It is time now to make that climb. To the bedroom. I wonder, if he touches me tonight, will I like it? Perhaps it is enough that I accept it. If I'm not too tired when he touches me, I may forgive him his stares and his self-portraits and whatever it was that made me so angry today.

Disorganization. That I am so disorganized. "Find a place for things and keep them there. Why don't you *think* about what you're doing sometimes?" he asked me. I held back an urge to say, "But if I did, I wouldn't be here," and thereby held off the inevitable fight. I may forgive him, if I'm not too tired.

He probably dreams of soft, supple virgins—innocently, in his sleep, for he is not a bad man. He is steady, moral, true. Still . . . willing, mindful girls eager to be the wife must haunt him.

I have tried. How could we, either of us, have known that I would become this discontent, this willful woman? Who is not mindful; who talks of independence and personhood and freedom; this closet feminist? Who often, of late, must be brought down? I was easy enough in the beginning, eager prey. Gave myself over to him thoroughly. Now, he says, and it's true, I've got these big ideas and all we do is fight. He must get at least as weary as I. Innocently, in his sleep, he must dream.

"*I'ma show that nigga*"—glass breaking—"*who he really messin' with.*" *The sounds of bludgeoning against metal and the metal denting, perhaps, but not breaking like the glass. Laughter. "See how he like the gray goose now. Yeah." Feet scratching in the glass. Footsteps dying down the street, heading away, and one voice, raw, epitaphic, shouting back, "I'm tired. I'm tired of people tryin' to mess ovah me!"*

I can understand that. I'm tired too. But I cannot concern myself with these things now. Tomorrow there's the wash, the floor, the kids and more disorganization.

The Bird Cage will take care of itself. Fire may sweep through it in the middle of the night. The birds it cages may find the reason to tear it down. The landlord may grow negligent and the city condemn it. But someday the Bird Cage will come down.

Then we hungry midnight birds will have our chance to swoop at a morning sky.

ALICE WALKER

Alice Walker is primarily known as a novelist and short story writer whose tragic and triumphant depictions of black women range from abused and ghostly figures suspended in the webs of an atavistic southern system to the strange, mysterious and defiant Meridian. At thirty-five, she has published two novels, *The Third Life of Grange Copeland* (1971) and *Meridian* (1977); a book of short stories, *In Love and Trouble* (1974); a collection of poems, *Revolutionary Petunias;* and a book for children, *Langston Hughes*. In Walker's fiction, one is aware of the black woman as part of an evolutionary spiral, moving from victimization to consciousness,[1] from the work-burdened, abused Mem Copeland to the dear-eyed, determined Meridian.

In addition to her achievements in fiction, Walker has written four landmark essays in black feminist criticism in the last five years. Considered together as a developing canon, they constitute the most comprehensive and authoritative statement on the role of black women in the arts. In the 1974 essay "In Search of Our Mothers' Gardens,"[2] Walker explores the history of the black woman's creativity as it existed in this country in the nineteenth and early twentieth century. In that essay she poses this heartbreaking and soul-searching dilemma: suppose there were black women born in the nineteenth century with a special talent. Suppose in these women there hungered the soul of a painter, the heart of a dancer, the spirit of a novelist. And we know that such creativity must have

[1] Paule Marshall also presents this sense of evolution in her characters' lives. At the end of each of her novels, the main characters undertake a symbolic journey to the past, and in a reverse replication of the Middle Passage, they begin in America and end in Africa.
[2] *Ms.*, May 1974.

existed. What happened to such a woman living in a century that did not even acknowledge her existence? Did she live

> under some ignorant and depraved white overseer's lash? Or was she required to bake biscuits for a lazy backwater tramp, when she cried out in her soul to paint watercolors of sunsets . . . Or was her body broken and forced to bear children . . . when her one joy was the thought of modeling heroic figures of Rebellion, in stone or clay?[3]

But to know the *herstory* of black women is to know more than tragedy and despair, is to recognize "the mute and inglorious ways" these nineteenth-century artists devised to retain their creativity. In quiltmaking, rootworking, storytelling, even cooking and gardening, they inscribed their artistic signatures. Walker comes to realize in the writing of this essay how much of the art of storytelling—and the very stories themselves—she has inherited from her own mother. This recognition of her mother's influence immediately summons the witness of Paule Marshall and Gayl Jones, who have also identified their mothers as sources of their aesthetic. As Marshall says of the women of her childhood, whose tales she absorbed in a Brooklyn kitchen where the women gathered after the day's work as domestics:

> They didn't know it, nor did I at the time, but they were carrying on a tradition as ancient as Africa, centuries old oral mode by which the culture and history, the wisdom of the race had been transmitted.[4]

For Walker there is a spiritual as well as artistic dimension to this legacy; for, in the commitment to their own creative expression, however unlikely as art, they handed down to their generations "respect for the possibilities—and the will to grasp them."

[3] "In Search of Our Mothers' Gardens," p. 66.
[4] "Shaping the World of My Art," in *New Letters* 40 (Autumn 1973), p. 103.

In spite of the subversive ways these black women laid claim to some means of artistic expression, the black woman artist still suffers greatly from the absence of models. In the 1975 essay, "Saving the Life That Is Your Own: The Importance of Models in the Artist's Life,"[5] Walker issues a condemnation of the forced isolation and alienation of the black woman artist as a function of a white male ideology which indoctrinates us into believing that only their writing is worth reading. In order to develop the intrepid faith in her own work, the courage to defy restraint or convention or stigma, the artist is desperate for the nourishment and sustenance that come from community, from connectedness, from "a dialogue with brave and imaginative women who came before."[6]

It is intolerable that such a model should vanish from the world of letters with scarcely a trace. Zora Neale Hurston wrote consistently for over a thirty-year period, immersed herself in the study of black folklore and provided a nearly complete record of her life. Still her fate was the same as if she had written only a paragraph—by ignorance utterly banished from the consideration of male scholars, inadequate as they were to judge her. Walker's quest to restore Zora Hurston to recognition has resulted in a two-part essay, "In Search of Zora Neale Hurston," published in *Ms.* magazine and an anthology of Hurston's writing, *I Love Myself When I Am Laughing . . . And Then Again When I Am Looking Mean and Impressive*, published by Feminist Press in 1979. In the Dedication[7] of that anthology Walker concludes that Zora suffered indifference and hostility because she was an independent and autonomous woman, scorning the approval

---

[5] Paper given November 11, 1975, as part of the Reid Lectureship at Barnard College Women's Center.
[6] Adrienne Rich, "Conditions for Work," in *On Lies, Secrets, and Silence: Selected Prose, 1966–1978*, Virago Press, 1980, p. 205.
[7] "On Being 'The Greatest' in a Country You Did Not Design," in *I Love Myself When I Am Laughing—And Then Again When I Am Looking Mean and Impressive: A Zora Neale Hurston Reader*, Feminist Press, 1979.

of a male elite. The power of such models to save lives is
only logical: against the insanity of a patriarchal system,
which falsifies reality, they teach black women the value
of their lives.

In her efforts to analyze the obstacles against the black
woman writer, Walker comes full circle with an essay
written in 1979, entitled "One Child of One's Own: A
Meaningful Digression Within the Work(s)."[8] The question Walker puts to herself is this: is a child a hindrance
to the artist at work? The answer is emphatically *no*. The
obstacles are frighteningly familiar—racism and powerless-
ness. But in this final quarter of the twentieth century,
there is a new twist to the old humiliations. White women
scholars—putative feminists, Barbara Smith calls them—are
as free as white males to treat the black woman as "Other,"
excluding them from anthologies, including them as tokens, considering white women as the standard for the female experience.[9] As Adrienne Rich put it, it is a strange
feminism indeed that allows white women to be more alien
to the literature and lives of black women than to centuries of the literature and history of white men.[10] And
since few white feminists are familiar with the literature
of blacks—women or men—there continues to be what
Susan McHenry calls "the edge" between black and white
feminists. Walker's essay denounces the easy feminism that
lays the problems of women on motherhood while ignoring
the hard problem of subtle and insidious racism perpet-
uated by feminists.

Alice Walker's story "Laurel" poses questions about the

[8] Published in *Ms.*, August 1979.
[9] A good example of this disregard for black women's lives as
representative is the current crop of so-called feminist movies.
Although there is not a single black woman in any of them—not
even in a minor role of neighbor or friend—these movies are still
touted as serious and authentic reflections of "the woman's"
experience. Or the number of books which use the word *woman*
in the title or as the subject and have not a single black woman
in them.
[10] "Disloyal to Civilization: Feminism, Racism, Gynephobia
(1978)," in *On Lies, Secrets, and Silence*, p. 307.

nature of interracial relationships and the need to take risks, about marriage and the need for safety and security. Two kinds of relationships are set in juxtaposition to each other in "Laurel"; the black woman's love affair with Laurel literally risks her life—there were laws against such couples in that still deeply segregated South. In contrast to the lusty, springtime, youthful affair with Laurel, the narrator's marriage is tranquil, safe, a refuge from the emotional extremes she has once known and which, even within the protective matrimonial bonds, she is not able to restrain.

Walker's second story in this anthology, "Advancing Luna and Ida B. Wells," involves an interracial friendship between two women who were active during the ferment of the Civil Rights movement.

Luna, a young white woman, and the narrator, a black southern woman, are drawn South to the student protest movement of the sixties. A year after their summer of civil rights activities and interracial sex, they are reunited in New York, where Luna recalls that she was raped by a black man during that summer. The rape becomes a third presence in the story; for rape is at once the blood-tie among all women, as well as the bloody specter haunting black men in the South, where even the suspicion of it wreaked unspeakable atrocities. For the black woman, this blood-knot interlacing the lives of all three is the bond that unites and the bond that constricts.

Walker presumes no easy answers in "Luna"; neither does she flee the deep angers and disturbing contradictions between black and white women. But sisterhood and innocence cannot co-exist. It is Walker's courage and insight that raise the moral and political questions that are as critical to feminism in the seventies as they were for the black struggle of the sixties.

Laurel

BY ALICE WALKER

It was also during that summer in the mid-sixties that I met Laurel.

There was a new radical Southern newspaper starting up . . . it was only six months old at the time, and was called *First Rebel*. The title referred, of course, to the black slave who was rebelling all over the South long before the white rebels fought the Civil War. Laurel was in Atlanta to confer with the young people on its staff, and, since he wished to work on a radical, racially mixed newspaper himself, to see if perhaps *First Rebel* might be it.

I was never interested in working on a newspaper, however radical. I agree with Leonard Woolf that to write against a weekly deadline deforms the brain. Still, I attended several of the editorial meetings of *First Rebel* because while wandering out of the first one, fleeing it, in fact, I'd bumped into Laurel, who, squinting at me through cheap, fingerprint-smudged blue and gray bifocals, asked if I knew where the meeting was.

He seemed a parody of the country hick; he was tall, slightly stooped, with blackish hair cut exactly as if someone had put a bowl over his head. Even his ears stuck out, and were large and pink.

Really, I thought.

Though he was no more than twenty-two, two years older than me, he seemed older. No doubt his bifocals added to this impression, as did his nonchalant gait and slouchy posture. His eyes were clear and brown and filled with an appropriate country slyness. It was his voice that held me. It had a charming lilt to it.

"Would you say that again?" I asked.

"Sure," he said, making it two syllables, the last syllable a higher pitch than the first. "I'm looking for where *First Rebel*, the newspaper, is meeting. What are *you* doing?"

The country slyness was clumsily replaced by a look of country seduction.

Have mercy! I thought. And burst into laughter.

Laurel grinned, his ears reddening.

And so we became involved in planning a newspaper that was committed to combating racism and other violence in the South . . . (until it ran out of funds and folded three years and many pieces of invaluable investigative journalism later).

Laurel's was not a variation of a Southern accent, as I'd at first thought. It was Americanized French-Dutch. His ancestors, a religious sect akin to the Amish of Pennsylvania, had immigrated to the United States in the early 1800s. They had settled in the Finger Lakes region of upstate New York because there they could grow the two things they liked growing best: winegrapes and apples.

I'd never heard anything like Laurel's speech. He could ask a question like "How d'you happen t'be here?" and it sounded as if two happy but languid children were slowly jumping rope under apple trees in the sun. And, on Laurel himself, while he spoke, I seemed to smell apples and the faint woodruffy bouquet of May wine.

He was also effortlessly complimentary. He would say, as we went through the cafeteria line, "You're beaut-ti-ful, reel-i," and it was like hearing it and caring about hearing it, for the first time.

Laurel, who loved working among the grapes, and had done so up to the moment of leaving the orchards for Atlanta, had dirt, lots of it, under his nails.

That's it, I thought. I can safely play here. No one brings such dirty nails home to dinner. That was Monday. By Tuesday I thought that dirty nails were just the right non-bourgeois attribute and indicated a lack of personal concern for appearances that included the smudged bifocals and the frazzled but beautifully fitting jeans; in a back pocket of which was invariably a half-rolled, impressively battered paperback book. It occurred to me that I could not look at Laurel without wanting to make love with him.

He was the same.

For a while, I blamed it on Atlanta in the spring . . . the cherry trees that blossomed around the campus buildings, the wonderful honeysuckle smells of our South, the excitement of being far away from New York City and its never-to-be-gotten-used-to dirt. But it was more: If we both walked into a room from separate doors, even if we didn't see each other, a current dragged us together. At breakfast neither of us could eat, except chokingly, so intense was our longing to be together. Minus people, table, food.

A veritable movie.

Throughout the rest of the week we racked our brains trying to think of a place to make love. But the hotels were still segregated, and once, after a Movement party at somebody's house, we were severely reprimanded for walking out into the Southern night, blissfully hand in hand.

"Don't you know this is outrageous?" a young black man (now, I hear, a textile workers' organizer) asked us, pulling us into his car, where I sat on Laurel's lap in a kind of sensual stupor—hearing his words, agreeing with them, knowing the bloody History behind them . . . but not caring in the least.

In short, there was no place for us to make love, as that term is popularly understood. We were housed in dormitories. Men in one. Women in another. Interracial couples were under surveillance wherever the poor things raised their heads anywhere in the city. We were reduced to a kind of sexual acrobatics on a bench close beside one of the dormitories. And, as lovers know, acrobatics of a sexual sort puts a strain on one's powers of physical ingenuity while making one's lust all the more a resident of the brain, where it quickly becomes all-pervading, insatiable and profound.

The state of lust itself is not a happy one if there is no relief in sight. Though I am happy enough to enter that state whenever it occurs, I have learned to acknowledge its many and often devastating limitations. For example, the most monumental issues fade from one's consciousness as if erased by a swift wind. Movements of great social and political significance seem but backdrops to one's daily exchanges—be they ever so muted and circumscribed—with The Object of One's Desire. (I at least was not yet able to articulate how the personal is the political, as was certainly true in Laurel's and my case. Viz., nobody wanted us to go to bed with each other, except us, and they had made laws to that effect. And of course whether we slept together or not was nobody's business, except ours.)

The more it became impossible to be with Laurel, to make love fully and naturally, the more I wanted nothing but that. If the South had risen again during one of our stolen kisses—his hands on my breasts, my hands on his (his breasts were sensitive, we discovered quite by acrobatic invention and accident)—we would have been hard pressed to notice. This is "criminal" to write, of course, given the myths that supposedly make multi-racial living so much easier to bear, but it is quite true. And yet, after our week together—passionate, beautiful, haunting and never, never to be approximated between us again, our desire to make love never to be fulfilled (though we did not know this then)—we went our separate ways. Because in fact, while we kissed and said Everything Else Be Damned! the South *was* rising again. *Was* murdering people. Was imprisoning our colleagues and friends. Was keeping us from strolling off to a clean, cheap hotel.

It was during our last night together that he told me about his wife. We were dancing in a local Movement-oriented nightclub. What would today be called a disco. He had an endearing way of dancing, even to slow tunes (during which we clung together shamelessly); he did a sort of hop, fast or slow depending on the music, from one foot to the other, almost in time with the music—and that

was dance to him. It didn't bother me at all. Our bodies
easily found their own rhythms anyway, and touching
alone was our reason for being on the floor. *There* we
could make a sort of love, in a dark enough corner, that
was not exactly grace but was not, was definitely not, acrobatics.

He peered at me through the gray-blue framed glasses.
"I've got a wife back home."

What I've most resented as "the other woman" is being
made responsible for the continued contentment and hap-
piness of the wife. On our last night together, our lust un-
diminished and apparently not to be extinguished, given
our surroundings, what was I supposed to do with this information?

All I could think was, "She's not *my* wife."

She was, from what little he said, someone admirable.
She was away from home for the summer, studying for an
advanced degree. He seemed perplexed by this need of
hers to continue her education instead of settling down on
the farm to have his children, but lonely rather than
bitter.

So it was *just sex* between us, after all, I thought.

(To be fair, I was engaged to a young man in the
Peace Corps. I didn't mind if it *was* just sex, since by that
time our mutual lust had reached a state of profundity
and almost of mysticism.)

Laurel, however, was tormented.

(I never told him about my engagement. As far as I
was concerned, it remained to be seen whether my engagement was relevant to my relationships with others. I
thought not, but realized I was still quite young.)

That night, Laurel wrung his hands, pulled his
strangely cut hair and cried, as we brazenly walked out
along Atlanta's dangerous, cracker-infested streets.

I cried because he did, and because in some odd way it
relieved my lust. Besides, I enjoyed watching myself pre-
tend to suffer. . . . Such moments of emotional dishon-
esty are always paid for, however, and that I did not

know this at the time attests to my willingness to believe
our relationship would not live past the moment itself.

And yet.

There was one letter from him to me after I'd settled in
a small Georgia town to a.) picket the jailhouse where a
local schoolteacher was under arrest for picketing the
jailhouse where a local parent was under arrest for picketing the jailhouse where a local child was under arrest for
picketing . . . and b.) to register voters.

He wrote that he missed me. He wanted a separation
from his wife.

I missed him. He was the principal other actor in all my
fantasies. I wrote him I was off to Africa, but would continue to write. I gave him the address of my school, to
which he could send letters.

Once in Africa, my fiancé (who was conveniently in the
next country from mine and free to visit) and I completed
a breakup that had been coming for our entire two-year
period of engagement. He told me, among other things,
that it was not uncommon for Peace Corps men to sleep
with ten-year-old African girls. *At that age, you see, they
were still attractive.* I wrote about that aspect of the Peace
Corps's activities to Laurel, as if I'd heard about it from a
stranger.

Laurel, I felt, would never take advantage of a ten-
year-old child. And I loved him for it.

Loving him, I was not prepared for the absence of letters from him, back at my school. Three months after my
return I still had heard nothing. Out of depression over
this and the distraction schoolwork provided, I was a
practicing celibate. Only rarely did I feel lustful, and then
of course I always thought of Laurel, as of a great opportunity, much missed. I thought of his musical speech and
his scent of apples and May wine with varying degrees of
regret and tenderness. However, our week of passion—
magical, memorable, but far too brief—gradually assumed
a less than central place even in my most sanguine recol-
lections.

In late November, six months after Laurel and I met, I received a letter from his wife.

My first thought, when I saw the envelope, was: she has the same last name as him. It was the first time their marriage was real for me. I was also frightened that she wrote to accuse me of disturbing her peace. Why else would a wife write?

She wrote that on July 4 of the previous summer (six weeks after Laurel and I met) Laurel had had an automobile accident. He was driving his van, delivering copies of *First Rebel*. He had either fallen asleep at the wheel or been run off the road by local rebels of the other kind. He had sustained a broken leg, a fractured back and a severely damaged brain. He had been in a coma for the past four months. Nothing could rouse him. She had found my letter in his pocket. Perhaps I would come see him?

(I was never to meet Laurel's wife, but I admired this gesture then, and I admire it now.)

It was a small Catholic hospital in Laurel's hometown. In the entryway a bloody, gruesome, ugly Christ the color of mashed rutabaga stood larger than life. Nuns dressed in black and white habits reminded one of giant flies. Floating moonlike above their "wings" their pink, cherubic faces were kind and comical.

Laurel's father looked very much like Laurel. The same bifocals, the same plain country clothing, the same open-seeming face—but on closer look, wide rather than open. The same lilt to his voice. Laurel's sister was also there. She, unaccountably, embraced me.

"We're so glad you came," she said.

She was like Laurel too. Smaller, pretty, with short blond hair and apple cheeks.

She reached down and took Laurel's hand.

Laurel alone did not look like Laurel. He who had been healthy, firm-fleshed, virile, lay now on his hospital bed a skeleton with eyes. Tubes entered his body everywhere. His head was shaved, a bandage covering the hole that had been drilled in the top. His breathing was hardly a whistle through a hole punched in his throat.

I took the hands that had given such pleasure to my breasts, and they were bones, unmoving, cold, in mine. I touched the face I'd dreamed about for months as I would the face of someone already in a coffin.

His sister said, "Annie is here," her voice carrying the lilt.

Laurel's eyes were open, jerking, twitching, in his head. His mouth was open. But he was not there. Only his husk, his shell. His father looked at me—as he would look at any other treatment. Speculatively. Will it work? Will it revive my son?

I did not work. I did not revive his son. Laurel lay, wheezing through the hole in his throat, helpless, insensate. I was eager to leave.

Two years later, the letters began to arrive. Exactly as if he thought I still waited for them at my school.

"My darling," he wrote, "I am loving you. Missing you and out of coma after a year and everybody given up on me. My brain damaged. Can you come to me? I am still bedridden."

But I was not in school. I was married, living in the South.

"Tell him you're married now," my husband advised. "He should know not to hurt himself with dreaming."

I wrote that I was not only married but "happily."

My marital status meant nothing to Laurel.

"Please come," he wrote. "There are few black people here. You would be lonesome but I will be here loving you."

I wrote again. This time I reported I was married, pregnant, and had a dog for protection.

"I dream of your body so luscious and fertile. I want so much to make love to you as we never could do. I hope you know how I lost part of my brain working for your people in the South I miss you. Come soon."

I wrote: "Dear Laurel, I am so glad you are better. I'm sorry you were hurt. So sorry. I cannot come to you because I am married. I love my husband. I cannot bear to come. I am pregnant—nauseous all the time and anxious because of the life I/We lead. Etc. etc."

To which he replied: "You married a jew. [I had published a novel and apparently reviewers had focused on my marriage instead of my work as they often did.] There are no jews here either. I guess you have a taste for the exotic tho I was not exotic only american a boy of the soil. I am a cripple now with part of my brain in somebody's wastepaper basket. We could have children if you will take the responsibility for bringing them up. I can not be counted on. Ha Ha."

I asked my husband to intercept the letters that came to our house. I asked the president of my college to collect and destroy those sent to me there. I dreaded seeing them.

"I dream of your body, so warm and brown, whereas mine is white and cold to me now. I could take you as my wife here the people are prejudiced against blacks they were happy martin luther king was killed. I want you here. We can be happy and black and beautiful and crippled and missing part of my brain together. I want you but I guess you are tied up with that jew husband of yours. I mean no disrespect to him but we belong together you know that."

"Dear Laurel, I am a mother [I hoped this would save me. It didn't.] I have a baby daughter. I hope you are well. My husband sends his regards."

Most of Laurel's letters I was not shown. Assuming that my husband confiscated his letters without my consent, Laurel telegraphed: "Annie, I am coming by greyhound bus don't let your dog bite me Laurel."

My husband said: "Fine, let him come. Let him see that you are not the woman he remembers. His memory is frozen on your passion for each other. Let him see how happy you and I are."

I waited, trembling.

It was a cold, clear evening. Laurel hobbled out of the

taxi on crutches, one leg shorter than the other. He had regained his weight and, though pale, was almost handsome. He glanced at my completely handsome husband once and dismissed him. He kept his eyes on me. He smiled on me happily, pleased with me.

I knew only one dish then, chicken tarragon; I served it.

I was frightened. Not of Laurel, exactly, but of feeling all the things I felt.

(My husband's conviction notwithstanding, I suspected marriage could not keep me from being, in some ways, exactly the woman Laurel remembered.)

I woke up my infant daughter and held her, disgruntled, flushed, and ludicrously alert, in front of me.

While we ate, Laurel urged me to recall our acrobatic nights on the dormitory bench, our intimate dancing. Before my courteous husband, my cheeks flamed. Those nights that seemed so far away to me seemed all he clearly remembered; he recalled less well how his accident occurred. Everything before and after that week had been swept away. The moment was real to him. I was real to him. Our week together long ago was very real to him. But that was all. His speech was as beautifully lilting as ever, with a zaniness that came from a lack of connective knowledge. But he was hard to listen to: he was both overconfident of his success with me—based on what he recalled of our mutual passion—and so intense that his gaze had me on the verge of tears.

Now that he was here and almost well, I must drop everything, including the baby on my lap—whom he barely seemed to see—and come away with him. Had I not flown off to Africa, though it meant leaving the very country in which he lived?

Finally, after the riddles within riddles that his words became (and not so much riddles as poems, and disturbing ones), my husband drove Laurel back to the bus station. He had come over a thousand miles for a two-hour visit.

My husband's face was drawn when he returned. He

loved me, I was sure of that. He was glad to help me out. Still, he wondered.

"*It lasted a week!*" I said. "Long before I met you!"

"I know," he said. "Sha, sha, baby," he comforted me. I had crept into his arms, trembling from head to foot. "It's all right. We're safe."

But *were we?*

And Laurel? Zooming through the night back to his home? The letters continued. Sometimes I asked to read one that came to the house.

"I am on welfare now. I hate being alive. Why didn't my father let me die? The people are prejudiced here. If you came they would be cruel to us but maybe it would help them see something. You are more beautiful than ever. You are so sexy you make me ache—it is not only because you are black that would be racism but because when you are in the same room with me the room is full of color and scents and I am all alive."

He offered to adopt my daughter, shortly after he received a divorce from his wife.

"She is getting another degree and seeing other men she is happy I am wanting you to come."

After my husband and I were divorced (some seven years after Laurel's visit and thirteen years after Laurel and I met), we sat one evening discussing Laurel. He recalled him perfectly, with characteristic empathy and concern.

"If I hadn't been married to you I would have gone off with him," I said. "Maybe."

"Really?" He seemed surprised.

Out of habit I touched his arm. "I loved him, in a way."

"I know," he said, and smiled.

"A lot of the love was lust. That threw me off for years until I realized lust can be a kind of love."

He nodded.

"I felt guilty about Laurel. When he wrote me I became anxious. When he came to visit us I was afraid."

"He was not the man you knew."

"I don't think I knew him well enough to tell. Even so, I was afraid the love and lust would come flying back, along with the pity. And that even if they didn't come back, I would run off with him anyway, because of the pity—*and for the adventure.*"

It was the word "adventure" and the different meaning it had for each of us that finally separated us. We had come to understand that, and to accept it, without bitterness.

"I wanted to ask you to let me go away with him, for just a couple of months," I said.

"*to let me go . . .*"

"He grew steadily worse, you know. His last letters were brutal. Even after he was committed, he wrote, blaming you for everything, even the accident, accusing you of awful, nasty things. He became a sick, bitter, vindictive man."

He knew me well enough to know I heard this and I did not hear it.

He sighed. "It would have been tough for me," he said. "Tough for our daughter. Tough for you. Toughest of all for Laurel."

(*"Tell me it's all right that I didn't go!"* I wanted to plead, but didn't.)

"Right," I said instead, shrugging, and turning our talk to something else.

The politics of sex

Advancing Luna and
Ida B. Wells

BY ALICE WALKER

I met Luna the summer of 1965 in Atlanta where we both attended a political conference and rally. It was designed to give us the courage, as temporary civil rights workers, to penetrate the small hamlets farther South. I had taken a bus from Sarah Lawrence in New York and gone back to Georgia, my home state, to try my hand at registering voters. It had become obvious from the high spirits and sense of almost divine purpose exhibited by black people that a revolution was going on, and I did not intend to miss it. Especially not this summery, student-studded version of it. And I thought it would be fun to spend some time on my own in the South.

Luna was sitting on the back of a pickup truck, waiting for someone to take her from Faith Baptist, where the rally was held, to whatever gracious black Negro home awaited her. I remember because someone who assumed I would also be traveling by pickup introduced us. I remember her face when I said, "No, no more back of pickup trucks for me. I know Atlanta well enough, I'll

Luna and Freddie Pye are composite characters, and their names are made up. This is a fictionalized account suggested by a number of real events.

walk." She assumed of course (I guess) that I did not
wish to ride beside her because she was white, and I was
not curious enough about what she might have thought to
explain it to her. And yet I was struck by her passivity,
her *patience* as she sat on the truck alone and ignored, because someone had told her to wait there quietly until it
was time to go.

This look of passively waiting for something changed
very little over the years I knew her. It was only four or
five years in all that I did. It seems longer, perhaps because we met at such an optimistic time in our lives. John
Kennedy and Malcolm X had already been assassinated,
but King had not been and Bobby Kennedy had not been.
Then too, the lethal, bizarre elimination by death of this
militant or that, exiles, flights to Cuba, shoot-outs between
former Movement friends sundered forever by lies planted
by the FBI, the gunning down of Mrs. Martin Luther
King, Sr., as she played the Lord's Prayer on the piano in
her church (was her name Alberta?), were still in the happily unfathomable future.

We believed we could change America because we
were young and bright and held ourselves *responsible* for
changing it. We did not believe we would fail. That is
what lent fervor (revivalist fervor, in fact; we would
revive America!) to our songs, and lent sweetness to our
friendships (in the beginning almost all interracial), and
gave a wonderful fillip to our sex (which, too, in the beginning, was almost always interracial).

What first struck me about Luna when we later lived
together was that she did not own a bra. This was curious
to me, I suppose, because she also did not need one. Her
chest was practically flat, her breasts like those of a child.
Her face was round, and she suffered from acne. She
carried with her always a tube of that "skin-colored" (if
one's skin is pink or eggshell) medication designed to dry
up pimples. At the oddest times—waiting for a light to
change, listening to voter registration instructions, talking
about her father's new girlfriend she would apply the
stuff, holding in her other hand a small brass mirror the

size of her thumb, which she also carried for just this purpose.

We were assigned to work together in a small, rigidly segregated South Georgia town whose city fathers, incongruously and years ago, had named Freehold, Georgia. Luna was slightly asthmatic and when overheated or nervous she breathed through her mouth. She wore her shoulder-length black hair with bangs to her eyebrows and the rest brushed behind her ears. Her eyes were brown and rather small. She was attractive, but just barely and with effort. Had she been the slightest bit overweight, for instance, she would have gone completely unnoticed, and would have faded into the background where, even in a revolution, fat people seem destined to go. I have a photograph of her sitting on the steps of a house in South Georgia. She is wearing tiny pearl earrings, a dark sleeveless shirt with Peter Pan collar, Bermuda shorts, and a pair of those East Indian sandals that seem to adhere to nothing but a big toe.

The summer of '65 was as hot as any other in that part of the South. There was an abundance of flies and mosquitoes. Everyone complained about the heat and the flies and the hard work, but Luna complained less than the rest of us. She walked ten miles a day with me up and down those straight Georgia highways, stopping at every house that looked black (one could always tell in 1965) and asking whether anyone needed help with learning how to vote. The simple mechanics: writing one's name, or making one's "X" in the proper column. And then, though we were required to walk, everywhere, we were empowered to offer prospective registrants a car in which they might safely ride down to the county courthouse. And later to the polling places. Luna, almost overcome by the heat, breathing through her mouth like a dog, her hair plastered with sweat to her head, kept looking straight ahead, and walking as if the walking itself was her reward.

I don't know if we accomplished much that summer. In retrospect, it seems not only minor, but irrelevant. A bunch of us, black and white, lived together. The black people who took us in were unfailingly hospitable and kind. I took them for granted in a way that now amazes me. I realize that at each and every house we visited I *assumed* hospitality, I *assumed* kindness. Luna was often startled by my "boldness." If we walked up to a secluded farmhouse and half a dozen dogs ran up barking around our heels and a large black man with a shotgun could be seen whistling to himself under a tree, she would become nervous. I, on the other hand, felt free to yell at this stranger's dogs, slap a couple of them on the nose, and call over to him about his hunting.

That month with Luna of approaching new black people every day taught me something about myself I had always suspected: I thought black people superior people. Not simply superior to white people, because even without thinking about it much, I assumed almost everyone was superior to them; but to everyone. Only white people, after all, would blow up a Sunday school class and grin for television over their "victory," *i.e.*, the death of four small black girls. Any atrocity, at any time, was expected from them. On the other hand, it never occurred to me that black people *could* treat Luna and me with anything but warmth and concern. Even their curiosity about the sudden influx into their midst of rather ignorant white and black Northerners was restrained and courteous. I was treated as a relative, Luna as a much welcomed guest.

Luna and I were taken in by a middle-aged couple and their young school-age daughter. The mother worked outside the house in a local canning factory, the father worked in the paper plant in nearby Augusta. Never did they speak of the danger they were in of losing their jobs over keeping us, and never did their small daughter show any fear that her house might be attacked by racists because we were there. Again, I did not expect this family to complain, no matter what happened to them because of us. Having understood the danger, they had assumed the risk. I did not think them particularly brave, merely typical.

I think Luna liked the smallness—only four rooms—of the house. It was in this house that she ridiculed her mother's lack of taste. Her yellow-and-mauve house in Cleveland, the eleven rooms, the heated garage, the new car every year, her father's inability to remain faithful to her mother, their divorce, the fight over the property, even more so than over the children. Her mother kept the house and the children. Her father kept the car and his new girlfriend, whom he wanted Luna to meet and "approve." I could hardly imagine anyone disliking her mother so much. Everything Luna hated in her she summed up in three words: *"yellow-and-mauve."*

I have a second photograph of Luna and a group of us being bullied by a Georgia state trooper. This member of Georgia's finest had followed us out into the deserted countryside to lecture us on how misplaced—in the South—was our energy, when "the Lord knew" the North (where he thought all of us lived, expressing disbelief that most of us were Georgians) was just as bad. (He had a point that I recognized even then, but it did not seem the point where we were.) Luna is looking up at him, her mouth slightly open as always, a somewhat dazed look on her face. I cannot detect fear on any of our faces, though we were all afraid. After all, 1965 was only a year after 1964 when three civil rights workers had been taken deep into a Mississippi forest by local officials and sadistically tortured and murdered. Luna almost always carried a flat black shoulder bag. She is standing with it against her side, her thumb in the strap.

At night we slept in the same bed. We talked about our schools, lovers, girlfriends we didn't understand or missed. She dreamed, she said, of going to Goa. I dreamed of going to Africa. My dream came true earlier than hers: an offer of a grant from an unsuspected source reached me one day as I was writing poems under a tree. I left Freehold, Georgia, in the middle of summer, without regrets, and flew from New York to London, to Cairo, to Kenya, and finally, Uganda, where I settled among black people with the same assumptions of welcome and

kindness I had taken for granted in Georgia. I was taken
on rides down the Nile as a matter of course, and accepted all invitations to dinner, where the best local
dishes were superbly prepared in my honor. I became, in
fact, a lost relative of the people, whose ancestors had
foolishly strayed, long ago, to America.

I wrote to Luna at once.

But I did not see her again for almost a year. I had
graduated from college, moved into a borrowed apartment
in Brooklyn Heights, and was being evicted after a month.
Luna, living then in a tenement on East Ninth Street, invited me to share her two-bedroom apartment. If I had
seen the apartment before the day I moved in I might
never have agreed to do so. Her building was between
Avenues B and C and did not have a front door. Junkies,
winos, and others often wandered in during the night
(and occasionally during the day) to sleep underneath the
stairs or to relieve themselves at the back of the first-floor
hall.

Luna's apartment was on the third floor. Everything in
it was painted white. The contrast between her three
rooms and kitchen (with its red bathtub) and the grungy
stairway was stunning. Her furniture consisted of two
large brass beds inherited from a previous tenant and
stripped of paint by Luna, and a long, high-backed
church pew which she had managed somehow to bring up
from the South. There was a simplicity about the small
apartment that I liked. I also liked the notion of extreme
contrast, and I do to this day. Outside our front window
was the decaying neighborhood, as ugly and ill-lit as a
battleground. (And allegedly as hostile, though somehow
we were never threatened with bodily harm by the His-
panics who were our neighbors, and who seemed, more
than anything, *bewildered* by the darkness and filth of
their surroundings.) Inside was the church pew, as
straight and spare as Abe Lincoln lying down, the white
walls as spotless as a monastery's, and a small, unutterably
pure patch of blue sky through the window of the back

bedroom. (Luna did not believe in curtains, or couldn't afford them, and so we always undressed and bathed with the lights off and the rooms lit with candles, causing rather nun-shaped shadows to be cast on the walls by the long-sleeved high-necked nightgowns we both wore to bed.)

Over a period of weeks, our relationship, always marked by mutual respect, evolved into a warm and comfortable friendship which provided a stability and comfort we both needed at that time. I had taken a job at the Welfare Department during the day, and set up my typewriter permanently in the tiny living room for work after I got home. Luna worked in a kindergarten, and in the evenings taught herself Portuguese.

It was while we lived on East Ninth Street that she told me she had been raped during her summer in the South. It is hard for me, even now, to relate my feeling of horror and incredulity. This was some time before Eldridge Cleaver wrote of being a rapist/revolutionary; of "practicing" on black women before moving on to white. It was also, unless I'm mistaken, before LeRoi Jones (as he was then known; now of course Imamu Baraka, which has an even more presumptuous meaning than "the King") wrote his advice to young black male insurrectionaries (women were not told what to do with *their* rebelliousness): "Rape the white girls. Rape their fathers." It was clear that he meant this literally and also as: to rape a white girl *is* to rape her father. It was the misogynous cruelty of this latter meaning that was habitually lost on black men (on men in general, actually), but nearly always perceived and rejected by women of whatever color.

"Details?" I asked.

She shrugged. Gave his name. A name recently in the news, though in very small print.

He was not a Movement star or anyone you would know. We had met once, briefly. I had not liked him because he was coarse and spoke of black women as "our" women. (In the early Movement, it was pleasant to think of black men wanting to own us as a group; later it be-

came clear that owning us meant exactly *that* to them.)
He was physically unattractive, I had thought, with something of the hoodlum about him: a swaggering, unnecessarily mobile walk, small eyes, rough skin, a mouthful of wandering or absent teeth. He was, ironically, among the first persons to shout the slogan everyone later attributed solely to Stokeley Carmichael—Black Power! Stokeley was chosen as the originator of this idea by the media, because he was physically beautiful and photogenic and articulate. Even the name—Freddie Pye—was diminutive, I thought, in an age of giants.

"What did you do?"

"Nothing that required making a noise."

"Why didn't you scream?" I felt I would have screamed my head off.

"You know why."

I did. I had seen a photograph of Emmett Till's body just after it was pulled from the river. I had seen photographs of white folks standing in a circle roasting something that had talked to them in their own language before they tore out its tongue. I knew why, all right.

"What was he trying to prove?"

"I don't know. Do you?"

"Maybe you filled him with unendurable lust," I said.

"I don't think so," she said.

Suddenly I was embarrassed. Then angry. Very, very angry. *How dare she tell me this!* I thought.

Who knows what the black woman thinks of rape? Who has asked her? Who *cares?* Who has even properly acknowledged that *she* and not the white woman in this story is the most likely victim of rape? Whenever interracial rape is mentioned, a black woman's first thought is to protect the lives of her brothers, her father, her sons, her lover. A history of lynching has bred this reflex in her. I feel it as strongly as anyone. While writing a fictional account of such a rape in a novel, I read Ida B. Wells's autobiography three times, as a means of praying to her spirit to forgive me.

My prayer, as I turned the pages, went like this: *"Please forgive me. I am a writer."* (This self-revealing statement alone often seems to me sufficient reason to require perpetual forgiveness; since the writer is guilty not only of always wanting to know—like Eve—but also of trying—again like Eve—to find out.) *"I cannot write contrary to what life reveals to me. I wish to malign no one. But I must struggle to understand at least my own tangled emotions about interracial rape. I know, Ida B. Wells, you spent your whole life protecting, and trying to protect, black men accused of raping white women, who were lynched by white mobs, or threatened with it. You know, better than I ever will, what it means for a whole people to live under the terror of lynching. Under the slander that their men, where white women are concerned, are creatures of uncontrollable sexual lust. You made it so clear that the black men accused of rape in the past were innocent victims of white criminals that I grew up believing black men literally did not rape white women. At all. Ever. Now it would appear that some of them, the very twisted, the terribly ill, do. What would you have me write about them?"*

Her answer was: *"Write nothing. Nothing at all. It will be used against black men and therefore against all of us. Eldridge Cleaver and LeRoi Jones don't know who they're dealing with. But you remember. You are dealing with people who brought their children to witness the murder of black human beings, falsely accused of rape. People who handed out, as trophies, black fingers and toes. Deny! Deny! Deny!"*

And yet, I have pursued it, *"some black men themselves do not seem to know what the meaning of raping someone is. Some have admitted rape in order to denounce it, but others have accepted rape as a part of rebellion, of 'paying whitey back.' They have gloried in it."*

"They know nothing of America," she says. *"And neither, apparently, do you. No matter what you think you know, no matter what you feel about it, say nothing. And to your dying breath!"*

Which, to my mind, is virtually useless advice to give to a writer.

Freddie Pye was the kind of man I would not have looked at then, not even once. (Throughout that year I was more or less into exotica: white ethnics who knew languages were a peculiar weakness; a half-white hippie singer; also a large Chinese mathematician who was a marvelous dancer and who taught me to waltz.) There was no question of belief.

But, in retrospect, there was a momentary *suspension* of belief, a kind of *hope* that perhaps it had not really happened; that Luna had made up the rape, "as white women have been wont to do." I soon realized this was unlikely. I was the only person she had told.

She looked at me as if to say: "I'm glad *that* part of my life is over." We continued our usual routine. We saw every interminable, foreign, depressing, and poorly illuminated film ever made. We learned to eat brown rice and yogurt and to tolerate kasha and odd-tasting teas. My half-black hippie singer friend (now a well-known reggae singer who says he is from "de *I*-lands" and not Sheepshead Bay) was "into" tea and kasha and Chinese vegetables.

And yet the rape, the knowledge of the rape, out in the open, admitted, pondered over, was now between us. (And I began to think that perhaps—whether Luna had been raped or not—it had always been so; that her power over my life was exactly the power *her word on rape* had over the lives of black men, over *all* black men, whether they were guilty or not, and therefore over my whole people.)

Before she told me about the rape, I think we had assumed a lifelong friendship. The kind of friendship one dreams of having with a person one has known in adversity; under heat and mosquitoes and immaturity and the threat of death. We would each travel, we would write to each other from the three edges of the world.

We would continue to have an "international list" of

lovers whose amorous talents or lack of talents we would continue (giggling into our dotage) to compare. Our friendship would survive everything, be truer than everything, endure even our respective marriages, children, husbands—assuming we *did*, out of desperation and boredom someday, marry, which did not seem a probability, exactly, but more in the area of an amusing idea.

But now there was a cooling off of our affection for each other. Luna was becoming mildly interested in drugs, because everyone we knew was. I was envious of the open-endedness of her life. The financial backing to it. When she left her job at the kindergarten because she was tired of working, her errant father immediately materialized. He took her to dine on scampi at an expensive restaurant, scolded her for living on East Ninth Street, and looked at me as if to say: "Living in a slum of this magnitude must surely have been your idea." As a cullud, of course.

For me there was the welfare department every day, attempting to get the necessary food and shelter to people who would always live amid the dirty streets I knew I must soon leave. I was, after all, a Sarah Lawrence girl "with talent." It would be absurd to rot away in a building that had no front door.

I slept late one Sunday morning with a painter I had met at the welfare department. A man who looked for all the world like Gene Autry, the singing cowboy, but who painted wonderful surrealist pictures of birds and ghouls and fruit with *teeth*. The night before, three of us—me, the painter, and "an old Navy buddy" who looked like his twin and who had just arrived in town—had got high on wine and grass.

That morning the Navy buddy snored outside the bedrooms like a puppy waiting for its master. Luna got up early, made an immense racket getting breakfast, scowled at me as I emerged from my room, and left the apartment, slamming the door so hard she damaged the lock. (Luna had made it a rule to date black men almost exclusively.

My insistence on dating, as she termed it "anyone," was incomprehensible to her, since in a politically diseased society to "sleep with the enemy" was to become "infected" with the enemy's "political germs." There is more than a grain of truth in this, of course, but I was having too much fun to stare at it for long. Still, coming from Luna it was amusing, since she never took into account the risk her own black lovers ran by sleeping with "the white woman," and she had apparently been convinced that a summer of relatively innocuous political work in the South had cured her of any racial, economic, or sexual political disease.)

Luna never told me what irked her so that Sunday morning, yet I remember it as the end of our relationship. It was not, as I at first feared, that she thought my bringing the two men to the apartment was inconsiderate. The way we lived allowed us to *be* inconsiderate from time to time. Our friends were varied, vital, and often strange. Her friends especially were deeper than they should have been into drugs.

The distance between us continued to grow. She talked more of going to Goa. My guilt over my dissolute if pleasurable existence coupled with my mounting hatred of welfare work, propelled me in two directions. South, or to West Africa. When the time came to choose, I discovered that *my* summer in the South had infected me with the need to return, to try to understand, and write about, the people I'd merely lived with before.

We never discussed the rape again. We never discussed, really, Freddie Pye or Luna's remaining feelings about what had happened. One night, the last month we lived together, I noticed a man's blue denim jacket thrown across the church pew. The next morning, out of Luna's bedroom walked Freddie Pye. He barely spoke to me—possibly because as a black woman I was expected to be hostile toward his presence in a white woman's bedroom. I was too surprised to exhibit hostility, however, which was only a part of what I felt, after all. He left.

Luna and I did not discuss this. It is odd, I think now,

that we didn't. It was as if he were never there; as if he and Luna had not shared the bedroom that night. A month later, Luna went alone to Goa, in her solitary way. She lived on an island and slept, she wrote, on the beach. She mentioned she'd found a lover there who protected her from the local beachcombers and pests.

Several years later, she came to visit me in the South and brought a lovely piece of pottery which my daughter much later dropped and broke, but which I glued back together in such a way that the flaw improves the beauty and fragility of the design.

Afterwards, Afterwords
SECOND THOUGHTS

That is the "story." It has an "unresolved" ending. That is because Freddie Pye and Luna are still alive, as am I. However, one evening while talking to a friend, I heard myself say that I had, in fact, written two endings. One, which follows, I considered appropriate for such a story published in a country truly committed to justice, and the one above, which is the best I can afford to offer a society in which lynching is still reserved, at least subconsciously, as a means of racial control.

I said that if we in fact lived in a society committed to the establishment of justice for everyone ("justice" in this case encompassing equal housing, education, access to work, adequate dental care, et cetera), thereby placing Luna and Freddie Pye in their correct relationship to each other, i.e., that of brother and sister, compañeros, then the two of them would be required to struggle together over what his rape of her had meant.

Since my friend is a black man whom I love and who loves me, we spent a considerable amount of time discussing what this particular rape meant to us. Morally wrong, we said, and not to be excused. Shameful; politically cor-

rupt. Yet, as we thought of what might have happened to
an indiscriminate number of innocent young black men in
Freehold, Georgia, had Luna screamed, it became clear
that more than a little of Ida B. Wells's fear of probing
the rape issue was running through us, too. The implications of this fear would not let me rest, so that months and
years went by with most of the story written but with me
incapable, or at least unwilling, to finish or to publish it.

In thinking about it over a period of years, there occurred a number of small changes, refinements, puzzles, in
angle. Would these shed a wider light on the continuing
subject? I do not know. In any case, I returned to my
notes, hereto appended for the use of the reader.

LUNA: IDA B. WELLS—DISCARDED NOTES

Additional characteristics of Luna: At a time when many
in and out of the Movement considered "nigger" and
"black" synonymous, and indulged in a sincere attempt to
fake Southern "hip" speech, Luna resisted. She was the
kind of WASP who could not easily imitate another's eth-
nic style, nor could she even exaggerate her own. She was
what she was. A very straight, clear-eyed, coolly observant
young woman with no talent for existing outside her own
skin.

IMAGINARY KNOWLEDGE

Luna explained the visit from Freddie Pye in this way:
    *"He called that evening, said he was in town, and did I
know the Movement was coming North? I replied that I
did know that."*
    When could he see her? he wanted to know.
    "Never," she replied.
    *He had burst into tears, or something that sounded like
tears, over the phone. He was stranded at wherever the*

evening's fund-raising event had been held. Not in the place itself, but outside, in the street. The "stars" had left, everyone had left. He was alone. He knew no one else in the city. Had found her number in the phone book. And had no money, no place to stay.

Could he, he asked, crash? He was tired, hungry, broke —and even in the South had had no job, other than the Movement, for months. Et cetera.

When he arrived, she had placed our only steak knife in the waistband of her jeans.

He had asked for a drink of water. She gave him orange juice, some cheese, and a couple of slices of bread. She had told him he might sleep on the church pew and he had lain down with his head on his rolled-up denim jacket. She had retired to her room, locked the door, and tried to sleep. She was amazed to discover herself worrying that the church pew was both too narrow and too hard.

At first he muttered, groaned, and cursed in his sleep. Then he fell off the narrow church pew. He kept rolling off. At two in the morning she unlocked her door, showed him her knife, and invited him to share her bed.

Nothing whatever happened except they talked. At first, only he talked. Not about the rape, but about his life.

"He was a small person physically, remember?" Luna asked me. (She was right. Over the years he had grown big and, yes, burly, in my imagination, and I'm sure in hers.) "That night he seemed tiny. A child. He was still fully dressed, except for the jacket and he, literally, hugged his side of the bed. I hugged mine. The whole bed, in fact, was between us. We were merely hanging to its edges."

At the fund-raiser—on Fifth Avenue and Seventy-first Street, as it turned out—his leaders had introduced him as the unskilled, barely literate, former Southern fieldworker that he was. They had pushed him at the rich people gathered there as an example of what "the system" did to "the little people" in the South. They asked him to tell about the 37 times he had been jailed. The 35 times he had been beaten. The one time he had lost consciousness in the "hot" box. They told him not to worry about his grammar. "Which, as you may recall," said Luna, "was horrible." Even so, he had tried to censor his "ain'ts" and his "us'es." He had been painfully aware that he was on exhibit, like Frederick Douglass had been for the Abolitionists. But unlike Douglass he had no oratorical gift, no passionate language, no silver tongue. He knew the rich people and his own leaders perceived he was nothing: a broken man, unschooled, unskilled at anything . . .

Yet he had spoken, trembling before so large a crowd of rich, white Northerners—who clearly thought their section of the country would never have the South's racial problems—begging, with the painful stories of his wretched life, for their money.

At the end, all of them—the black leaders, too—had gone. They left him watching the taillights of their cars, recalling the faces of the friends come to pick them up: the women dressed in African print that shone, with elaborately arranged hair, their jewelry sparkling, their perfume exotic. They were so beautiful, yet so strange. He could not imagine that one of them could comprehend his life. He did not ask for a ride, because of that, but also because he had no place to go. Then he had remembered Luna.

Soon Luna would be required to talk. She would mention her confusion over whether, in a black community surrounded by whites with a history of lynching blacks, she had a right to scream as Freddie Pye was raping her. For her, this was the crux of the matter.

And so they would continue talking through the night.

This is another ending, created from whole cloth. If I believed Luna's story about the rape, and I did (had she told anyone else I might have dismissed it), then this reconstruction of what might have happened is as probable an accounting as any is liable to be. Two people have now become "characters."

I have forced them to talk until they reached the stumbling block of the rape, *which they must remove themselves,* before proceeding to a place from which it will be possible to insist on a society in which Luna's word alone on rape can never be used to intimidate an entire people, and in which an innocent black man's protestation of innocence of rape is unprejudicially heard. Until such a society is created, relationships of affection between black men and white women will always be poisoned—from within as from without—by historical fear and the threat of violence, and solidarity among black and white women is only rarely likely to exist.

POSTSCRIPT: HAVANA, CUBA, NOVEMBER, 1976

I am in Havana with a group of other black American artists. We have spent the morning apart from our Cuban hosts bringing each other up to date on the kind of work (there are no apolitical artists among us) we are doing in the United States. I have read "Luna."

High above the beautiful city of Havana I sit in the Havana Libre pavilion with the muralist/photographer in our group. He is in his mid-thirties, a handsome, brown, erect individual whom I have known casually for a number of years. During the sixties he designed and painted street murals for both SNCC and the Black Panthers, and in an earlier discussion with Cuban artists he showed impatience with their explanation of why we had seen no murals covering some of the city's rather dingy walls: Cuba, they had said, unlike Mexico, has no mural tradition. "But the point of a revolution," insisted Our Muralist, "is to make new traditions!" And he had pressed his argument with such passion for the *usefulness,* for revolutionary communication, of his craft, that the Cubans were both exasperated and impressed. They drove us around the city for a tour of their huge billboards, all advancing socialist thought and the heroism of men like Lenin, Ca-

milo, and Che Guevara, and said, "These, *these* are our
'murals'!"

While we ate lunch, I asked Our Muralist what he'd
thought of "Luna." Especially the appended section.

"Not much," was his reply. "Your view of human weakness is too biblical," he said. "You are unable to conceive
of the man without conscience. The man who cares nothing about the state of his soul because he's long since sold
it. In short," he said, "you do not understand that some
people are simply evil, a disease on the lives of other people, and that to remove the disease altogether is prefera-
ble to trying to interpret, contain, or forgive it. Your
'Freddie Pye,'" and he laughed, "was probably raping
white women on the instructions of his government."

Oh ho, I thought. Because, of course, for a second, during which I stalled my verbal reply, this comment made
both very little and very much sense.

"I *am* sometimes naïve and sentimental," I offered. I
am sometimes both, though frequently by design. Admission in this way is tactical, a stimulant to conversation.

"And shocked at what I've said," he said, and laughed
again. "Even though," he continued, "you know by now
that blacks could be hired to blow up other blacks, and
could be hired *by someone* to shoot down Brother Malcolm, and hired *by someone* to provide a diagram of Fred
Hampton's bedroom so the pigs could shoot him easily
while he slept, you find it hard to believe a black man
could be hired *by someone* to rape white women. But
think a minute, and you will see why it is the perfect
disruptive act. Enough blacks raping or accused of raping
enough white women and any political movement that
cuts across racial lines is doomed.

"Larger forces are at work than your story would indicate," he continued. "You're still thinking of lust and rage,
moving slowly into aggression and purely racial hatred.
But you should be considering money—which the rapist
would get, probably from your very own tax dollars, in
fact—and a maintaining of the status quo; which those hiring the rapist would achieve. I know all this," he said,

"because when I was broke and hungry and selling my blood to buy the food and the paint that allowed me to work, I was offered such 'other work.'"

"But you did not take it."

He frowned. "There you go again. How do you know I didn't take it? It paid, and I was starving."

"You didn't take it," I repeated.

"No," he said. "A black and white 'team' made the offer. I had enough energy left to threaten to throw them out of the room."

"But even if Freddie Pye *had been* hired *by someone* to rape Luna, that still would not explain his second visit."

"Probably nothing will explain that," said Our Muralist. "But assuming Freddie Pye *was* paid to disrupt—by raping a white woman—the black struggle in the South, he may have wised up enough later to comprehend the significance of Luna's decision not to scream."

"So you are saying he *did have* a conscience?" I asked.

"Maybe," he said, but his look clearly implied I would never understand anything about evil, power, or corrupted human beings in the modern world.

But of course he is wrong.

NTOZAKE SHANGE

Any consideration of the work of Ntozake Shange must necessarily begin with her choreopoem, "for colored girls who have considered suicide when the rainbow is enuf," not just because it was a successful 1976 Broadway hit and nationally and internationally acclaimed, but because never in the history of American theater have we seen an entire drama devoted to powerful and recognizable images of black women. Black women have never seen so much of themselves on the American stage. In this work Shange took some of the central realities of black women's lives and shaped them with the vocabulary, the grammar, the rhythms and the sensitivities of black women. What emerges is not a single monolithic view of *the black woman* but fourteen stories of fourteen different black women speaking each in her unique voice but reflecting an experience shared by thousands of other women. From a wild teen-aged graduation night party to the agonies of abortion and failed love affairs, "for colored girls . . ." communicates lyrically and passionately the sound and fury of black women's lives.

Though Shange's choreopoem has earned some tough criticism as being apolitical and ahistorical,[1] and to some

[1] In her critique "Considering Suicide," Andrea Benton Rushing says the play is "shockingly ahistorical" in its failure to show racism as the major cause of black women's oppression. Rushing's most potent criticism of "for colored girls" is that the women in the play exist in isolation from the twin axes of black culture—the extended family and the black church:

The women in "For Colored Girls" are single. Except for Crystal, they don't have children . . . They don't have brothers, fathers, or uncles; . . . the ladies of the rainbow have no mothers, aunties, grandmothers, sisters, cousins, godmothers, play aunts, or play sisters. They have no christenings, funerals or weddings to go to and be buoyed extent male-oriented, since the women's destinies seem to be determined by the bad or good behavior of men, the power of this drama is undeniable. From New York to San Francisco, the women in the audience laughed, cried and shouted their recognition and approval. Hardly anyone was unmoved. Clearly, Shange has done what Adrienne Rich has challenged the woman artist to do in her essay "When we Dead Awaken": to convert "female anger and the furious awareness of the Man's power over her" into the materials of poetry.[2] From the opening moments of the play when the lady in red announces that she is ending an affair with a man who "has been of no assistance" to her to the song of solidarity all the women sing together at the end, "for colored girls" is driven by a woman's pain, a woman's anger, a woman's need to survive, to demand her space in the world: "this is a woman's trip & i need my stuff."

In her Introduction to a new book of poems, *nappy edges*,[3] Shange says that for the past three years her work has been entirely woman-centered. The time she has spent in a close community with other women artists is helping her to break through the ignorance about women's realities, to find the common symbols that women share, to clarify women's needs:

> *the collective recognition of certain realities that are female can still be hampered, diverted, diluted by a masculine presence. yes. i segregated my work & took it to women. much like i wd take fresh water to people stranded in the mohave desert. i wdnt take a camera crew to observe me. i wdnt ask the people*

and challenged by, no neighborhood's pride to push them on to college, no families (nuclear or extended) to harass and nourish and soothe them. They are isolated and alienated as the typical, middle-class, single white woman in contemporary urban America and that is probably part of the reason the play succeeds with white audiences.

[2] In *Woman As Writer*, ed. Jeannette L. Webber and Joan Grumman, Houghton Mifflin Company, 1978, p. 125.

[3] St. Martin's Press, 1978.

> *who had never known thirst to come watch the thirsty
> people drink*[4]

Nourished and shaped by her artistic collaboration with
women, Shange is emerging as an even more forceful and
uncompromising spokesperson for women's liberation. She
is totally clear about what happens when women demand
artistic validity for their own personal symbols:

> *i mean a man can get personal in his work when he
> talks politics or bout his dad/but women start alla
> this foolishness bout their bodies & blood & kids
> & what's really goin on at home/well & that ain't
> poetry/that's goo-ey gaw/female stuff*[5]

In spite of the opposition, or perhaps because of it, and
with the help of other women, Shange has developed a
formidable stance:

> *these stains & scars are mine
> this is my space
>   i am not movin*

The two stories in this anthology indicate that Shange
locates much of women's oppression in the sexual arena.
In "comin to terms," Mandy's growing need to be solitary[6]
is only a prologue to the demand for selfhood. Because of
the weight of her own assertions, she finds a man's body, a
man's incessant demands and needs an intolerable burden.
The refusal of sex is merely the ground level in the con-
struction of a new relationship between them. Like any
other builders they will have to "come to terms" before
a new edifice can be erected, and there will be no assumptions.

[4] From Introduction to *nappy edges*, p. 22.
[5] *nappy edges*, p. 13.
[6] The solitary woman, sitting alone at night with coffee and
cigarette, the children asleep in the bedroom, grabbing a few
precious moments for herself in the still hours of night, is a re-
curring figure in women's fiction. It appears in Marilyn French's
The Women's Room, Paule Marshall's "Reena," and Tillie Olsen's "Tell Me a Riddle," to name only three.

In "aw, babee, you so pretty" there are larger social and political implications. The men in the story are poor and black living in any Caribbean country where they exist as colonized subjects. In the lobbies of hotels, they accost the young black women tourists, plying their trade —which is essentially selling themselves in exchange for a chance to leave the Islands. In New York the same ritual is played out by a brilliant but starving sculptor who, of course, needs a place to stay. The ending is different this time, as the woman is admonished to resist the cheap come-on, instead of melting into a romantic fantasy. To the soft, fake, male flattery she is urged to answer in tones of steel and caution and thereby recover her own perspective.

aw, babee,
you so pretty

BY NTOZAKE SHANGE

not only waz she without a tan, but she held her purse
close to her hip like a new yorker or someone who rode
the paris métro. she waz not from here, but from there.

there some coloureds, negroes, blacks, cd make a living
big enough to leave there to come here: but no one went
there much any more for all sorts of reasons. the big
reason being immigration restrictions & unemployment.
nowadays, immigration restrictions of every kind apply to
any non-european persons who want to go there from
here. just like unemployment applies to most non-
european persons without titles of nobility or north american university training. some who want to go there from
here risk fetching trouble with the customs authority
there. or later with the police, who can tell who's not from
there cuz the shoes are pointed & laced strange/the pants
be for august & yet it's january/the accent is patterned for
port-au-prince, but working in crown heights. what makes
a person comfortably ordinary here cd make him dangerously conspicuous there.

so some go to london or amsterdam or paris, where they
are so many no one tries to tell who is from where. still
the far right wing of every there prints lil pamphlets that
say everyone from here shd leave there & go back where
they came from.

anyway the yng woman i waz discussing waz from
there & she was alone. that waz good. cuz if a man had no
big brother in groningen. no aunt in rouen. no sponsor in
chicago. this brown woman from there might be a good
idea. everybody knows that rich white girls are hard to

find. some of them joined the weather underground, some the baader-meinhof gang. a whole bunch of them gave up men entirely. so the exotic-lover-in-the-sun routine becomes more difficult to swing/if she wants to talk abt plastic explosives & the resistance of the black masses to socialism insteada giving head as the tide slips in or lending money just for the next few days. is hard to find a rich white girl who is so dumb, too.

anyway, the whole world knows, european & non-european alike, the whole world knows that nobody loves the black woman like they love farrah fawcett-majors. the whole world dont turn out for a dead black woman like they did for marilyn monroe. (actually, the demise of josephine baker waz an international event, but she waz also a war hero) the worldwide un-beloved black woman is a good idea, if she is from there & one is a yng man with gd looks, piercing eyes, knowledge of several romantic languages, the best dancing spots, the hill where one can see the entire bay at twilight, the beach where the seals & pelicans run free, the hidden "local" restaurants; or in paris, a métro map. in mexico city the young man might know where salsa is played, not that the jalisco folklorico is not beautiful. but if she is from there & black she might want to dance a dance more familiar. such a yng man with such information exists in great numbers everywhere. he stops a yng woman with her bag on her hip, demanding she come to his house for dinner that night. (they are very hospitable) when the black woman from there says she must go to antwerp at 6:oo/ he says, then, when she comes back. his friends agree. (they are persistent) he asks, as he forces his number into her palm, are you alone. this is important. for the yng man from here with designs on a yng woman from there respects the territorial rights of another man, if he's in the country.

that is how the approach to the black woman works in the street. "aw babee/ you so pretty" begins often in the lobby of hotels where the bright handsome yng men wd be loiterers were they not needed to tend the needs of the black women from there. tourists are usually white people or asians who didnt come all this way to meet a black woman who isnt even foreign. so the hotel managers wink an eye at the yng men in the lobby or by the bar who wd be loitering, but they are going to help her have a gd time. maybe help themselves, too.

everybody in the world, everybody knows the black woman from there is not treated as a princess, as a jewel, a cherished lover. that's not how sapphire got her reputation, nor how mrs. jefferson perceives the world. "you know/ babee/ you dont act like them. aw babee/ you so pretty."

the yng man in the hotel watches the yng black woman sit & sit & sit, while the european tourists dance with one another & the dapper local fellas mambo frenetically with secretaries from arizona. in search of the missing rich white girl. so our girl sits & sits & sits & sits. maybe she is courageous & taps her foot. maybe she is bold & enjoys the music, smiling, shaking shoulders. let her sit & know she is unwanted. she is not white and she is not from here. let her know she is not pretty enough to dance the next merengue. then appear, mysteriously, in the corner of the bar. stare at her. just stare. when stevie wonder's song "isn't she lovely" blares thru the red-tinted light, ask her to dance & hold her as tyrone power wda. hold her & stare. dance yr ass off. she has been discovered by the non-european fred astaire. let her know she is a surprise . . . an event. by the look on yr face you've never seen anyone like this. black woman from there. you say, "aw/ you not from here?" totally astonished. she murmurs that she is from there. as if to apologize for her unfortunate place of birth, you say, "aw babee/ you so pretty." & it's all over.

a night in a pension near the sorbonne. pick her up from the mattress. throw her gainst the wall in a show of exotic temper & passion: *"maintenant, tu es ma femme. nous nous sommes mariés."* unions of this sort are common wherever the yng black women travel alone. a woman travelling alone is an affront to the non-european man, who is known the world over, to european & non-european

alike, for his way with women, his sense of romance, how
he can say "aw babee/ you so pretty" & even a beautiful
woman will believe no one else ever recognized her loveli-
ness, till he came along.

he comes to a café in willemstad in the height of the
sunset. an able-bodied, sinewy yng man who wants to buy
one beer for the yng woman. after the first round, he discovers he has run out of money. so she must buy the next
round, when he discovers what beautiful legs she has,
how her mouth is like the breath of tiger lilies. the taxi
driver doesnt speak english, but he knows to drop his
countryman off before he takes the yng woman to her
hotel. the tab is hers.

but hers are, also, the cheeks that grandma pinches, if
the yng man has honorable intentions. all the family will
meet the yng black woman from there. the family has
been worried abt this yng man for a while. non-european
families dont encourage bachelors. bachelorhood is a career we associate with the white people: dandies on the
order of errol flynn, robert de niro. the non-european men
have women. some women they marry & stay with forever. get chicken on sunday (chicken fricassee, arroz con
pollo, poulet grillee, smothered chicken, depending on
what kinda black woman she is & whether she is from
here or there). then some women they just are with for
years or a day. but our families do expect a yng man to
waltz in with somebody at sometime. & if she's from there,
the family's very excited. they tell the yng woman abt
where they are from & how she cd almost be from the
same place, except she is from there. but more rousing
than coincidental genealogical traits is the torrid declara-
tion: "we shall make love in the . . . how you call it/ yes
in the earth, in the dirt. i will have you . . . in my . . .
how you say . . . where things grow . . . aw/ yes. i will
have you in the soil." probably under the stars & smelling
of wine an unforgettable international affair can be con-
summated.

at 11:30 one evening i waz at the port authority, new
york, united states, myself. now i was there & i spoke eng-

lish & i waz holding approximately $7 american currency, when a yng man from there came up to me from the front of the line of people waiting for the princeton new jersey united states local bus. i mean to say, he gave up his chance for a good seat to come say to me: "i never saw a black woman reading nietzsche." i waz demure enough, i said i had to for a philosophy class. but as the night went on i noticed this yng man waz so much like the yng men from here who use their bodies as bait & their smiles as passport alternatives. anyway the night did go on. we were snuggled together in the rear of the bus going down the jersey turnpike. he told me in english/ which he had spoken all his life in st. louis/ where he waz raised/ that he had wanted all his life to meet someone like me/ he wanted me to meet his family, who hadnt seen him in a long time, since he left missouri looking for opportunity/ opportunity to sculpt. he had been everyplace, he said, & i waznt like any black woman he had ever met anywhere. there or here. he had come back to new york cuz of immigration restrictions & high unemployment among black american sculptors abroad.

just as we got to princeton, he picked my face up from his shoulder where i had been fantasizing like mad & said: "aw babee/ you so pretty." i believe that night i must have looked beautiful for a black woman from there. though a black woman from anywhere cd be asked at any moment to tour the universe. to climb a six-story walk-up with a brilliant & starving painter. to share kadushi. to meet mama. to getta kiss each time the swing falls toward the willow branch. to imagine where he say he from. & more/ she cd/ she cd have all of it/ she cd not be taken/ long as she dont let a stranger be the first to say: "aw babee/ you so pretty." after all, immigration restrictions & unemployment cd drive a man to drink or to lie. so if you know yr beautiful & bright & cherishable awready. when he say, in whatever language, "aw babee/ you so pretty," you cd say, "i know, thank you." & then when he asks yr name again cuz yr answer was inaudible. you cd

say: "difficult." then he'll smile. & you'll smile. he'll say:
"what nice legs you have." you can say: "yes. they run in
the family."

"aw babee/ i've never met any one like you."

"that's strange. there are millions of us."

"the suspect is black & always in his early 20's"

FRENCHY HODGES

Born in Dublin, Georgia, in 1940, Frenchy Hodges lived nearly all her growing-up years in the rural South. She went to school in Georgia, including two years at Clark College, in Atlanta. She graduated from Fort Valley State College, in Fort Valley, Georgia. During her college years she spent summers in the North at domestic jobs that the college summer program provided. After two years of teaching English in Georgia, Hodges migrated North in 1966 to Detroit, where she taught English and creative writing in inner-city junior and senior high schools. In 1977 she returned South and is now teaching in Atlanta.

Knowing the various migrations of Frenchy Hodges is essential to understanding her poetry and fiction, because her unique sensibility is a hybrid: a black, southern, rural sensibility transplanted to the North. One of her most anthologized poems, *Belle Isle* (in *Black Wisdom*, Broadside Press, 1971) reveals that duality. Belle Isle, a park in Detroit that in the 1960s became a summer haven for the city's black and mostly poor population, is used to symbolize their ability to transcend the harsh urban reality. The park is transformed by the warmth, wit, and coping power of the folk who use it, and it becomes a surrogate for the front porch they left in the South.

Remembering what front porches meant to blacks in the South is part of Hodges' search for forgotten folk idioms. In another poem, entitled *Piece de Way Home*, from a book by the same title, Hodges recalls that that particular folk expression meant not only that you were grown up enough to go part of the way home with someone but it also announced your gaining a degree of independence from home. This remembrance of things past is not simply self-indulgent nostalgia. It is essential to her vision to re-establish connections with the values that nourish and strengthen her.

The failure of that vision is what assures the death of the young black man in Hodges' story "Requiem for Willie Lee." Because of the misuse of the earth and "good growing things," people like Willie Lee are not able to transcend their fate. Willie Lee is Bigger Thomas, Black Boy, Bobo, Big Boy—all the young blacks of this country whose very inheritance is to be repressed by physical and psychic violence. In "Requiem," Willie Lee is as threatening to the black middle-class schoolteacher as he once was to whites. The act of reconciliation between the schoolteacher and Willie Lee is a recurrent theme in black literature, from Ellison's *Invisible Man* to Paule Marshall's *Brown Girl, Brownstones.* Since all the Willie Lees of this society have been erased from history, it is the most profound act of recognition to see them. To see these invisible ones means confronting the terror of one's own invisibility. The schoolteacher-narrator knows Willie Lee but does not want to acknowledge him. She wants her vacation. She wants to be unmolested. In the story, she achieves sight when the fate of Willie Lee becomes more important than the luxury resort, rustic cabins, and sunning in leisure, when in fact she realizes that her fate and that of Willie Lee are one.

Requiem for Willie Lee

BY FRENCHY HODGES

I teach you know, and it was summer, one of the few times
we get to be like children again. Summers we pack up
and go somewhere that only rich folk year-round can afford. And if we can only afford a day and a night, we take
what we can get and do not count the loss. For twenty-
four hours we groove fine on the dollar we have to spend,
and in my purse with the credit cards was exactly eighteen
dollars: a ten, a five, and three ones.

El Habre is a rustic resort area halfway between Los
An and Sanfran. Not a swanky place, but fronting two
miles of the most beautiful oceanic view, the junglic-
beach is splattered with endless numbers of summer-
camp type cabins whitewashed and dingy gray measuring
about nine by nine and most of them claiming five sleeping places. Crowded with beds, they can only be used for
sleeping. Such is El Habre.

But El Habre has one thing more. El Habre has one
of the most popular clubhouses in the world and people
who have no intention of ever seeing the cabins—some
never even knowing they exist—come to enjoy the fun, the
food, and the fine show of stars. So, one lazy summer afternoon near the end of my vacation, Gaile (my hostess) and
I and her little girl Donaile set out in my trusty old Mer-
cedes for remote El Habre.

Now we, like many people, didn't know of the need for
reservations and we experienced a foreboding of the wait
to come when we saw the acres and acres of cars in the
Temporary Guests' parking lot. We parked and were ushered by red-coated attendants through a multi-turnstile

entrance to a waiting room as we cracked private jokes about the three of us and the only occasional dark faces in evidence among the sea of white. The waiting room was a comfortable no-nonsense place with white straight-backed chairs placed everywhere. There were perhaps a hundred people or more. Only three others were black, an older couple looking for all the world like contented grand-parents, which in fact they were, as we learned from the restless little boy of about four who was with them. To my right were two hippie couples making jokes and telling stories about places they'd been and things they'd done. Most of the people were encouraging them to keep up this light show by laughing animatedly at every joke and story punch line. I was sorta enjoying them myself, exchanging "ain't-they-sick" glances with Gaile as we kept a wary eye on Donaile across the room playing with the little grand-boy.

Somewhere in the middle of all this, the door burst open and in came Willie Lee, tall, lean, reed-slender, country-sun-and-rain-black, and out of place. In his right hand was a little girl's. With his left he closed the door. He then thrust this hand to some hidden place in the bosom of his black denim jacket and stood for a moment deliberately surveying the room. Though he had a pleasant mischievous schoolboy face, he seemed to be about twenty-two or three. Right away I knew him. Well, not *him,* but from some wellspring of intuition I knew into him and sensed some sinister intent enter that room in the winsome grin and bold arresting gaze that played around the room.

Silence played musical chairs around the group and the hippies were *it,* ending a story that was just begun. All eyes were on the man and the child at the door.

He swaggered Saturday-night-hip-style to a seat across the room from Gaile and me, sat, and the little girl leaned between his knees looking smug and in-the-know about something she knew and we did not. Willie Lee his name was, he said, but somewhere later I heard the child call him Bubba.

Oh, Willie Lee, where did you come from and why are you here where you don't belong with that do-rag on your head, and those well-worn used-to-be-bright-tan riding boots on your feet, and that faded blue sweat shirt and those well-worn familiar-looking faded dungarees? Willie Lee, why did you come here and I know it's a gun or a knife in your jacket where your left hand is and you ain't gonna spoil my last-of-summer holiday!

"What do you think?" *sotto voce,* I said to Gaile.

"Methinks the deprived has arrived," *sotto voce,* her reply.

From the time he entered, he took over.

"Don't let me stop nothing, gray boys," he said to the storytellers. "We just come to have some fun. Yeah! Spread around the goodwill!" He threw back his head and laughed.

That was when I noticed fully the little girl. She was watching him, laughing to him like she knew what was to come and was deliciously waiting, watching him for the sign. She seemed to be about nine. He stuck out his hand and carefully looked at his watch.

"Yeah!" he said, stretching out his legs from some imaginary lounge chair. "Whatcha say, Miss Schoolteacher?" He laughed, looking boldly amused at me.

Years of teaching and I knew him. Smart, a sharp mind, very intelligent and perceptive but reached by so many forces before me, yet coming sometimes and wanting something others had not given, others who didn't know how, some not knowing he needed, grown in the street and weaned on corners, in alleys, and knowing only a wild creative energy seeking something all humans need. I knew him, looked in his eyes and perceived the soul lost and wandering inside.

"I say forget it, Willie Lee. That's what I say."

A momentary look of recognition crossed his face and when he realized what we both knew, he laughed a laugh of surprise that even here some remnant of his failed past jumped out to remind him of the child he'd been, yet appreciating too, I think, that here it was he in charge, not I.

Gaile had tensed as I spoke. "Come here a minute, Baby," she called to Donaile, but the child was already on her way to her mother, and quickly positioned herself between her legs. She stood facing this newly arrived pair and stared at them. The little girl, Willie's sister he said, made a face at the smaller child who then hid her face in her mother's lap. Still, I looked at Willie Lee. Then I looked away, regretting having acknowledged his person only to have that acknowledgement flung laughingly back in my face, and I resolved to have no more to say to him but to try and figure out what his plan was and how to escape it unharmed.

Again, he must have read my mind.

"Folks," he said, "my sister and I just come to have a little fun. She's had a little dry run of what to expect, and it's coming her birthday and I told her, 'Donna,' I say, 'I'ma let you have a little piece of the action up at El Habre.' She'll be seven next week, you know, and well, it's good to learn things while you young." He laughed again.

Then turned to a flushed-looking man sitting on his left.

"Hey, Pops, how's business on Wall Street?" That laugh again.

The poor man looked for help around the room and finding none in the carefully averted eyes, finally perceived Willie Lee waiting soberly for his answer.

"Nnnnn-not in the ssss-stockmarket," he said, to which Willie Lee guffawed.

I found myself looking intently at that laughing face, trying to figure out what to do and how to do it. I reviewed the entrance from the parking lot. We'd come through a turnstile such as large amusement parks have and we'd been ushered to this side room to wait for reservations. Now where were those uniformed ushers who'd directed us here? One had come and called out a party of five about forty minutes ago. I decided to give up my waiting position and be content to read about this fiasco in tomorrow's paper.

So deciding, I stood up resolutely, took Donaile's hand

and said to Gaile, "Let's go," and started for the door.
The whole room stumbled from its trance to begin the
same pilgrimage.

Coldly, "Stop where you are, *everybody!*" he said,
arresting us, and we turned to look at him standing and
calmly holding a gun.

Defeated, I dropped the child's hand and stood there
watching the others return to their original seats.

You will not hurt me, Willie Lee. I stood still, looking
at him.

"Slim, you and the sister can go if you want to," he
said looking levelly at me. Dreamlike I saw a little lost
boy sitting in my class, wanting something—love maybe
—but too lost, misguided and misbegotten and too far
along on a course impossible to change and too late if we
but knew how.

"Thank you," I said, and Gaile and I went out the door,
each of us holding one of Donaile's hands.

Something was wrong at the turnstiles, and the sky had
turned cloudy and dark. Instead of the neatly dressed
ushers we'd seen coming in, there were two do-rags-under-
dingy-brim-hatted fellows wearing old blue denims and
black denim jackets calmly smoking in the graying day.

When they saw us, I felt the quick tension as cigarettes
were halted in midair.

"Where y'all going, Sistuhs?" the short pudgy one said.

"We got tired of waitin' and *he* said we could go," I
answered, standing still and looking at them intently.

They looked at each other a moment.

Then, "I think y'all better wait a while longer," the tall
droopy-eyed one said.

Some sixth sense told me we'd be safer inside, and then
I saw the bulge of the gun at the pudgy one's side stick-
ing from the waist of his pants.

"You're probably right," I said, and with studied cas-
ualness, we turned and went back to the room we'd just
left.

Things had started to happen inside. Willie Lee was

brandishing the little black and sinister gun as he methodically went to each person collecting any valuables people were wearing and money from pockets and bags.

"Get your money out, Slim," he said to me as we came back inside.

Distinctly, I remember returning to my seat, locating my billfold, extracting eight dollars—the five and three ones, thinking I'd not give any more than I *had* to and holding the three ones in my hand and stashing the five in my skirt pocket.

He was snatching watches from wrists and rings from fingers and making people empty their pockets and purses to him and putting these things in a dingy little laundry bag with a drawstring. People seemed dazed in their cooperation while the little girl, Donna, carted booty from all over the room in wild and joyful glee. The room was hot and deathly quiet. Then her hand was in my skirt pocket and she was gone to him and his bag with my three singles and the five.

Gaile was just sitting there and Donaile was leaning quietly between her legs. And I was thinking. Where is everybody? What have they done to them? We'd heard nothing before *he* came. Then I heard something. I heard the sirens and my mouth dropped open. Oh, no! Don't come now. I sat wishing they had not come just then with Willie's job unfinished and the child in the throes of her wild pre-birthday glee!

Then he was standing in front of me.

"I'm sorry, Slim, but you see how it is!" he said with amused resolution.

He grabbed the not-on-Wall-Street man, pushed him roughly toward the door.

"Okay, everybody out," he said.

Things got confusing then. Outside we vaguely heard shouts and what I guess was gunfire, and not the holiday fireworks it sounded like. We all went rushing to the door. The door got jammed, then was not. More shots were heard and screams and cries. Outside, amid rushing legs, a turnstile smoker lay groaning and bleeding on the ground. The child Donna ran screaming to where he groaned and lay. Holding tight to Donaile's hand, Gaile and I ran toward the turnstile amid wild and crowded confusion. Then someone was holding me.

"Let me go!"

"Bitch, come with me!" a mean voice said. "You too, Bitch, and bring the kid!" This to Gaile.

We were shoved and pushed into the rear seat of a Scaporelli's Flower Delivery station wagon. Crowded next to us were the two hippie girls clinging to each other and crying. The back doors were slammed, and Willie Lee hustled the pleading Wall Street man in the front seat, jumping in behind him. And Droopy-Eye of the turnstile jumped in the driver's seat, and started the car. Donaile was crying and clinging to Gaile. The course we took was bizarre and rash because people were running everywhere. And still more people were running from the gilded entrance of the El Habre Clubhouse to scatter confusedly along the course we sped. Too many people scattered along this fenced-in service drive where running people and a racing car should never be. He tried to dodge them at first, blowing his horn, but they would not hear and heed, so soon he was knocking them down, murdering his way toward a desperate freedom. The blond hippie girl began to heave and throw up on her friend. I closed my eyes begging the nightmare end. And then I smelled the flowers. Looking back, I saw them silently sitting there.

I looked at the back of Willie Lee's head, where he, hunched forward, gun in hand, tensely peered ahead.

"Willie Lee, it just won't work." I kept my eyes on the back of his head.

"Shut up, Bitch," Droopy-Eye said.

Willie Lee looked back to me.

"Man, that's Miss Schoolteacher. She knows *everything*," he exaggerated. "Slim, it'll work 'cause *you* part of our exit ticket now, since Ol' Sam here brought y'all in."

"Willie Lee, give it up," I said.

"Man, let's dump the dizzy bitch! I was just grabbing

anybody," he excused himself. Then as an afterthought, "I never did like schoolteachers no way."

Then up ahead they saw the gate.

"Hey, Sam, crash that gate. No time to stop," Willie said, peering behind.

"Man, ain't no cops gonna run down no people. You got time to open that gate!" This from a man who'd run people down.

Willie Lee peered again through the flowers at the road behind.

"Willie Lee, the road will end when you reach the gate. It's a dirt road then where you have to go slow, unless," I added, "you're ready to die and meet your maker."

"Damn, this bitch think she know everything!" Droopy-Eye said while Willie Lee just looked at me.

Donaile was crying still. Gaile was too. Wall Street was now quietly sitting there, just sitting and staring straight ahead. The hippie girls were crying.

I turned around and looked behind. The running people had receded in the distance, framed in stage-like perspective by the big El Habre Clubhouse where we'd been going to enjoy an afternoon show. And tomorrow my vacation would end, if my life didn't end today.

Droopy-Eye stopped the car and Willie Lee got out and opened the gate. Now began dust and sand as the station wagon plowed too fast down the gravelly, dusty road. Down before us, we could see the ocean's white-capped waves. And between us and the ocean was the circular courtyard flanked by four or five small buildings and one other building larger than the rest.

"The road will end at those buildings," I said. "What you gonna do then, Willie Lee?"

"I'ma chunk yo' ass in the ocean, Bitch, if you don't shut up."

I kept looking levelly at Willie Lee. He kept hunched forward looking down the slowly ending road. We reached the courtyard entrance, a latticed, ivy-covered archway, and Droopy drove the station wagon through.

"Oh, shit, the road *do* end!" Droopy moaned as he stopped the car.

When the motor was cut, we heard the ocean's waves, and back in the distance, the people running and screaming behind. Why are they coming this way, I wondered, remembering the time we kids ran home to our burning house. They must be cabin dwellers, I thought.

"What now, Willie Lee?" I said.

Willie and Droopy jumped out of the car.

"Okay, everybody out!" Willie directed.

When Wall Street, the last, had finally climbed out, Willie shouted, "Okay, Slim, y'all take off. Sam, you take Wall Street, and the two girls come with me." And they began to hustle the three toward the bigger building with the cafeteria sign.

Thank you, Willie Lee, for letting me free. Gaile and Donaile ran toward the woods where the cabins were and where beyond was the busy sea. As I ran behind them, I looked back to see Sam and Willie crashing in the cafeteria door, dragging and pushing the man and the girls inside, just as a Wonder Bread truck began to enter the courtyard from behind. It was filled with guns-ready police. I screamed to Gaile to wait for me.

When we'd reached the bottom of the hill, we heard shouting and gunfire. We ran on cutting right to a service path that led through the green woods lush with undergrowth. About every fifty feet on either side of the path were the cabins, whitewashed, dank and gray. Running and running, stopping some to breathe and rest and to try and soothe the terrified child. *You shouldn't have come here, Willie Lee, bringing your sister to see you fail.* Soon we heard others coming, loud and excited in the tragedy of this day.

Why couldn't you stop, Willie Lee, when it started going wrong and kept on going that way? You're not a fool, because I know you from each year you've been in my classes, and when I've tried to teach you, reach you, touch you, love you, you've snarled "Take your hands off me"

*and I've kept myself to myself and tried my best to forget
every one of you and this afternoon at El Habre was part
of my plan to get as far away from you as I can and here
you are set on tearing up my turf. Will I never get away
from you?*

Once while I stopped resting, some people passed.

"They killed the one with the droopy-eyes," they said,
"but the other was only wounded and got away."

"He's coming this way, they say."

Then another: "I got my gun in the cabin. When I git
it, I'ma help hunt'im and I hope I get to blow'im away."

"They say he's looking for his girlfriend, a teacher or
somebody that got away."

*Willie Lee, why are you looking for me? Why don't you
give yourself up and die? Will I never get away from you?*

"Gaile, I've got to go find him," I said. "You take
Donaile and try to get away."

I didn't stay for her protest but started walking resolutely back over the path we'd come. The day was dark
and the woods were dark and the clouds were dark in
the sky. I met and passed people who looked curiously
at me. He is looking for me, I thought, and maybe they
wondered, thought they knew. I had visions of him knocking people down, shooting anyone trying to stop him, keep
him from having his way. Still, why *was* he looking for
me? And then I knew. For the same reason I was now
looking for him. He was my student who'd failed and I
was the teacher who'd failed him. Not for hostage, not
for harm, but to die! To die near me who knew him. Well,
not *him*, but knew into him just the same. He, who's going to die. Is dying. And now he knows. And I'm the only
person who knows him and can love the little boy hurting inside.

His jacket was gone and so was his do-rag and blood
was caked in his straightened unkempt hair. His eyes un-
seeing, he peered ahead and stumbled dying past me.

"Willie Lee," I called his name.

He stopped and in slow motion, semi-crouched, gun
half-raised, he turned, peering at me through time. In the

green-gray light, I opened wide my arms and silently bade him come. He dropped his gun and came paining into my arms.

It was another world then. People continued to run by bumping us as they did. Glancing about, I saw a cabin nearby.

"Let's go in here," I said.

"Yeah, this what I want," he said. "Someplace to stop."

I looked inside and saw the cabin was bare except for the beds. I climbed through the door and helped him in, leading him to the one double bed. Two singles above and one single below on the side.

"What is this place?" he asked in wonder as our eyes grew accustomed to the darker inside. Drab even in this darkened day.

"This is one of the resort cabins," I said. "Part of El Habre too."

"What do they *do* here?" he asked.

"Sun and swim and sleep," I said. "Hear the ocean on the beach below?"

"And for this, shit, people *pay?*" He gestured around the room in unbelieving wonder.

"Yes," I said, "for this, *Shit,*" I looked to him and was held by his waiting eyes, "people pay. For the sun and the earth and the good growing things and the moon, and the dawn and the dew, people take their hard-earned bread and come here and stay and pay. *They pay!*"

Until then, I had been calm. *Steady, Teach, or you'll lose again.* I softer added, "*We* pay. We all pay."

He was quiet then and dropped his head. He looked at his hands and then at his feet. Then he looked at me.

Soberly, "Well, I spoiled it for them today, didn't I? I spoiled it today real bad," he chuckled, "didn't I?" Then he threw back his head and laughed and laughed.

And I threw back my head and just laughed and laughed hugging him.

"Yes, you did!" I said. "Yes, you really did!"

Perhaps our laughter called the people. And there they were outside the cabin windows peering and laughing in.

I went to the windows then and gently pulled the shades and as best I could, I comforted the dying man, making a requiem for him, for myself, and for all the world's people who only know life through death.

Remember Him a Outlaw

BY ALEXIS DEVEAUX

remember him a outlaw. living in the bowery. didnt hardly work. he couldnt he roars. tobacco smiles. in baggy dove-colored khaki pants and big orange workboots. he is slew-foot. doing his wine walk. hips swaying west down 112 street. he tips his cap to the women. he grins at stoops. talking loud to other bums old friends. the sky or garbage. up the street at the corner of 5th & 112 he stops. to salute cars. to wait. to cross. his sober eye always leary. he crosses to our corner.

ma! ma! here come uncle willie! ma!
hey uncle willie!

mommie from somewhere inside the house runs to the window on instinct. she pops out. relief spreads over her yellow face. we run and climb at uncle willie. a mountain to jump on.

take me for a piggy-back uncle willie!
take me first!
look! i got on your hat uncle willie oooooh what you got in your pocket is that candy??

a long face melts in his shoulder cage. on his head hair beads. eyes like stars and rot-gut wine. medicine for his thick smooth lips. he sweats. his black skin wet tar. a reflection to look at and never see in. a cherub. an old womans son. uncle willie wasnt 43.

he is drunk. desperate to hold all of us. at the same time. he throws a few jabs to odell. ducks. fat vickie is teased. rosie runs to him. hugging me round the neck. twins we walk together. booboo and nell squint their eyes to look up. the sun has a new face.

up to the stoop uncle willie is a father who visits. knows we love him boisterous. he stops to see mommie in the 2nd floor window. she shakes her head and grins. glad to see him. saying nothing saying

willie nigger when you gon change?

uncle willie rears back in the heat. he sways. wipes sweat in a dingy rag from his neck. he throws back his head to talk

hey mae! mae! where you get all those ugly children from?
oh shut up. what you got in your pockets willie what you done stole?

the stoop is crowded with our friends. they stare and giggle. they are kidnapped. cannot play ball or rope. fascinated children at a circus. he is their uncle and pied piper. willie breaks up to laugh. he bends over. slaps his knees. we feel his pockets with silent permission. he winks at mommie

now mae you know i dont steal. borrows well what you borrowed?

we already know. cherries and penny-candies flow from his pockets. it is a stream. it cannot stop.

lord ha' mercy willie. they gon catch you one day on that market.
look mae. this my family. my nieces an nefew.
hope yall dont make no faggot outta him. they know uncle willie always gon bring them something they know uncle willie dont steal. yall give some to your lil friends.

we are bombarded from the ringside. fingers poke my face hungry. odell wants more candy. he is searching. he discovers in a back pocket. spanish neighbors snicker and point. in the window mommie laughs

willie! odell got your stuff!

odell is an imp running. his thin brown-body flies over the sidewalk. over cracks and cans. he cackles. escaping uncle willies chase

come back here boy! dont you fall and break my jug!
if you do ill break both your legs
come here boy!

odell stops to be caught. his miniature face a pearl shining sweat. uncle willie blows a sigh of relief. he chuckles. glad to have the pint of purple-wine back safe.

aint he something? dont know where you found that
one at mae. listen momma- im taking rose an lex on
the avenue. buy the kids some ice cream.
we be right back. rest of yall stay here.

we walk on 5th avenue with uncle willie. he stops every 2 feet. dudes who ran with his brother in 45 and then. numbers runners. fathers. enemies. remember when niggers wore clothes made in italy and talked mafia. up and down lenox avenue. on 5th. numbers. getting over the war of. the good cocaine guineas brought up town the year before real dope came. jim-jam is dead. 8th avenue turned dope. tried to cheat georgie out some pay off money. found him in the elevator. no head. remember the lames busted. still in there. old playmates. couldnt get high no more off gin or jonnie walker red.

uncle willie pulls us from behind him. marshmallow fingers squeeze and held our shy hands. we sweat and are introduced celebrities.

richie in the joint man. yeah. got a pound jack.
blew a nigger in 2 114 street. he dont play jack.
my brother. these his kids. dont they look like him?
mean an black just like they daddy.

richie kids? didnt know that yeah look just like richie
spit!
nawww man
sure they do
here honey. yall buy yourself something

coins roll out our hands to the sidewalk. silver dimes and
quarters run curving in circles. fall on their faces in the
gutter. uncle willie chases a nickel. under his boot its freedom is squashed.

we move from one stoop-crowd to another. down the
line uncle willie waves. talks. here is black-father the watermelon man. and miss king. always dressed in black.
summer or winter. old miss goldberg in the door of her
laundromat. spit creeps from a corner of her mouth. she
puffs a corn pipe. in front of her uncle willie stops. uncle
willie feels her dead tits. leaves. he makes her hairy face
turn pink for him. she dribbles as he walks away. she
dreams on one day having him. right in the laundromat.
on the ground me and rosie are hiding giggles.

uncle willie steps inside the ice cream place. on the big
stools our sandaled feet dangle high off the floor. uncle
willie reaches to kiss a big woman behind the counter.

nigger where you been? dont put your greasy lips on
me. much as you smell.
you know you like it. stop actin so funny.
your nigger must be somewhere in here. listen flossy-
let me have 6 cones. yeah 6. these richie kids. whats
the damage on that? put it on my bill you aint got no
bill here
long as this your store momma- i got me a bill

flossy looks at him. she smiles. her mouth pauses in a day
like this before. when uncle willie walked thru the
door. young and polished. he teases her. he waits for closing time. waits to claim the chocolate gold his night for
love.

the sun melts our ice cream-on-credit. outside uncle
willie hurries us to the block. we are 3 hurries. careful to

hold the melting vanilla drips over our fingers. against our
clothes. the 2 scoops disappear in to 1. we lick the sweet
cream from our hands. as it runs we turn the corner. back.

> ok mae   take care momma. im going over to see
> grammie. everybody got ice cream. uncle willie dont
> have nothing. dont get no kiss?

odell is always first to him. i am always last. we walk back
to the corner. watch as he fades across the street in colors
and noises up the west side. uncle willie moves. hips like a
swan. he stops to bum a cigarette. he shares his purple
magic and continues. the beginning of our sunset.

and after that when he moved out the bowery grammie
took him back. we moved to the bronx. always saw him
on saturdays 114 street. in front of 216. uncle willie
sweats. looking for a womans packages to carry up. to
collect his jug-money. tip his cap. downstairs he waits. he
spots me. grabs my hand. proud to own me. his sho-nuff
blood. rushed upstairs to see grammie. she pleads with me
not to stay long but to stay a virgin. she gives me my allowance. she kisses me behind the door. i say goodbye
and go. downstairs uncle willie is waiting.

> come on baby   ill walk you to the subway.
> momma give you your money? dont say nothing.
> shhh

we tip to 7th avenue. grammie rattles in the window. the
veins of her small throat strain and pop. she yells

> willie willie! dont you take that child money!
> dont worry about nothing momma!
> i aint gon take her money just walking to the train
> station. dont want none a these low niggers putting
> they hands on her thats all!

at the liquor store where grammie cannot see i give uncle
willie his 50 cent allowance. and wait briefly outside as he
turns my quarters into purple-sweet juice. he is a magi-
cian. war counselor. he is my main man. coming out grin-

ning. he clutches my shoulder. in his hand is love. we walk. for a quick taste he steps in a hallway. out of respect for me. it was easy to peep. him his head bent backwards. wine drops from his mouth. he jams his magic in a favorite pocket. uncle willie flows back into the light. every saturday our sacred routine. every year uncle willie and me.

til the week or summer richie came home. back to the pit. go down make it rich. to snort more poison. to infest his begging matter. hustle his mother. anybody. make a flunkie of his brothers love. for him uncle willie runs the street. collects his old boys together. spreads news richies out. boasting with pride when richie got his eldorado. never let uncle willie sit in the front seat. gratefully taking the 5s and 10s richie shoved at him saying

nigger you need to buy yourself some new clothes man raggidty as you is

pretty little black man. richie hill is a name. like 8th avenue. the powder he peddles. between niggers he shot and the .38 under his left arm pit. sharp fists that splattered a nigger jaw. richie is power over the dope-sick. a fox is a vulture. slick hair nigger back out the joint. black-berry face in skin the color of new coal around smooth lips like uncle willie.

friday is a carnival afternoon 114 street. a vacuum sucks the souls of its people in the nauseous heat. buildings squat together an infinite line of faces. and bodies chatter hanging from the windows. to feel the breezes that never come. women shout from one side of the narrow street to the other. mating calls. and stray husbands in search of the number or gossip. wasting time. pasted on stoops hordes of people. little ones. ½ naked tar-babies run from the spray and coldness of a fire hydrant. they are laughing. people fill every empty space here fleeing from the shit poor.

uncle willie prances up and down in front of 216. he grins and sweats. he is fresh and clean. his head is inflated. his eyes strut. in an unnatural fashion he is clean.

in shoes of alligator green. italian knit sweater. silk green
pants hang loose against his hips. not use to the rich feel
of soft fiber. uncle willie is a dream in green. leather cap
and green socks silk. the new pants have no back pocket
to carry anything. uncle willie sees me. coconut eyes run
to him.

> *hey uncle willie! hey man you looking too good!*
> *when did you fall into this*
> *yeah momma im moving up. now that richie out-*
> *you working for him or something?*
> *make me a cupla bills   you know.*
> *nothing too tough. no more days niggers out here*
> *gon run over me   who that lil monster*
> *you was talking to on the corner.*
> *who. duck?*
> *baby i know you take care of yourself but if one of*
> *these chumps out here mess around we straighten*
> *him out. know none a them wanna run up on richie.*
> *he wanna see you.*
> *momma showed us your picture in the paper black as*
> *you is. always knew you be the one lex. told mae and*
> *momma. mae always fussing cause you in a book.*
> *uncle willie was the first one to recognize you   so*
> *they give you 8-grand for your college huh? where is*
> *it*
> *cornell university. upstate next to the farms*
> *what you gon take up momma*
> *everything. psychology. i dont know*
> *when you leaving?*
> *tuesday night it all begins*
> *uncle willie been waiting a long time to see this*
> *baby. im prouda you. gon cut that picture out an put*
> *it right in my new wallet. show all the niggers my*
> *niece going to one the best colleges.*
> *richard around?*
> *yeah got a place 111 street. him an his man red.*
> *told me to bring you over there soon as you came.*
> *hes prouda you momma.*

uncle willies new shoes clop a hollow sound. thru the
tribes the faces of poets and whores tangled together we
move. up the block to 8th avenue the air is a vise no one
can escape. bloated junkies in packs like wolves pace
down and up. their nervous eyes glitter. at 6:00 the sun
cooks the street. smells of chicken and watermelon mix
with us. 8th avenue spreads gangrehea. it is us. rhythms
are gospel from the dark cool bars. fingers pop. bop. in
the heats beat. a toothless woman stops. in the middle of
the street. her hips move like a snake charmed. she is
voodoo. she is happy. while the cars and buses scream.
they are in a hurry. they do not understand. she is free.

at the corner of 111 street we turn. up the long stairs of
a ½ condemned building we stop on the 6th floor. knock
and puff at the 2nd door. hear feet slowly answer the
noise we make.

red! red! willie. open up. i got lexie.
richie here?

the doors eye opens and closes.

yeah   hes in the front. richie! wake up man!
you got company

down the empty-blue hallway hear glass knock against
glass on the floor. a fan hums low. jazz whispers in the
walls. it is hot like the street. smell wolves here. red walks
behind us. he is skinny. his red bare chest a map of battle
scars.

in the tiny front-room 2 chairs and a love seat are
squeezed. a big coffee table you step over to get by is covered with coke bottles and cigarette ash.

hey richard. whats happn

in a coarse voice the black-berry face speaks.

hi   stuff. scuse me for not having my clothes on.
so hot in this room

he has been sleeping.
he is asleep.

come here baby. let me see you. watch yourself!
willie! get a broom. sweep this mess out the way!
you want her to think we pigs? hey red aint she
grown up stuff? baby red is my right arm.

uncle willie is a maid. he sweeps the floor. he wipes the
coffee table. he sweats in brown garbage bags. he is glad
to help. i open a window. the telephone rings in another
tiny room richie answers

yeah i got it sucka. just have your man there
when? right now?? no im waiting for sugar. sent him
crosstown. wont be back til 7. cant send red man.
need him here. what??
just lay cool. youll get it in 20 minutes.
ill send willie. yeah man   yeah.

the telephone is quiet. richie stands in the doorway. he
looks at uncle willie. he lights a cigarette.

red! get that thing together. nigger over there cant
wait. look at that lame! gave him 200 dollars. look
what the nigger do. probably bought a case of pluck
by now. willie. willie! pull yourself together man.
need you for something

red goes to the kitchen. his eyes are sealed in sweat-
covers. he sleeps. from the pink kitchen he returns. he
shoves pork chops and frozen hamburgers in a shopping
bag.

here it is richie. maybe i should put it in 2 bags.
yeah, willie got enough sense to carry it—just be his
luck to break it. wake up man!
yeah jack yeah. i hear you. what you want me to do
go over to 108 street central park west. where we
stopped off yesterday? the orange stoop. 1st floor left
in the back-
the bald head chump   richie?
uhhuh. suckas name is randolph. the one-hand dude.
owe him a grand. he get it when im ready.

dont know who the lame think he dealing with.
tell him to meet me in joe-blo about 9.
shouldnt take you more than 15 minutes willie.
take it straight there.

red gives the fat shopping bag to uncle willie.

you kidding me   richie??
bulls out there gon think i took off some supermarket.
this randolph cat a butcher jack?
salready dripping blood on me.
take the thing an get back man!
here baby. put this in your pocket. 50 dollars
enough? make sure you come by an see me. take you
downtown monday night. we hang out together.
momma said you leaving tuesday. let me know if you
need some dust. make sure she get to the subway
willie. take care of yourself baby.

hustled out the door   blood comes after business. out-side uncle willie stoops to wipe pale-red juice from his shoes. down the street we are conspicuous. on the side-walk pork chops run away. the shopping bag is too full. 50 dollars causes a fire in my skirt pocket. hear the siren scream. red city-wagons surround me. pink faces in gas masks and plastic coats drown me. laughing because i am a fire. smoke puffs. sail away over roof tops. wonder where my 50 dollars is. i pat my pocket for an answer.

uncle willie you dont have to walk me to the subway.
go ahead. to 108 street. that bag might break.
nawwwww momma. uncle willie can handle this.
must be something for your father to give away all
this meat. sure you can make it to the train?
tell mae you saw richie. wheres your money keep
your hands on it. chumps out here.
aww aint no body thinking about getting me uncle
willie. ill see you monday or tuesday
before i go.
alright momma get home safely

down 8th avenue uncle willie goes away. he leans to one side walking. careful to dodge blood drops from the bag. he is a green dream. he is gone.

i am out. back from the subways and downtown. saturday is ½ spent. the paper money in my pocket just change left over from the boxes and bags i carry up stairs. climb 3 flights to #9. the door kicks open. a trumpet is assaulted. trumped by a strange smell. the air is cold. coming out. hollow sound. dont go in. see gray. see mommie quiet. her eyes at me quiver in their sockets. a whisper drips

> *lexie? close the door an come here*
> *put those things there an sit down*

sit. do not move. the couch wants to speak. what i do now. it wasnt me ma. how come vickie is crying? brought home some change just like you told me. whats wrong with rosie? dont ask. choke. think. ithaca. hallucinate new life. grow up. think. in the ivy league wonderland. a cow grows milk from a tree. tuesday bus ticket #94376. fly brown butterfly. farms are cartoon in storybooks. sunsets are black.

> *mommie your eyes have turned in*
> *mommie where are your lips*

> *uncle willie died*

burst firecracker. burst. blop. blop. what? too much too many. blop. blop. what?? cows dont grow on trees. huh? speak slow. huh. leave uncle willie? dead. i am in ithaca. white lake in the pink sun. a sable moonface. you kidding me?? mommie i am going apart.

> *no   it isnt cold.*
>   *no more wine.*
> *this is september.*
>   *it aint cold.*

stand up. sit down. my belly is a fever humming. the world spins around.

play trumpet. say.
play. screech. screech. trumpet.
scream notes.

crack my head. mommie is a spiritual

allah, allah
damn!
allah
this is quicksand
stop
dont tell me
grammie called. not too long ago. say police found
him early this morning. on some roof 108 street. ice
box-cold. just his pants an wallet. laid up there. dont
know what he was doing. willie never bes over there.
didnt use that stuff.
willie was too afraid. somebody drew out his blood
seem like   an shot him full of poison.
gets in your blood
makes you fly
  black dot
  heart drops

thats ridiculous. i see uncle willie right now. saw him yesterday. talk. shine. walk. in purple magic. long face i love
you. head of hair beads. eye of stars and rot-gut. medicine
wine for his thick smooth lips

lexie-

mommie he sweats-

no-

mommie i see him

they will lock you in a box
will they give me to the worms?
they will make you dust   in green

remember him   a outlaw.

These "wild and holy women"

GAYL JONES

Gayl Jones was born in Lexington, Kentucky, November 23, 1949. She attended grade school and high school in Lexington, received a scholarship to Connecticut College in New London, Connecticut, and completed a master's degree in creative writing at Brown University. For the last four years she has been teaching Afro-American literature and creative writing at the University of Michigan.

She published her first novel *Corregidora* when she was only twenty-six and since then has published a second novel, *Eva's Man* (1976), a book of short stories, *White Rat* (1977), and is working on a third novel, *Palmares*, which is about the fugitive slave settlements in Brazil in the seventeenth and eighteenth centuries. The main character in *Palmares* is a slave woman named Almeyda who journeys into the interior of Brazil searching for her husband. According to Jones, Almeyda is a more heroic woman character than the ones she has written about in earlier stories. The black woman as hero—as opposed to the woman who is sexually abused and powerless—represents Jones' attempt to achieve greater balance in her work.

Gayl Jones is the third generation of black women writers in her family. Her grandmother, Amanda Wilson, wrote plays for church programs and schools. Her mother, Lucille Jones, is a published writer. One of Jones' early memories is of her mother sitting at the kitchen table writing at night after working during the day as a domestic. She also wrote stories for Gayl and her brother and read them aloud when they were children. Then, like many women with families to care for, she stopped writing early in the fifties, but recently, with her daughter's encouragement, she has published several stories in *Obsidian* (Spring 1977). In an interview with her mother, Jones admits the similarities of style and tone between her writing and her mother's[1]—there is the flat conversational tone, stories of desperation and tragedy hidden beneath the ordinariness of everyday life, the sense of psychic and sexual abuse of women. In the *Obsidian* stories, Lucille Jones writes about a young girl kidnapped by white men and forced into prostitution, a wife who slices her husband's jaw with an ax when she finds him with another woman, and a father and son competing in a jealous rivalry for the same woman. These are the kinds of stories that also compel the imagination of her daughter, Gayl.

The influence of the mother on her daughter's writing is significant for many reasons. First because it is a special and rare phenomenon for a black woman to have her mother as a literary model. For Gayl Jones it has unquestionably meant that she has suffered less than most women from "contrary instincts"[2]—those psychological and social hindrances to a woman devoting herself to a writing career. Without question, conflict or doubt, she is a writer:

> *I used to have an image of myself when I grew up . . . I was this independent woman, I never saw myself as being married or having children or anything like that, and I was always traveling, particularly to Spanish-speaking places,* and I was a writer.[3]

From her mother, Jones also learned the tradition of oral storytelling, which is so much in evidence in her writing. Jones is insistent upon the importance of words being heard, being said aloud, so that the rhythms and patterns of a language are preserved and the integrity of the oral tradition is maintained. When her characters speak, they are also documenting the experience of black people, utilizing the original language of the people, drawing on the

[1] "Interview with Lucille Jones," *Obsidian.*
[2] Virginia Woolf coined this phrase in *A Room of One's Own.*
[3] Interview with Michael Harper in *Massachusetts Review,* XVIII (Autumn 1977), p. 711.

storehouse of folklore which expresses the attitudes and morality contained in that folklore.

> *"If that nigger loved me he wouldn't've throwed me down the steps," I called.*

> *"What?" She came to the door.*

> *"I said if that nigger loved me he wouldn't've throwed me down the steps."*

> *"I know niggers love you do worse than that," she said.*[4]

This is Ursa speaking to her friend Catherine in Jones' first novel, *Corregidora*. Spoken aloud, the lines are obviously based on the rhythm and pattern of the three-line blues song. The first line is repeated with slight variation in the second line, the repetition holding us in momentary suspense as we wait for the "resolution" or "answer" in the last line. Catherine's "answer" to Ursa is wise and knowing and calls on a woman's experience with men and love: she is saying that people can love deeply and still hurt each other and one does not necessarily preclude the other.

In all of her writing so far Gayl Jones has performed the ritual of the blues as Ralph Ellison has defined it:

> *the impulse to keep the painful details and episodes of a brutal experience alive in one's aching consciousness . . . and to transcend it, not by the consolation of philosophy, but by squeezing from it a near-tragic, near-comic lyricism.*[5]

In "Jevata," a fifty-year-old woman lives with her eighteen-year-old lover named Freddy. The story is told through Jevata's middle-aged friend, Mr. Floyd, a direct descendant of the itinerant blues singer. Something of a wanderer, homeless and without family, he is considered a

[4] *Corregidora*, pp. 36–37.
[5] "Richard Wright's Blues," in *Shadow and Act*, Random House, 1953, p. 90.

fool by the community because he loves Jevata and gives her money and friendship without any sexual favors in return; but Mr. Floyd conveys to the reader a true empathy for Jevata. Because he is attracted to her sixteen-year-old daughter, Floyd acknowleges his own hidden and unacceptable urges, thus exposing his own vulnerable humanity and Jevata's pathetic and unarticulated need. When Floyd tries to get her to explain why she tried to kill Freddy, she gives the heart-wrenching answer of a person who is emotionally mute. She cannot explain her feelings because "It always have took me a long time, Floyd."

Again in "Asylum" the black woman being treated in a hospital for mental patients is unable to defend herself with words. Against a powerful and baffling and painful reality she retaliates with hostility and calculated belligerence. The white hospital is a cold, alien, implacable force—a world in control of her, with names to define her sickness and thus the power to imprison her. Her last question to the doctors shows that she too understands the nature of institutional power and the terms she must submit to if she wants to be freed. These are the painful details of brutal experiences, endured without consolation.

In preserving the memory of the black past—both the personal and historical past—Jones uses the language, the symbols, the myths generated by that tradition. Those specific forms, as Ellison tells us, represent profoundly a particular group's attempt to humanize the world.[6] Only a few black writers like Jones have this ability to recall a past which even now is fleeting. I recall a picture in *Corregidora* of a woman doing hair in the kitchen telling a girl to hold her ear, so she won't burn her when she straightens the edges, and I realized I had almost forgotten that ritualistic scene. Images of torn pages, records destroyed, blacks being cheated out of their land are historical images selected by Jones as she carries out the task of preserving the evidence.

If critics are hard on Jones for what they do not ap-

[6] "The Art of Fiction: An Interview," in *Shadow and Act*, p. 172.

prove of or understand, it is because they understand so little about black life. Diane Johnson said in *The New York Review of Books* that a white reader, like herself, could not relate to such dehumanized pictures of black life and lamented that all of Jones' women characters were brutalized and dull. As in the blues, Jones' people do not often transcend their lives; they struggle, they cope, they accept the bittersweet irony of their lives and do not expect resolutions. As in the blues, there is little of conventional morality or middle-class American ideals in these lives. Jones' characters drift into or out of marriage or living arrangements without regard for society's standards, they refer to sexual acts in raw street terms; they speak without delicate pretensions. The wild words of the black woman in "Asylum" are an indictment of the white doctor's middle-class hypocrisy: "He writes about my sexual amorality because I wouldn't let that other doctor see my pussy." Perhaps the genteel reader or critic will, like the doctor, want to cringe at this woman's crudeness but only at the risk of avoiding the deeper question Jones is forcing us to face: how do freedom and love survive a brutal history?

One wishes for the heroic voice, for the healing of the past; but it is presumptuous to demand that these things appear before their time. The blues certainly do not encompass the entire black American experience, nor do they admit all of its complexities, but they allow bitterness, infidelity, promiscuity and pain (as well as humor) to exist. For now Gayl Jones' voice is a blues voice. Some of her people cannot speak standard English and so sound stupid to the outsider, some are emotionally withdrawn, some still have generations of exploitation to extricate themselves from. She is their voice. Their past is in her blood.

Asylum

BY GAYL JONES

When the doctor coming? When I'm getting examined?

They don't say nothing all these white nurses. They walk around in cardboard shoes and grin in my face. They take me in this little room and sit me up on a table and tell me to take my clothes off. I tell them I won't take them off till the doctor come.

Then one of them says to the other, You want to go get the orderly?

She might hurt herself.

Not me, I won't get hurt.

Then they go out and this big black woman comes in to look after me. They sent her in because they think I will behave around her. I do. I just sit there and don't say nothing. She acts like she's scared. She stands next to the door.

You know, I don't belong here, I start to say, but don't. I just watch her standing up there.

The doctor will come in to see you in a few minutes, she says.

I nod my head. They're going to give me a physical examination first. I'm up on the table but I'm not going to take my clothes off. All I want them to do is examine my head. Ain't nothing wrong with my body.

The woman standing at the door looks like somebody I know. She thinks I'm crazy, so I don't tell her she looks like somebody I know. I don't say nothing. I know one thing. He ain't examining me down there. He can examine me anywhere else he wants to, but he ain't touching me down there.

The doctor's coming. You can go to the bathroom and empty your bladder and take your clothes off and put this on.

I already emptied my bladder. The reason they got me here is my little nephew's teacher come and I run and got the slop jar and put it in the middle of the floor. That's why my sister's daughter had me put in here.

I take my clothes off but I leave my bloomers on cause he ain't examining me down there.

The doctor sticks his head in the door.

I see we got a panty problem.

I say, Yes, and it's gonna stay.

He comes in and looks down in my mouth and up in my nose and looks in my ears. He feels my breasts and my belly to see if I got any lumps. He starts to take off my bloomers.

I ain't got nothing down there for you.

His nose turns red. I stare at the black woman who's trying not to laugh. He puts a leather thing on my arm and tightens it. He takes blood out of my arm.

I get dressed and the big nurse goes with me down the hall. She doesn't talk. She doesn't smile. Another white man is sitting behind a desk. He is skinny and about my age and he attaches some things to my head and tells me to lay down. I lay down and see all the crooked lines come out. I stare at circles and squares and numbers and move them around and look at little words and put them together anyway I want to, then they tell me to sit down and talk about anything I want to.

How I do?

I can't tell you that, but we can tell you're an intelligent person even though you didn't have a lot of formal education.

How can you tell?

He doesn't say nothing. Then he asks, Do you know why they brought you here?

I peed in front of Tony's teacher.

Did you have a reason?

I just wanted to.

You didn't have a reason?
I wanted to.
What grade is Tony in?
The first.
Did you do it in front of the little boy?
Yeah, he was there.

He doesn't comment. He just writes it all down. He says tomorrow they are going to have me write words down, but now they are going to let me go to bed early because I have had a long day.

It ain't as long as it could've been.

What do you mean?

I look at his blue eyes. I say nothing. He acts nervous. He tells the nurse to take me to my room. She takes me by the arm. I tell her I can walk. She lets my arm go and walks with me to some other room.

Why did you do it when the teacher came?

She just sit on her ass and fuck all day and it ain't with herself.

I write that down because I know they ain't going to know what I'm talking about. I write down whatever comes into my mind. I write down some things that after I get up I don't remember.

We think you're sociable and won't hurt anybody and so we're going to put you on this floor. You can walk around and go to the sun room without too much supervision. You'll have your sessions every week. You'll mostly talk to me, and I'll have you write things down everyday. We'll discuss that.

I'll be in school.

He says nothing. I watch him write something down in a book. He thinks I don't know what he put. He thinks I can't read upside down. He writes about my sexual amorality because I wouldn't let that other doctor see my pussy.

My niece comes to visit me. I have been here a week. She acts nervous and asks me how I'm feeling. I say I'm feeling real fine except everytime I go sit down on the toilet this long black rubbery thing comes out a my bowels. It looks like a snake and it scares me. I think it's something they give me in my food.

She screws up her face. She doesn't know what to say. I have scared her and she doesn't come back. It has been over a month and she ain't been back. She wrote me a letter though to tell me that Tony wanted to come and see me but they don't allow children in the building.

I don't bother nobody and they don't bother me. They put me up on the table a few more times but I still don't let him look at me down there. Last night I dreamed I got real slender and turned white like chalk and my hair got real long and the black woman she helped them strap me down because the doctor said he had to look at me down there and he pulled this big black rubbery thing look like a snake out of my pussy and I broke the stirrups and jumped right off the table and I look at the big black nurse and she done turned chalk white too and she tells me to come to her because they are going to examine my head again. I'm scared of her because she looks like the devil, but I come anyway, holding my slop jar.

If the sounds fit put them here.

They don't fit.

How does this word sound?

What?

Dark? Warm? Soft?

Me?

He puts down: libido concentrated on herself.

What does this word make you feel?

Nothing.

You should tell me what you are thinking?

Is that the only way I can be freed?

Jevata

BY GAYL JONES

I didn't see Jevata when she ran Freddy away from her house, but Miss Johnny Cake said she had a hot poker after him, and would have killed him too, if he hadn't been faster than she was. Nobody didn't know what made her do it. I didn't know either then, and I'm over there more than anybody else is. Now I'm probably the onliest one who know what did happen—me and her boy David. Miss Johnny Cake don't even know, and it seem like she keep busier than anybody else on Green Street. People say what make Miss Johnny so busy is the Urban Renewal come and made her move out of that house she was living in for about forty years, and all she got to do now is sit out there on the porch and be busy. Once she told me she felt dislocated, and I told Jevata what she said, and Jevata said she act dislocated.

Miss Johnny Cake aint the onliest one talking about Jevata neither. All up and down Green Street they talking. They started talking when Jevata went up to Lexington and brought Freddy back with her, and they aint quit. They used to talk when I'd come down from Davis town to visit her. Then I guess they got used to me. I called myself courting her then. We been friends every since we went over to Simmons Street School together, and we stayed friends. I guess all the courting was on my side though, cause she never would have me. I still come to see about her though. I was coming to see about her all during the time that Freddy was living with her.

"I don't see what in the world that good-lookin boy see in her," Miss Johnny Cake would say. "If I was him and eighteen, I wouldn't be courting the mama, I be courting the daughter. He ain't right, is he, Mr. Floyd?"

I wouldn't say anything, just stand with my right foot up on the porch while she sat rocking. She was about seventy, with her gray hair in two plaits.

"I don't see what they got in common," Miss Johnny said.

"Same thing any man and woman got in common," I said.

"Aw, Mr. Floyd, you so nasty."

Before Freddy came, Jevata used to have something to say to people, but after he came she wouldn't say nothing to nobody. She used to say I was the only one that she could trust, because the others always talked about her too much. "Always got something to say about you. Caint even go pee without them having something to say about you." She would go on by and wouldn't say nothing to nobody. People said she got stuck up with that young boy living with her. "Woman sixty-five going with a boy eighteen," some of the women would say. "You seen her going up the street, didn't you? Head all up in the air, that boy trailin behind her. Don't even look right. I be ashamed for anybody to see me trying to go with a boy like that. Look like her tiddies fallen since he came, don't it? But you know she always have been like 'at though, always looking after boys. I stopped Maurice from going down there to play. But you know if he was like anybody else he least be trying to get some from the daughter too."

Now womens can get evil about something like that. Wasn't so much that Jevata was going with Freddy, as she wouldn't say nothing to them while she was doing it. Now if she'd gone over there and said something to them, and let them all in her business and everything, they would felt all right then, and they wouldn't a got evil with her. "Rest of us got man trouble, Miss Jevata must got boy trouble," they'd laugh.

Now the boy's eighteen, but Jevata ain't sixty-five though, she's fifty, cause I ain't but two years older than her myself. I used to try to go with her way back when

we was going to Simmons Street School together, but she
wouldn't have me then, and she won't have me now. She
married some nigger from Paris, Kentucky, one come out
to Dixieland dance hall that time Dizzy Gillespie or Cab
Calloway come out there. Name was Joe Guy. He stayed
with her long enough to give her three children. Then he
was gone. I was trying to go with her after he left, but she
still wouldn't have me. She mighta eventually had me if
he hadn't got to her, but after he got to her, seem like she
wouldn't look at no mens. Onliest reason she'd look at me
was because we'd been friends for so long. But first time I
tried to get next to her right after he left, she said, "Shit,
Floyd, me and you friends, always have been and always
will be." I asked her to marry me, but she looked at me
real evil. I thought she was going to tell me I could just
quit coming to see her, but she didn't. After that she just
wouldn't let me say nothing else about it, so I just come
over there every chance I get. She got three childrens.
Cynthy the oldest. She sixteen. Then she got a boy fourteen, name David, and a little boy five, name Pete. Sometime she call him Pete Junebug, sometime Little Pete.

Don't nobody know where in Lexington she went and
got Freddy. Some people say she went down to the re-
form school they got down there and got him. It ain't that
he's bad or nothing, it's just that they think something's
wrong with him. I didn't know where she got him myself,
because it was her business and I figured she tell me
when she wanted to, and if she didn't wont to, she
wouldn't.

Miss Johnny Cake lives over across the street from
Jevata, and everytime I pass by there, she got to call me
over. Sometimes I don't even like to pass by there, but I
got to. She thinks I'm going to say something about Jevata
and Freddy, but I don't. I just listen to what she's got to
say. After she's said her piece, sometimes she'll look at me
and say, "Clarify things to me, Mr. Floyd." I figure she
picked that up from Reverend Jackson, cause he's always
saying, "The Lord clarified this to me, the Lord clarified
that to me." I ain't clarified nothing to her yet.

"He's kinda funny, ain't he?" she said one day. That was when Freddy and Jevata was still together. It seemed like Miss Johnny Cake just be sitting out there waiting for me to come up the street, because she would never fail to call me over. Sitting up there, old seventy-year-old woman, couldn't even keep her legs together. One a the men on the street told me she been in a accident, and something happened to that muscle in her thighs, that's supposed to help you keep your legs together. I believed him till he started laughing, and then I didn't know whether to believe him or not.

"That boy just don't act right, do he? He ain't right, is he, Mr. Floyd? Something wrong with him, ain't it?" She waited, but not as if she expected an answer. I guess she'd got used to me not answering. "You reckon he's funny? Naw, cause he wouldn't be with her if he was funny, would he? I guess she do something for him. She must got something he wont. God knows I don't see it. Mr. Floyd, you just stand up there and don't say nothing. Cat got your tongue, and Freddy got hers." She looked at me grinning. I blew smoke between my teeth. "If you wonted to, I bet you could tell me everything that go on in that house."

I said I couldn't.

"Well, I know she sixty-five, cause she used to live down 'ere on Poke Street when I did. She might look like she forty-five, and tell everybody she forty-five, but she ain't. Now, if that boy was *right*, he be trying to go with Cynthy anyway. That's what a *right* boy would do. But he ain't right. He don't even *look* right, do he, Mr. Floyd?"

I told her he didn't look no different fom anybody else to me.

Miss Johnny grinned at me. "You just don't wont to say nothin' against her, do you? Ain't no reason for you to take up for him, though, cause he done cut you out, aint he?"

I said I was going across the street. She said she didn't see why I won't to take up for him, cut me out the way he did.

One day when I came down the street, Freddy was

standing out in the yard, his shirt sleeves rolled up, standing up against the post, looking across the street at Miss
Johnny, looking evil. I didn't think Miss Johnny would
bother me this time. I waved to her and kept walking. She
said, "Mr. Floyd, ain't you go'n stop and have a few words
with me? You got cute too?" I went over to her porch before I got a chance to say anything to Freddy. He was
watching us, though. Green Street wasn't a wide street,
and if she talked even a little bit as loud as she'd been
talking, he would have heard.

"Nigger out there," she said, almost at a whisper.
"Keep staring at me. Look at him."

She kept patting her knees. I didn't turn around to look
at him. I was thinking, "He see those bloomers you got
on."

"Look at him," she said, still low.

"Nice day, ain't it?" I said, loud.

"Fine day," she said, loud, too, then whispered, "I wish
he go in the house. I don't even like to look at him."

I said nothing. I lit a cigarette. She started rocking back
and forth in her rocker, and closed her eyes, like she was
in church. Or like I do when I'm in church.

"You have you a good walk?" she asked, her eyes still
closed.

I said, "OK."

We were talking moderate, now.

"You a fool you know that? Walk all the way out here
from Davis town, just to see that woman. She got what
she need, over there."

I hoped he hadn't heard, but I knew he had. I wondered if I was in his place, if I would have come over and
said something to her.

"You know you a fool, don't you?" she asked again, still
looking like she was in church.

I didn't answer.

"You know you a fool, Mr. Floyd," she said. She rocked
a while more then she opened her eyes.

"But I reckon you say you been a fool a long time, ain't
no use quit now."

I turned a little to the side so I could see out of the corner of my eye. He was still standing there. I couldn't tell if he was watching or not. I felt awkward about crossing the street now. I gave Miss Johnny a hard look before I crossed. She only smiled at me.

"Mr. Floyd," Freddy said. He always called me "Mr. Floyd." He was still looking across the street at Miss Johnny. I stood with my back to her. He asked me to walk back around the yard with him. I did. I stood with my back against the house, smoking a cigarette.

"I caint stand that old woman," he said. "You see how she was setting, didn't you? Legs all open. I never could stand womens sit up with their legs all open. 'Specially old women."

I said they told me she couldn't help it.

"I had a aunt use to do that," he said. "She can help it. She just onry. Ain't nothin wrong with that muscle. She just think somebody wont to see her ass. Like my aunt. Used to think I wonted to see her ass, all the time."

I said nothing. Then I asked "How's Jevata . . . and the children?"

"They awright. Java and Junebug in the house. Other two at school."

I finished my cigarette and was starting in the house.

"Think somebody wont to see her ass," Freddy said. He stayed out in the yard.

Jevata was in the kitchen ironing. She took in ironing for some white woman lived out on Stanley Street.

"How you, Floyd?" she asked.

"Not complaining," I said. I sat down at the kitchen table. She looked past me out in the back yard where Freddy must have still been standing.

"What Miss Busy have to say about me today?" she asked, looking back at me.

"Nothin'."

"You can tell me," she said. "I won't get hurt."

"Miss Johnny wasn't doing nothing but out there talking bout the weather," I said.

"Weather over here?" she asked.

I smiled.

She looked back out in the yard. I thought Freddy was still standing out there, but when I turned around in my seat to look, he wasn't. He must have gone back around to the front of the house.

"How you been?" she asked me as if she hadn't asked before, or didn't remember asking.

She wasn't looking at me, but I nodded.

"I never did think I be doing this," she said. "You 'member that time I told you Joe and me went down to Yazoo, Mississippi and this ole, white woman come up to me and asked me did I iron, and I said, 'Naw, I don't iron.' I wasn't gonna iron for *her*, anyway."

I said nothing. I had already offered to help Jevata out with money, but she wouldn't let me. I worked with horses, and had enough left over to help. Now, I was thinking, she had *four* kids to take care of.

"He found a job yet?" I asked.

She looked at me, irritated. She was sweating from the heat. "I told him he could take his time. He ain't been here long. He need time to get adjusted."

I was wondering how much adjusting did he need. It was over half a year ago since she went and got him.

"You don't think Freddy's evil, do you?" she asked.

I looked at her. I didn't know why she asked that. I said, "Naw, I don't think he's evil." She went back to ironing. I just sat there in the kitchen, watching her. After a while Freddy came in through the back door. He didn't say anything. He passed by, and I saw him put his hand on her waist. She smiled but didn't turn around to look at him. He went on into the front of the house. I sat there about fifteen or twenty minutes longer, and then I got up and said I was going.

"Glad you stopped by," Jevata said.

I said I'd probably be back by sometime next week, then I went out the back way.

Miss Johnny not only caught me when I was coming to see Jevata, but she caught me when I was leaving.

"I never did think that bastard go in the house," she

said. "Sometime I wish the Urban Renewal come and move me away from here. They dislocate me once, they might as well do it again."

I was thinking she probably heard Reverend Jackson say, "When the devil dislocate you, the Lord relocate you."

"How's Miss Jevata doing?" she asked.

"She's awright," I said.

"Awright as you can be with a nigger like that on your hands. If it was me, I be ashamed for anybody see me in the street with him. If he wont to go with somebody, he ought to go with Cynthy. I didn't tell you what I seen them doing last night?"

"What?" I asked frowning.

"I seen 'em standing in the door. Standing right up in the door kissing. Thought nobody couldn't see 'em with the light off. But you know how you can see in people's houses. Tha's the only time I seen 'em though. But still if they gonna do something like that, they ought to go back in there where caint nobody see 'em, and do it. Cause 'at ain't right. Double sin as old as she is. And they sinned again, cause you spose to go in your closet and do stuff like that."

I said nothing.

"You know I'm right, Mr. Floyd."

I still said nothing.

"Naw, you prob'ly don't know if I'm right or not," she said.

I looked away from her, over across the street at Jevata's house.

"Tiddies all sinking in," she said. "I don't see what he see in her. Look like she ain't got no tiddies no more. I don't see what he see in her. You think I'm crazy, don't you? I just don't like to see no old womens trying to go with young boys like that. I guess y'all ripe at that age, though, ain't you?"

I said I couldn't remember back that far.

"Floyd, you just a nigger. You just mad cause you been trying to go with her yourself. I bet you thought y'all *was* going together, didn't you? Everybody else thought so too, but not me. I didn't."

I turned around to look at her. She kept watching me.

"Ain't no use you saying nothing neither, cause I know you wasn't. I can tell when a man getting it and when he aint."

I started to tell her I could tell when a woman wonts it and can't have it, but I just told her I'd be seeing her.

"You got a long walk back to Davis town, ain't you, Mr. Floyd?"

The next time I was down to Jevata's only the girl was at home. I asked her where her mama was. She said she and Freddy took Junebug downtown to get him some shoes. She told me Jevata had been mad all morning.

"Mad about what?" I asked.

"Mad cause Miss Johnny told Freddy to go up to the store for her."

"To get what?"

"A bottle of Pepsi Cola."

"Did he go?"

"Naw, he sent Davey." Then she said, "I don't know what makes that woman so meddlesome, anyway."

We were in the living room. I hadn't set down when I heard Jevata wasn't there. She was still standing, her arms folded like she was cold. She was frowning.

"What is it?" I asked.

"I guess I do know why she so meddlesome, why they all so meddlesome," she said.

I waited for her to go on.

"They talking about them, ain't they, Mr. Floyd? People all up and down the street talking, ain't they?" She didn't ask the question as if she expected an answer. She was still looking at me, frowning. She was a big girl for sixteen. She could've passed for eighteen. And she acted older than she was. She acted about twenty.

"Sometimes I'm ashamed to go to school. Kids on this street been telling everybody up at school. But you know

I wouldn't tell mama. I don't wont to hurt her. I wouldn't do anything to hurt her."

I was thinking Jevata probably already knew, or guessed that people who didn't even know her might be talking about her.

I didn't say anything.

"They saying nasty things," she said.

I still didn't say anything. She kept looking at me. I put my hand on her shoulder. She was the reason I understood how Jevata could feel about Freddy, those times I felt attracted to Cynthy, wanting to touch those big breasts. I took my hand away.

"Just keep trying not to hurt her," I said.

She was looking down at the floor. I kept watching her breasts. They were bigger than her mama's. I was thinking of Mose Mason, who they put out of church for messing with that little girl him and his wife adopted. The deacons came to the house and he said, "I ain't doing nothing but feeling around on her tiddies. I ain't doing nothin' y'all wouldn't do." They was mad, too. "They ack like they ain't never wont to feel on nobody," Moses told me when we was sitting over in Tiger's Inn. "Shit, I bet they do more feeling Saturday night than it take me a whole damn week to do. And then they come sit up under the pulpit on Sunday morning and play like they hands ain't never touched nothin' but the Holy Bible. Saying 'amen' louder than anybody. Shit, don't make me no difference, though, whether I'm with 'em or not cause the Baptist is sneaky, anyway. Sneak around and do they dirt."

"I can hear them," Cynthy said quietly. "I can hear her telling him to hold her. 'Hold me, Freddy,' she say. I can hear her telling him he's better to her than my daddy was."

I couldn't think of anything to tell her. I wanted to touch her again, but didn't dare.

When Jevata came in, she said, "Cynthy tell you what that bitch did?"

I nodded.

"I know what she wonts, bitch," she said. "I know just what she wonts with him."

She asked me if I wanted something to eat. I said, Naw, I'd better be going. I'd been just waiting around to see her.

"Why did she try to kill 'im, Mr. Floyd?" Miss Johnny asked. It was a couple of weeks after Jevata had gone after Freddy with the poker.

"I don't know," I said. I had my right foot up on the porch and was leaning on my knee, smoking.

"Got after Cynthy, didn't he? I bet that's what he did."

"He didn't bother Cynthy," I said, angry. But I didn't know whether he did or not.

"I bet tha's what he did. I bet she went somewhere and come back and found them in that house." She started laughing.

"I don't know what happened," I said.

"Seem like she tell you, if she tell anybody," Miss Johnny said.

I threw my cigarette down on the ground, and mashed it out.

"I wish she let me come over there and get some dandelions like I used to, so I can make me some wine out of 'em," she said.

"If Freddy was over there, you could tell him to get you some," I said.

"I wouldn't tell 'at nigger to do nothing for me," she said. She was angry. I looked at her for a moment, and then I walked out of the yard.

When I got to Jevata's, she was sitting in the front room with her housecoat on, the same dirty yellow one Cynthy said she was wearing the day she threatened to kill Freddy. Cynthy said she hadn't been out of the house since she chased Freddy out. I asked her if she was all right.

"Ain't complaining, am I?" she said. She said she had some Old Crow back there in the kitchen if I wanted some. I said, "Naw, thank you." She hadn't been drinking any herself, which surprised me. She didn't drink much anyway, but I thought maybe with Freddy gone, she might.

"Shit, Floyd, why you looking at me like that?" she asked.

"I didn't know I was looking at you any way," I said.

"Well, you was."

I said nothing.

"I seen Miss Bitch call you over there. What she wont this time?"

"She wonts to know why," I said.

"I ain't told *you* why."

"And you won't, will you?"

She looked away from me, then she said, "You know it always have took me a long time, Floyd."

She didn't say anything else, and I tried not to look at her the way I had been looking. She sat on the edge of the couch with her hands together, like she was nervous, or praying. Her shoulders were pulled together in a way that made her look like she didn't have any breasts.

Cynthy came in the front room, and asked me how I was.

"Awright."

"Mama, supper's ready," she said.

"Stay for supper, won't you, Floyd?" Jevata asked me.

"Yeah."

"Cynthy, where's Freddy?" Jevata asked suddenly.

Cynthy looked at me quickly, then back at Jevata.

"He's not here, Mama," Cynthy said.

"Floyd, you ain't seen Freddy, have you?" Jevata asked me.

I just looked at her. I couldn't even have replied as calmly as Cynthy had managed to. I just kept looking at her. Jevata laughed suddenly, a quick, nervous laugh, then said, "Naw, y'all, I don't mean Freddy, I mean where's Little Pete, y'all. I don't mean Freddy I feel like a fool now."

I said nothing.

"He's down the road playing with Ralph," Cynthy said.

"Well, tell him to come on up here and get his supper."

"What about David, Mama?"

"You take his plate in there to him. I don't wont to see him."

"Yes, m'am."

I looked at Cynthy, puzzled, then I said I would take it. Jevata looked at me, but said nothing.

David was lying on the bed. I set his plate down on the chair by the bed. He didn't say anything.

"You know something about this, don't you?" I asked. He still said nothing.

"I b'lieve you know what happened."

"Go way and leave me alone!" David said. "You ain't my daddy."

I stood looking at him for a moment. He still lay on his belly. He had half turned around when he was hollering, but he hadn't looked at me. I finally left the room. When I came back in the kitchen, Little Pete was sitting at the table and Cynthy was putting the food on the table.

"Where's Jevata?" I asked.

Cynthy said nothing.

"I just ask her when Freddy was coming back and then she start acting all funny. I didn't do nothin', Mr. Floyd."

"I know you didn't," I said.

Cynthy looked at me and sat my plate down on the table. I sat down with them. Jevata didn't come back.

"Don't you think you better take your mama a plate," I said to Cynthy.

"She said she didn't wont nothin'," she said.

I stood up.

"She looked like she didn't wont nothin', Mr. Floyd," Cynthy said.

I sat back down.

I knew there was one place I could find out where Freddy was. I took the bus to Lexington, then went over to the barber shop over in Charlotte Court, right off Georgetown Street.

"Any y'all know Freddy Coleman?" I asked.

They didn't answer. Then, one man sitting up in the

chair, getting his hair trimmed around the sides, cause he
didn't have any in the top, said, "What you got to do with
him?"

"Nothin'," I said. "I just wont to know where he is."

"I used to know. He used to keep the yard down here
at Kentucky Village."

Some of the other men started laughing. Kentucky Village was a school for delinquent boys. I asked what was
funny.

"Close to them KV boys, wasn't he?" one of the men
said.

The man in the chair started laughing. "He never did
do nothing. Just used to stand up there with the rake.
Womens be passing by looking. Didn't do 'em no good."
He asked me why I wanted him.

"I'm just looking for him," I said.

They looked at each other, like people who got a secret.
They were trying not to laugh again.

"You can try that liquor store up the street. They tell
me his baby hang out over there."

The rest of the men started laughing. I left them and
went up to the liquor store. Somebody told me Freddy was
living in an apartment up over some restaurant off Second
Street.

I found the place and went upstairs and knocked on the
door. He wasn't glad to see me.

"How you find me?" he asked.

I came in before he asked me to. I stayed standing.

"What do you wont?" he asked. "Finding out where I
am for *her?*"

"Naw, for myself," I said.

I looked around. The living room was small. Only a
couch and a couple of chairs, and a low coffee table. On
the coffee table was a hat with feathers on it. It was a
woman's hat. We were both standing. I didn't sit down
without him asking me to. He wasn't saying anything and
I wasn't. I was thinking he *was* a good-looking man, almost *too* good-looking. The onliest other man I knew was
that good-looking was Mr. Pindar, a fake preacher that

used to go around stealing people's money. He used to get drunks off the street and have them go before the congregation and play like he had changed their life. And people would believe it, too. He was so good-looking the women would believe it, and preached so good the men would believe it.

Freddy kept standing there looking at me. I kept looking at him.

"Where's my ostrich hat?" It was a man's voice, but somehow it didn't sound like a man.

Freddy looked embarrassed, he was frowning. He hollered he didn't know where it was.

"You seen my ostrich hat, honey?" the man asked again. He came in, like he was swaying, saw me and stopped cold. He said, "How do," snatched the hat from the table and went back in the other room.

Freddy wasn't looking at me. I said I'd better be going.

"He's crazy," Freddy said quickly. "He live down at Eastern State, and he's crazy."

Eastern State was the mental hospital.

"He got a room down at Eastern State," Freddy said. "They let him out everyday so he can get hisself drunk. That's all he do is get hisself drunk."

I said nothing. The man had come back in the room, and was standing near the door, pouting, his lower lip stuck out. Freddy hadn't turned to see him.

I started to go. Freddy reached out to put his hand on my arm, but didn't. He looked like he didn't want me to go.

"I was going to ask you to come back to her," I said, my eyes hard now. I ignored the man standing there, pouting. "I was going to tell you she needs you."

Freddy looked like he wanted to cry. "You know she kill me if I go back there," he said.

"Why?" I asked.

He said nothing.

I went toward the door again and he came with me. He still hadn't turned around to see the man. I asked him

why again. Then I wanted another why. I asked him why
did he go with her in the first place.

He said nothing for a long time, then he reached out to
touch my arm again. I don't know if he would have
stopped again this time, but I stood away from him.

"She was going to the carnival. You know the one they
have back behind Douglas Park every year, the one back
there. She was passing through Douglas Park and seen me
sitting up there all by myself. She ask me if I wont to go
to the carnival. I don't know why she did. Maybe she
thought I was lonesome, but I wasn't. I was sitting up
there all by myself. She took me with her, you know.
They had this man in this tent who was swallowing
swords and knives, you know like they do. She wanted to
take me there, so I went. We was standing up there
watching this man, up close to him. We was standing up
close to each other too, and then all a sudden Miss Jevata
kind of turned her head to me, you know, and said kind
of quiet like, 'You know, Miss Jevata could teach you how
to swallow lightning,' she said. That was all she said. She
didn't say nothing else and she didn't say that no more. I
don't even know if anybody else heard her. But I think
that's why I went back with her. That was the reason I
went with her."

I said nothing. When I closed the door, I heard something hit the wall.

"Freddy did something to David, didn't he," I asked
her.

"Naw, it wasn't David," Jevata said. She was sitting
with her hands together.

I frowned, watching her.

"Petie come and told me Freddy tried to throw him
down the toilet. I didn't believe him."

"If he tried he would've," I said. "What did him and
David do?"

She kept looking at me. I was waiting.

"I seen him go in the toilet," she said finally. "Him and
David went back in the toilet together. He didn't even

have his pants zipped up when he come back to the house."

I was over by her when she burst out crying. When she stopped, she asked me if I could do something for her. I told her all she had to do was ask. When she told me she still loved Freddy, that she wanted me to get him back for her, I walked out the door.

I thought I wouldn't see her again. When the farm I worked for wanted me to go up to New Hampshire for a year to help train some horses, I went. I told myself when I did come back, I was through going out there, but I didn't keep my promise to myself.

When I got there, Miss Johnny wasn't sitting out on her porch, but Jevata was sitting out on hers—with a baby, sitting between her breasts. She was tickling the baby and laughing. When she looked up at me, she was still laughing.

"Floyd, Freddy back," she said. "Freddy come back."

I didn't know what to say to her. I asked if Cynthy was at home. She said yes. I went in the house. Cynthy was standing in the living room. She must have seen me coming.

"Freddy back?" I asked.

She put her hands to her mouth, and drew me toward the kitchen.

"Naw, she mean the baby," she said. "She named the baby Freddy."

"Is it his?" I asked.

She hesitated, frowning, then she said, "Yes." She got farther into the kitchen and I went with her.

"She didn't wont to have him at first. At first she tried to get rid of him."

I kept looking at her. She was a grown woman now. I remembered when I first started coming there, right after her daddy left. Everytime I'd come, she'd get the broom and start sweeping around my feet, like she was trying to sweep me out of the house. Now she looked at me, still frowning, but I could tell she was glad to see me. She said she knew I'd been sending them the money, but Jevata thought Freddy had.

I said nothing. I stood there for a moment, then I said I'd better be going.

"You will come back to see us?" she asked quickly, apprehensively. "We've missed you."

I looked at her. I started to move toward her, then I realized that she meant I might be able to help Jevata.

"Yes, I'll be back," I said.

She smiled. I went out the door.

"You little duck, you little duck, Freddy, you little duck," Jevata said, tickling the baby, who was laughing. A pretty child.

"You be back to see us, won't you, Floyd?" she asked when I started down the porch.

"Yes," I said, without turning around to look at her.

"A thinking woman sleeps with monsters"

TONI MORRISON

---

*She was experimental. She was interested in herself.
You know Black women who were like Sula had to
go into show business if they wanted to do a creative
thing, didn't want to be married, didn't want to go to
church, didn't want to do whatever Black women
did. There was no place for them unless they had
some talent, they could sing or dance. Otherwise, if
she didn't have that, she would be like Sula. She was
determined to be whoever she was. To be totally
free. Which is a very dangerous thing, because you
have no commitment to anybody, and therefore no
responsibility to anybody.*[1]

What distinguishes Toni Morrison's second novel *Sula*
(1974) is not just that black life is dealt with on the
mythological level but that the mythical hero is a woman.
In all of the great myths that function in black literature
from the great migration, bondage to freedom, the con-
frontation with invisibility, the marginal black—the heroes
we have come to associate with those myths are, for the
most part, men. Of course that is because men have been
allowed and encouraged to be writers and have followed
the natural instinct to make their heroes male. What Morrison does in *Sula* is therefore of major importance because she allows us to see the black woman's experience
not only as valid but in larger mythic terms.

Sula concerns the friendship between two black girls,
Sula Peace and Nel Wright, as they grow into woman-
hood in the Black Bottom of a town called Medallion,
Ohio. In 1922 they are both twelve years old and part of

[1] Toni Morrison in "An Interview with Toni Morrison" by Ger-
ald Gladney, "The EASY Guide To Black Arts," September 1,
1976, p. 8.

a black past that is all but extinct, a past which Morrison
insists we cannot abandon because we need the truth and
sustenance that came out of it. Those years between 1920
and 1945 when there was an identifiable and cohesive
black community, when no one in the Bottom was afraid
to leave the door unlocked, was also a time when a willing
and able-bodied worker in a little southern Ohio town
would not have been allowed to shovel gravel on a con-
struction yard. But if a black man in those times was reduced to menial work and itineracy he, at least, had the
choice of mobility, the respect of black women and the
fear of white men.

In a world that is both racist and male-centered Sula's
heroic energies are all the more remarkable. When she
and Nel "discovered years before that they were neither
white nor male, and that all freedom and triumph was forbidden to them, they had set about creating something
else to be."[2] Nel chooses respectability, prayer meetings,
keeping house, catering to a husband's whims. Sula
chooses to be a wanderer, a violator of the community's
standards. Self-invented, she lives by her own whim,
strangely independent but also impulsive, idle and dangerous. And though the black community, in desperate
need of a scapegoat to assuage its own sense of victimization, locates Sula as the source of disaster, we cannot accept Sula simply as the embodiment of evil. She is too
magical, too extraordinary, too heroic and proud. She is
the doer of deeds we dreamed of doing but dared not. She
defies convention, scorns mediocrity, refuses the sexual
role.

In all mythic tales there is an attempt to account for the
extraordinary capacities of the hero. The excerpt from
Sula in this anthology called "Eva Peace" is the story of
the two generations of black women which produced Sula
Peace. The creator in this myth is Eva, literally life-giver,
first woman. As mother of the Peace women she sits at the
top of the house she had built and directs lives. In her

[2] Sula, Chatto & Windus, 1980, p. 52

legendary past, it is believed, she sold her leg for $10,000 to take care of her children. She burns up her beloved son Plum because she cannot bear to see him die like some piss-stained junkie. As creator and sovereign, she gives and takes life.

Eva is not to be mixed up with some ridiculous notion of a black matriarch. She represents the resilience, the tenacity, the skill with which some black women learned to confront the meanness of poverty. She represents one definition of black womanhood. But Eva is crippled—she knows survival better than she will ever know love—and while the Peace women are as free a set of women as we have ever seen in literature, they are dangerously free because they are unconnected. When Sula overhears her mother telling a friend that she does not like her daughter, Sula is released even from her mother's love and then there are no boundaries to contain her.

Toni Morrison, author of two other novels, *The Bluest Eye* (1971) and *Song of Solomon* (1978), is at work on her fourth novel, *Tar Baby*, which continues her quest to collect the experiences of the black past, to extract from legend and oral history the meaning of the nightmares and of our lives.

Eva Peace

BY TONI MORRISON

Sula Peace lived in a house of many rooms that had been built over a period of five years to the specifications of its owner, who kept on adding things: more stairways—there were three sets to the second floor—more rooms, doors and stoops. There were rooms that had three doors, others that opened out on the porch only and were inaccessible from any other part of the house; others that you could get to only by going through somebody's bedroom. The creator and sovereign of this enormous house with the four sickle-pear trees in the front yard and the single elm in the back yard was Eva Peace, who sat in a wagon on the third floor directing the lives of her children, friends, strays, and a constant stream of boarders. Fewer than nine people in the town remembered when Eva had two legs, and her oldest child, Hannah, was not one of them. Unless Eva herself introduced the subject, no one ever spoke of her disability; they pretended to ignore it, unless, in some mood of fancy, she began some fearful story about it—generally to entertain children. How the leg got up by itself one day and walked on off. How she hobbled after it but it ran too fast. Or how she had a corn on her toe and it just grew and grew and grew until her whole foot was a corn and then it traveled on up her leg and wouldn't stop growing until she put a red tag at the top but by that time it was already at her knee.

Somebody said Eva stuck it under a train and made them pay off. Another said she sold it to a hospital for $10,000—at which Mr. Reed opened his eyes and asked,

"Nigger gal legs goin' for $10,000 a *piece?*" as though he could understand $10,000 a *pair*—but for *one?*

Whatever the fate of her lost leg, the remaining one was magnificent. It was stockinged and shod at all times and in all weather. Once in a while she got a felt slipper for Christmas or her birthday, but they soon disappeared, for Eva always wore a black laced-up shoe that came well above her ankle. Nor did she wear overlong dresses to disguise the empty place on her left side. Her dresses were mid-calf so that her one glamorous leg was always in view as well as the long fall of space below her left thigh. One of her men friends had fashioned a kind of wheelchair for her: a rocking-chair top fitted into a large child's wagon. In this contraption she wheeled around the room, from bedside to dresser to the balcony that opened out the north side of her room or to the window that looked out on the back yard. The wagon was so low that children who spoke to her standing up were eye level with her, and adults, standing or sitting, had to look down at her. But they didn't know it. They all had the impression that they were looking up at her, up into the open distances of her eyes, up into the soft black of her nostrils and up at the crest of her chin.

Eva had married a man named BoyBoy and had *three* children: Hannah, the eldest, and Eva, whom she named after herself but called Pearl, and a son named Ralph, whom she called Plum.

After five years of a sad and disgruntled marriage Boy-Boy took off. During the time they were together he was very much preoccupied with other women and not home much. He did whatever he could that he liked, and he liked womanizing best, drinking second, and abusing Eva third. When he left in November, Eva had $1.65, five eggs, three beets and no idea of what or how to feel. The children needed her; she needed money, and needed to get on with her life. But the demands of feeding her three children were so acute she had to postpone her anger for two years until she had both the time and the energy for it. She was confused and desperately hungry. There were very few black families in those low hills then. The Suggs, who lived two hundred yards down the road, brought her a warm bowl of peas, as soon as they found out, and a plate of cold bread. She thanked them and asked if they had a little milk for the older ones. They said no, but Mrs. Jackson, they knew, had a cow still giving. Eva took a bucket over and Mrs. Jackson told her to come back and fill it up in the morning, because the evening milking had already been done. In this way, things went on until near December. People were very willing to help, but Eva felt she would soon run her welcome out; winters were hard and her neighbors were not that much better off. She would lie in bed with the baby boy, the two girls wrapped in quilts on the floor, thinking. The oldest child, Hannah, was five and too young to take care of the baby alone, and any housework Eva could find would keep her away from them from five thirty or earlier in the morning until dark—way past eight. The white people in the valley weren't rich enough then to want maids; they were small farmers and tradesmen and wanted hard-labor help if anything. She thought also of returning to some of her people in Virginia, but to come home dragging three young ones would have to be a step one rung before death for Eva. She would have to scrounge around and beg through the winter, until her baby was at least nine months old, then she could plant and maybe hire herself out to valley farms to weed or sow or feed stock until something steadier came along at harvest time. She thought she had probably been a fool to let BoyBoy haul her away from her people, but it had seemed so right at the time. He worked for a white carpenter and toolsmith who insisted on BoyBoy's accompanying him when he went West and set up in a squinchy little town called Medallion. BoyBoy brought his new wife and built them a one-room cabin sixty feet back from the road that wound up out of the valley, on up into the hills and was named for the man he worked for. They lived there a year before they had an outhouse.

Sometime before the middle of December, the baby,

Plum, stopped having bowel movements. Eva massaged his stomach and gave him warm water. Something must be wrong with my milk, she thought. Mrs. Suggs gave her castor oil, but even that didn't work. He cried and fought so they couldn't get much down his throat anyway. He seemed in great pain and his shrieks were pitched high in outrage and suffering. At one point, maddened by his own crying, he gagged, choked and looked as though he was strangling to death. Eva rushed to him and kicked over the earthen slop jar, washing a small area of the floor with the child's urine. She managed to soothe him, but when he took up the cry again late that night, she resolved to end his misery once and for all. She wrapped him in blankets, ran her finger around the crevices and sides of the lard can and stumbled to the outhouse with him. Deep in its darkness and freezing stench she squatted down, turned the baby over on her knees, exposed his buttocks and shoved the last bit of food she had in the world (besides three beets) up his ass. Softening the insertion with the dab of lard, she probed with her middle finger to loosen his bowels. Her fingernail snagged what felt like a pebble; she pulled it out and others followed. Plum stopped crying as the black hard stools ricocheted onto the frozen ground. And now that it was over, Eva squatted there wondering why she had come all the way out there to free his stools, and what was she doing down on her haunches with her beloved baby boy warmed by her body in the almost total darkness, her shins and teeth freezing, her nostrils assailed. She shook her head as though to juggle her brains around, then said aloud, "Uh uh. Nooo." Thereupon she returned to the house and her bed. As the grateful Plum slept, the silence allowed her to think.

Two days later she left all of her children with Mrs. Suggs, saying she would be back the next day.

Eighteen months later she swept down from a wagon with two crutches, a new black pocketbook, and one leg. First she reclaimed her children, next she gave the surprised Mrs. Suggs a ten-dollar bill, later she started building a house on Carpenter's Road, sixty feet from BoyBoy's one-room cabin, which she rented out.

When Plum was three years old, BoyBoy came back to town and paid her a visit. When Eva got the word that he was on his way, she made some lemonade. She had no idea what she would do or feel during that encounter. Would she cry, cut his throat, beg him to make love to her? She couldn't imagine. So she just waited to see. She stirred lemonade in a green pitcher and waited.

BoyBoy danced up the steps and knocked on the door.

"Come on in," she hollered.

He opened the door and stood smiling, a picture of prosperity and good will. His shoes were a shiny orange, and he had on a citified straw hat, a light-blue suit, and a cat's-head stickpin in his tie. Eva smiled and told him to sit himself down. He smiled too.

"How you been, girl?"

"Pretty fair. What you know good?" When she heard those words come out of her own mouth she knew that their conversation would start off polite. Although it remained to be seen whether she would still run the ice pick through the cat's-head pin.

"Have some lemonade."

"Don't mind if I do." He swept his hat off with a satisfied gesture. His nails were long and shiny. "Sho is hot, and I been runnin' around all day."

Eva looked out of the screen door and saw a woman in a pea-green dress leaning on the smallest pear tree. Glancing back at him, she was reminded of Plum's face when he managed to get the meat out of a walnut all by himself. Eva smiled again, and poured the lemonade.

Their conversation was easy: she catching him up on all the gossip, he asking about this one and that one, and like everybody else avoiding any reference to her leg. It was like talking to somebody's cousin who just stopped by to saw howdy before getting on back to wherever he came from. BoyBoy didn't ask to see the children, and **Eva** didn't bring them into the conversation.

After a while he rose to go. Talking about his appointments and exuding an odor of new money and idleness, he danced down the steps and strutted toward the pea-green dress. Eva watched. She looked at the back of his neck and the set of his shoulders. Underneath all of that shine she saw defeat in the stalk of his neck and the curious tight way he held his shoulders. But still she was not sure what she felt. Then he leaned forward and whispered into the ear of the woman in the green dress. She was still for a moment and then threw back her head and laughed. A high-pitched big-city laugh that reminded Eva of Chicago. It hit her like a sledge hammer, and it was then that she knew what to feel. A liquid trail of hate flooded her chest.

Knowing that she would hate him long and well filled her with pleasant anticipation, like when you know you are going to fall in love with someone and you wait for the happy signs. Hating BoyBoy, she could get on with it, and have the safety, the thrill, the consistency of that hatred as long as she wanted or needed it to define and strengthen her or protect her from routine vulnerabilities. (Once when Hannah accused her of hating colored people, Eva said she only hated one, Hannah's father Boy-Boy, and it was hating him that kept her alive and happy.)

Happy or not, after BoyBoy's visit she began her retreat to her bedroom, leaving the bottom of the house more and more to those who lived there: cousins who were passing through, stray folks, and the many, many newly married couples she let rooms to with housekeeping privileges, and after 1910 she didn't willingly set foot on the stairs but once and that was to light a fire, the smoke of which was in her hair for years.

Under Eva's distant eye, and prey to her idiosyncrasies, her own children grew up stealthily: Pearl married at fourteen and moved to Flint, Michigan, from where she posted frail letters to her mother with two dollars folded into the writing paper. Sad little nonsense letters about minor troubles, her husband's job and who the children favored. Hannah married a laughing man named Rekus who died when their daughter Sula was about three years old, at which time Hannah moved back into her mother's big house prepared to take care of it and her mother forever.

With the exception of BoyBoy, those Peace women loved all men. It was manlove that Eva bequeathed to her daughters. Probably, people said, because there were no men in the house, no men to run it. But actually that was not true. The Peace women simply loved maleness, for its own sake. Eva, old as she was, and with one leg, had a regular flock of gentleman callers, and although she did not participate in the act of love, there was a good deal of teasing and pecking and laughter. The men wanted to see her lovely calf, that neat shoe, and watch the focusing that sometimes swept down out of the distances in her eyes. They wanted to see the joy in her face as they settled down to play checkers, knowing that even when she beat them, as she almost always did, somehow, in her presence, it was they who had won something. They would read the newspaper aloud to her and make observations on its content, and Eva would listen feeling no obligation to agree and, in fact, would take them to task about their interpretation of events. But she argued with them with such an absence of bile, such a concentration of manlove, that they felt their convictions solidified by her disagreement.

With other people's affairs Eva was equally prejudiced about men. She fussed interminably with the brides of the newly wed couples for not getting their men's supper ready on time; about how to launder shirts, press them, etc. "Yo' man be here direc'lin. Ain't it 'bout time you got busy?"

"Aw, Miss Eva. It'll be ready. We just having spaghetti."

"Again?" Eva's eyebrows fluted up and the newlywed pressed her lips together in shame.

Hannah simply refused to live without the attentions of

a man, and after Rekus' death had a steady sequence of
lovers, mostly the husbands of her friends and neighbors.
Her flirting was sweet, low and guileless. Without ever a
pat of the hair, a rush to change clothes or a quick application of paint, with no gesture whatsoever, barefoot in
the summer, in the winter her feet in a man's leather
slippers with the backs flattened under her heels, she
made men aware of her behind, her slim ankles, the dew-
smooth skin and the incredible length of neck. Then the
smile-eyes, the turn of her head—all so welcoming, light
and playful. Her voice trailed, dipped and bowed; she
gave a chord to the simplest words. Nobody, but nobody,
could say "hey sugar" like Hannah. When he heard it, the
man tipped his hat down a little over his eyes, hoisted his
trousers and thought about the hollow place at the base of
her neck. And all this without the slightest confusion
about work and responsibilities. While Eva tested and
argued with her men, leaving them feeling as though they
had been in combat with a worthy, if amiable, foe, Hannah rubbed no edges, made no demands, made the man
feel as though he were complete and wonderful just as he
was—he didn't need fixing—and so he relaxed and
swooned in the Hannah-light that shone on him simply
because he was. If the man entered and Hannah was carrying a coal scuttle up from the basement, she handled it
in such a way that it became a gesture of love. He made
no move to help her with it simply because he wanted to
see how her thighs looked when she bent to put it down,
knowing that she wanted him to see them too.

But since in that crowded house there were no places
for private and spontaneous lovemaking, Hannah would
take the man down into the cellar in the summer where it
was cool back behind the coal bin and the newspapers, or
in the winter they would step into the pantry and stand
up against the shelves she had filled with canned goods,
or lie on the flour sack just under the rows of tiny green
peppers. When those places were not available, she would
slip into the seldom-used parlor, or even up to her bedroom. She liked the last place least, not because Sula slept

in the room with her but because her love mate's tendency was always to fall asleep afterward and Hannah was fastidious about whom she slept with. She would fuck practically anything, but sleeping with someone implied for her a measure of trust and a definite commitment. So she ended up a daylight lover, and it was only once actually that Sula came home from school and found her mother in the bed, curled spoon in the arms of a man.

Seeing her step so easily into the pantry and emerge looking precisely as she did when she entered, only happier, taught Sula that sex was pleasant and frequent, but otherwise unremarkable. Outside the house, where children giggled about underwear, the message was different. So she watched her mother's face and the face of the men when they opened the pantry door and made up her own mind.

Hannah exasperated the women in the town—the "good" women, who said, "One thing I can't stand is a nasty woman"; the whores, who were hard put to find trade among black men anyway and who resented Hannah's generosity; the middling women, who had both husbands and affairs, because Hannah seemed too unlike them, having no passion attached to her relationships and being wholly incapable of jealousy. Hannah's friendships with women were, of course, seldom and short-lived, and the newly married couples whom her mother took in soon learned what a hazard she was. She could break up a marriage before it had even become one—she would make love to the new groom and wash his wife's dishes all in an afternoon. What she wanted, after Rekus died, and what she succeeded in having more often than not, was some touching every day.

The men, surprisingly, never gossiped about her. She was unquestionably a kind and generous woman and that, coupled with her extraordinary beauty and funky elegance of manner, made them defend her and protect her from any vitriol that newcomers or their wives might spill.

Eva's last child, Plum, to whom she hoped to bequeath everything, floated in a constant swaddle of love and affection, until 1917 when he went to war. He returned to the States in 1919 but did not get back to Medallion until 1920. He wrote letters from New York, Washington, D.C., and Chicago full of promises of homecomings, but there was obviously something wrong. Finally some two or three days after Christmas, he arrived with just the shadow of his old dip-down walk. His hair had been neither cut nor combed in months, his clothes were pointless and he had no socks. But he did have a black bag, a paper sack, and a sweet, sweet smile. Everybody welcomed him and gave him a warm room next to Tar Baby's and waited for him to tell them whatever it was he wanted them to know. They waited in vain for his telling but not long for the knowing. His habits were much like Tar Baby's but there were no bottles, and Plum was sometimes cheerful and animated. Hannah watched and Eva waited. Then he began to steal from them, take trips to Cincinnati and sleep for days in his room with the record player going. He got even thinner, since he ate only snatches of things at beginnings or endings of meals. It was Hannah who found the bent spoon black from steady cooking.

So late one night in 1921, Eva got up from her bed and put on her clothes. Hoisting herself up on her crutches, she was amazed to find that she could still manage them, although the pain in her armpits was severe. She practiced a few steps around the room, and then opened the door. Slowly, she manipulated herself down the long flights of stairs, two crutches under her left arm, the right hand grasping the banister. The sound of her foot booming in comparison to the delicate pat of the crutch tip. On each landing she stopped for breath. Annoyed at her physical condition, she closed her eyes and removed the crutches from under her arms to relieve the unaccustomed pressure. At the foot of the stairs she redistributed her weight between the crutches and swooped on through the front room, to the dining room, to the kitchen, swinging and swooping like a giant heron, so graceful sailing about

in its own habitat but awkward and comical when it
folded its wings and tried to walk. With a swing and a
swoop she arrived at Plum's door and pushed it open with
the tip of one crutch. He was lying in bed barely visible in
the light coming from a single bulb. Eva swung over to
the bed and propped her crutches at its foot. She sat
down and gathered Plum into her arms. He woke, but
only slightly.

"Hey, man. Hey. You holdin' me, Mamma?" His voice
was drowsy and amused. He chuckled as though he had
heard some private joke. Eva held him closer and began
to rock. Back and forth she rocked him, her eyes wandering around his room. There in the corner was a half-eaten
store-bought cherry pie. Balled-up candy wrappers and
empty pop bottles peeped from under the dresser. On the
floor by her foot was a glass of strawberry crush and a
Liberty magazine. Rocking, rocking, listening to Plum's
occasional chuckles, Eva let her memory spin, loop and
fall. Plum in the tub that time as she leaned over him. He
reached up and dripped water into her bosom and
laughed. She was angry, but not too, and laughed with
him.

"Mamma, you so purty. You so purty, Mamma."

Eva lifted her tongue to the edge of her lip to stop the
tears from running into her mouth. Rocking, rocking.
Later she laid him down and looked at him a long time.
Suddenly she was thirsty and reached for the glass of
strawberry crush. She put it to her lips and discovered it
was blood-tainted water and threw it to the floor. Plum
woke up and said, "Hey, Mamma, whyn't you go on back
to bed? I'm all right. Didn't I tell you? I'm all right. Go
on, now."

"I'm going, Plum," she said. She shifted her weight and
pulled her crutches toward her. Swinging and swooping,
she left his room. She dragged herself to the kitchen and
made grating noises.

Plum on the rim of a warm light sleep was still chuckling. Mamma. She sure was somethin'. He felt twilight.
Now there seemed to be some kind of wet light traveling

over his legs and stomach with a deeply attractive smell. It wound itself—this wet light—all about him, splashing and running into his skin. He opened his eyes and saw what he imagined was the great wing of an eagle pouring a wet lightness over him. Some kind of baptism, some kind of blessing, he thought. Everything is going to be all right, it said. Knowing that it was so he closed his eyes and sank back into the bright hole of sleep.

Eva stepped back from the bed and let the crutches rest under her arms. She rolled a bit of newspaper into a tight stick about six inches long, lit it and threw it onto the bed where the kerosene-soaked Plum lay in snug delight. Quickly, as the *whoosh* of flames engulfed him, she shut the door and made her slow and painful journey back to the top of the house.

Just as she got to the third landing she could hear Hannah and some child's voice. She swung along, not even listening to the voices of alarm and the cries of the deweys. By the time she got to her bed someone was bounding up the stairs after her. Hannah opened the door. "Plum! Plum! He's burning, Mamma! We can't even open the door! Mamma!"

Eva looked into Hannah's eyes. "Is? My baby? Burning?" The two women did not speak, for the eyes of each were enough for the other. Then Hannah closed hers and ran toward the voices of neighbors calling for water.

TONI CADE BAMBARA

In Toni Cade Bambara's first collection of short stories, the central consciousness of most of the stories is a young girl, an adolescent about ten years old, chafing at and defying the restrictions imposed by both racism and sexism. Nearly all the stories in her second short story collection, *The Sea Birds Are Still Alive* (1977), are about young and middle-aged women. Once again the conflict centers around the struggle of black women to free themselves from narrow, limiting choices, old images, from the victimization of old definitions.

The story "Medley" is an example of the themes Bambara is continually working out. The woman in this story is a free, self-defined, independent being. She is not in danger of living out any biologically, historically, or socially contrived role; but she comes up against the whole set of male rituals which intend to thwart her movement. Sweet Pea is a professional manicurist, financially successful and proud of her work. Eventually her respect for her work causes the break in her relationship with Larry. He is not actually jealous of her work, "just going through one of them obligatory male numbers, all symbolic, no depth." It is important to note how Bambara concludes this story because it indicates a definite shift in attitude toward the destinies of black women. Neither grimly tragic nor unbelievably heroic, Sweet Pea is simply a woman used to making her own decisions, depending on her own street-wise, level-headed good sense. She is making plans to leave a man no longer capable of respecting her.

The spirit of the blues and jazz singers informs these stories in several ways. In "Medley" the music of the black past is Sweet Pea's objective correlative, describing the reaches of her soul, depths she has sounded that take her way beyond the sad little scapegoat rituals with Larry.

Structurally the story is designed like an improvisational jazz composition. Bambara plays the melody at the beginning; we know that the main part of the story—its melodic line—is the deterioration of Sweet Pea's love affair with Larry. Then Bambara plays the middle section like a jazz riff: the melody is obscured, covered over, seemingly abandoned, as she explores all the details of these characters' lives that have bearing on their present circumstances. Sweet Pea's two other husbands, Larry's failure as a bass player, her job with Moody, snatches of conversations with her girlfriends—are all themes that must be played as though each instrument in a jazz combo were playing an individual improvisation around the main theme. At the end, these disparate parts are interwoven, directing us back to the melody, where we can now understand Sweet Pea's inexorable decision to leave Larry.

Music functions symbolically in Bambara's second story, "Witchbird," a story that is a commentary on the treatment of the black woman in art and in life. In both life and art, the black woman has been imprisoned in stereotypes, made to carry out the fantasies and perversions of whites and males. Honey, the main character, physically matches the image of the black matriarch: she's large, overweight, easygoing, and because she fits people's idea of the strong black mother, she is treated as such. She becomes everybody's fortress in time of trouble, a confidante and cook and maid, absolutely fearless and unquestionably sexless. She seems archetypally older than all other women, though she's barely forty; and she is always being cast in the plays she tries out for as an Aunt Jemima type. As Honey puts it, "Whole being entrapped, all possibly impaled, locked in some stereotype . . . Shit, I ain't nobody's mother."

Bambara gives a fictional directive to the new generation of black writers to unlock the black woman from this fatal imagery as the symbolic witchbird is screaming for Honey's release. The rage of the witchbird is Honey's own power pushing her beneath the outer core, making her attempt the transformation: "Bird make me think some singer locked up inside, hostage." Hungering for the song or the drama that can convey the pain and the beauty of who she is, that will carry her full self, the self that no one sees, or desires, or celebrates, Honey searches through the songs of the old blues singers (Bessie and Trixie Smith, and Ma Rainey) determined to find a way to express who she is. "So many women in them songs waiting to be released into the air again, freed to roam."

Witchbird

BY TONI CADE BAMBARA

I

Curtains blew in and wrecked my whole dressing-table arrangement. Then in he came, eight kinds of darkness round his shoulders, this nutty bird screechin on his arm, on a nine-speed model, hand brakes and all. Said, "Come on, we goin ride right out of here just like you been wantin to for long time now." Patting the blanket lassoed to the carrier, leaning way back to do it, straddling the bike and thrusting his johnson out in front, patting, thrusting, insinuating. Bird doing a two-step on the handle bars.

Damn if I'm riding nowhere on some bike. I like trains. Am partial to fresh-smelling club cars with clear windows and cushy seats with white linen at the top for my cheek to snooze against. Not like the hulking, oil-leaking, smoke-belching monstrosity I came home on when the play closed. Leaning my cheek against the rattling window-pane, like to shook my teeth loose. Cigar stench, orange peels curling on the window sills, balls of wax paper greasy underfoot, the linen rank from umpteen different hair pomades. Want the trains like before, when I was little and the porter hauled me up by my wrists and joked with me about my new hat, earning the five my mama slipped him, leisurely. Watching out for my person, saving a sunny seat in the dining car, clearing the aisle of perverts from round my berth, making sure I was in the no-drama section of the train once we crossed the Potomac.

"Well, we can cross over to the other side," he saying, "you in a rut, girl, let's go." Leaning over the edge of the

boat, trailing a hand in the blue-green Caribbean. No
way. I like trains. Then uncorking the champagne, the
bottle lodged between his thighs. Then the pop of the
cork, froth cascading all over his lap. I tell you I'm partial
to trains. "Well, all right," he sayin, stepping out his
pants. "We go the way you want, any way you want.
Cause you need a change," he saying, chuggin over my
carpet in this bubble-top train he suddenly got. Bird
shouting at me from the perch of eye-stinging white linen.
And I know something gotta be wrong. Cause whenever
I've asked for what I want in life, I never get it. So he got
to be the devil or some kind of other ugly no-good thing.

"Get on out my room," I'm trying to say, jaws stuck.
Whole right side and left paralyzed like I'm jammed in a
cage. "You tromping on my house shoes and I don't play
that. Them's the house shoes Heywood gave me for
Mother's Day." Some joke. Heywood come up empty-
handed every rent day, but that don't stop him from
boarding all his ex ole ladies with me freebee. But yellow
satin Hollywood slippers with pompoms on Mother's Day,
figuring that's what I'm here for. Shit, I ain't nobody's
mother. I'm a singer. I'm an actress. I'm a landlady look
like. Hear me. Applaud me. Pay me.

"But look here," he saying, holding up a pair of house
shoes even finer than mine. Holding em up around his
ears like whatshisname, not the Sambo kid, the other little
fellah. "Come on and take this ride with me."

All this talk about crossing over somewhere in dem
golden slippers doing something to my arms. They jiggling loose from me like they through the bars of the
cage, cept I know I'm under the covers in a bed, not a
box. Just a jiggling. You'd think I was holding a hazel
switch or a willow rod out in the woods witching for
water. Peach twig better actually for locating subter-
ranean springs. And I try to keep my mind on water,
cause water is always a good thing. Creeks, falls, founda-
tions, artesian wells. Baptism, candelight ablutions,
skinny-dipping in the lake, C&C with water on the side.
The root of all worthy civilizations, water. Can heal you.

Scrunched up under the quilts, the sick tray pushed to the side, the heal of rain washing against the window can heal you or make you pee the bed one, which'll wake you from fever, from sleep, will save you. Save me. Cause damn if this character ain't trying to climb into my berth. And if there's one thing I can do without, it's phantom fucking.

"Honey? You told me to wake you at dark. It's dark." Gayle, the brown-skin college girl my sometime pi-ano player—sometime manager—mosttime friend Heywood dumped on me last time through here, jiggling my arms. Looking sorrowful about waking me up, she knows how sacred sleep can be, though not how scary.

"Here," she says, sliding my house shoes closer to the bed. "You know Heywood was all set to get you some tired old navy-blue numbers. I kept telling him you ain't nobody's grandma," she says, backing up to give me room to stretch, looking me over like she always does, compar-ing us I guess to flatter her own vanity, or wondering maybe if it's possible Heywood sees beyond friend, col-league, to maybe woman. All the time trying to pry me open and check out is there some long ago Heywood-me history. The truth is there's nothing to tell. Heywood spot him a large, singing, easygoing type woman, so he dumps his girl friends on me is all. I slide into the cold slippers. They're too soft now and give no support. Cheap-ass shoes. Here it is only Halloween, and they falling apart al-ready. I'm sucking my teeth but can't even hear myself good for the caterwauling that damn bird's already set up in the woods, tearing up the bushes, splitting twigs with the high notes. Bird make me think some singer locked up inside, hostage. Cept that bird ain't enchanting, just an-noying.

"Laney's fixing a plate of supper for Miz Mary," Gayle is saying, sliding a hand across my dressing-table scarf like she dying to set her buns down and mess in my stuff. My make-up kit ain't even unpacked, I'm noticing, and the play been closed for over a month. I ain't even taken the time to review what that role's done to my sense of balance, my sense of self. But who's got time, what with all of Heywood's women cluttering up my house, my life? Prancing around in shorty nightgowns so I don't dare have company in. A prisoner in my own house.

"Laney say come on, she'll walk to the shop with you, Honey. Me too. I think my number hit today. Maybe I can help out with the bills."

Right. I'd settle for some privacy. Had such other plans for my time right in through here. Bunch of books my nephew sent untouched. Stacks of *Variety* unread under the kitchen table. The new sheet music gathering dust on the piano. Been wanting to go over the old songs, the ole Bessie numbers, Ma Rainey, Trixie Smith, early Lena. So many women in them songs waiting to be released into the air again, freed to roam. Good time to be getting my new repertoire together too instead of rushing into my clothes and slapping my face together just because Laney can't bear walking the streets alone after dark, and Gayle too scared to stay in the place by herself. Not that Heywood puts a gun to my head, but it's hard to say no to a sister with no place to go. So they wind up here, expecting me to absorb their blues and transform them maybe into songs. Been over a year since I've written any new songs. Absorbing, absorbing, bout to turn to mush rather than crystallize, sparkling.

II

Magazine lady on the phone this morning asked if I was boarding any new up-and-coming stars. Very funny. Vera, an early Heywood ex, had left here once her demo record was cut, went to New York and made the big time. Got me a part in the play, according to the phone voice contracted to do a four-page spread on Vera Willis, Star. But that ain't how the deal went down at all.

"I understand you used to room together" was how the phone interview started off. Me arranging the bottles and jars on my table, untangling the junk in my jewelry boxes. Remembering how Vera considered herself more guest than roommate, no problem whatsoever about leaving all the work to me, was saving herself for Broadway or Hollywood one. Like nothing I could be about was all that important so hey, Honey, pick up the mop. Me sitting on the piano bench waiting for Heywood to bring in a batch of cheat sheets, watching Vera in the yard with my nieces turning double dudge. Then Vera gets it in her mind to snatch away the rope and sing into the wooden handle, strolling, sassy, slinky between the dogwoods, taking poses, kicking at the tail of the rope and making teethy faces like Heywood taught her. The little girls stunned by this performance so like their own, only this one done brazenly, dead serious, and by a grown-up lady slithering about the yard.

Staring out the window, I felt bad. I thought it was because Vera was just not pretty. Not pretty and not nice. Obnoxious in fact, selfish, vain, lazy. But yeah she could put a song over, though she didn't have what you'd call musicianship. Like she'd glide into a song, it all sounding quite dull normal at first. Then a leg would shoot out as though from a split in some juicy material kicking the mike cord out the way, then the song would move somewhere. As though the spirit of music had hovered cautious around her chin thinking it over, looking her over, then liking that leg, swept into her mouth and took hold of her throat and the song possessed her, electrified the leg, sparked her into pretty. Later realizing I was staring at her, feeling bad because of course she'd make it, have what she wanted, go everywhere, meet everybody, be everything but self-deserving.

First-class bitch was my two cents with the producers, just to make it crystal clear I didn't intend riding in on her dress tails but wanted to be judged by my own work, my reputation, my audition. Don't nobody do me no favors, please, cause I'm the baddest singer out here and one of the best character actressses around. And just keeping warmed up till a Black script comes my way.

Wasn't much of a part, but a good bit at the end. My daddy used to instruct, if you can't be the star of the show, aim for a good bit at the end. People remember that one good line or that one striking piece of business by the bit player in the third act. Well, just before the end, I come on for my longest bit in the play. I'm carrying this veil, Vera's mama's veil. The woman's so grief-stricken and whatnot, she ain't even buttoned up right and forgot to put on her veil. So here I come with the veil, and the mourners part the waves to give me a path right to the grave site. But once I see the coffin, my brown-sugar honey chile darlin dead and boxed, I forget all about the blood mama waiting for her veil. Forget all about maintaining my servant place in the bourgy household. I snatch off my apron and slowly lift that veil, for I am her true mother who cared for her and carried her through. I raise the hell outta that veil, transforming myself into Mother with a capital M. I let it drape slowly, slowly round my corn rolls, slowly lower it around my brow, my nose, mouth opening and the song bursting my jaws asunder as the curtain—well, not curtain, but the lights, cause we played it in the round, dim. Tore the play up with the song.

Course we did have a set-to about the costume. The designer saw my point—her talents were being squandered copying the pancake box. Playwright saw my point too, why distort a perfectly fine character just cause the director has mammy fantasies. An African patchwork apron was the only concession I'd make. Got to be firm about shit like that, cause if you ain't some bronze Barbie doll type or the big fro murder-mouth militant sister, you Aunt Jemima. Not this lady. No way. Got to fight hard and all the time with the scripts and the people. Cause they'll trap you in a fiction. Breath drained, heart stopped, vibrancy fixed, under arrest. Whole being entrapped, all possibility impaled, locked in some stereotype. And how you look trying to call from the box and be heard much less be understood long enough to get out and mean something useful and for real?

Sometimes I think I do a better job of it with the bogus scripts than with the life script. Fight harder with directors than with friends who trap me in their scenarios, put a drama on my ass. That's the problem with friends sometimes, they invest in who you were or seem to have been, capture you and you're through. Forget what you had in mind about changing, growing, developing. Got you typecasted. That's why I want some time off to think, to work up a new repertoire of songs, of life. So many women in them songs, in them streets, in me, waiting to be freed up.

Dozing, drifting into sleep sometime, the script sliding off the quilts into a heap, I hear folks calling to me. Calling from the box. Mammy Pleasant, was it? Tubman, slave women bundlers, voodoo queens, maroon guerrillas, combatant ladies in the Seminole nation, calls from the swamps, the tunnels, the classrooms, the studios, the factories, the roofs, from the doorway hushed or brassy in a dress way too short but it don't mean nuthin heavy enough to have to explain, just like Bad Bitch in the Sanchez play was saying. But then the wagon comes and they all rounded up and caged in the Bitch-Whore-Mouth mannequin with the dead eyes and the mothball breath, never to be heard from again. But want to sing a Harriet song and play a Pleasant role and bring them all center stage.

Wives weeping from the pillow not waking him cause he got his own weight to tote, wife in the empty road with one slipper on and the train not stopping, mother anxious with the needle and thread or clothespin as the children grow either much too fast to escape the attention of the posse or not fast enough to take hold. Women calling from the lock-up of the Matriarch cage. I want to put some of these new mother poems in those books the nephew sends to music. They got to be sung, hummed, shouted, chanted, swung.

Too many damn ransom notes fluttering in the window, or pitched in through the glass. Too much bail to post. Too many tunnels to dig and too much dynamite to set. I read the crazy scripts just to keep my hand in, cause I knew these newbreed Bloods going to do it, do it, do it. But meanwhile, I gotta work . . . and hell. Then read one of them books my nephew always sending and hearing the voices speaking free not calling from these new Black poems. Speaking free. So I know I ain't crazy. But fast as we bust one, two loose, here come some crazy cracker throwing a croaker sack over Nat Turner's head, or white folks taking Malcolm hostage. And one time in Florida, dreaming in the hotel room about the Mary McLeod Bethune exhibit, I heard the woman calling from some diary entry they had under glass, a voice calling, muffled under the gas mask they clamped on hard and turned her on till she didn't know what was what. But calling for Black pages.

Then waking and trying to resume the reading, cept I can't remember just whom I'm supposed to try to animate in those dead, white pages I got to deal with till a Blood writes me my own. And catch myself calling to the white pages as I ripple them fast, listening to the pages for the entrapped voices calling, calling as the pages flutter.

Shit. It's enough to make you crazy. Where is my play, I wanna ask these new Bloods at the very next conference I hear about. Where the hell is my script? When I get to work my show?

"A number of scandalous rumors followed the run of the play, taking up an inordinate amount of space in the reviews," the lady on the phone was saying, me caught up in my own dialogue. "I understand most of the men connected with the play and Vera Willis had occasion to . . ."

There was Heywood, of course. Hadn't realized they'd gotten back together till that weekend we were packing the play off to New York. Me packing ahead of schedule and anxious to get out of D.C. fast, cause Bradwell, who used to manage the club where I been working for years, had invited me to his home for the weekend. For old times' sake, he'd said. Right. He'd married somebody else, a singer we used to crack on as I recall, not a true note in her, her tits getting her over. And now she'd left him rolling around lonely in the brownstone on Edgecombe Avenue she'd once thought she just had to have. I went out and bought two hussy nightgowns. I was gonna break out in a whole new number. But never did work up the nerve. Never did have the occasion, ole Bradwell crying the blues about his wife. So what am I there for—to absorb, absorb, and transform if you can, ole girl. Absorb, absorb and try to convert it all to something other than fat.

Heywood calling to ask me to trade my suite near the theater for his room clear cross town.

"You can have both," I said, chuckling. "I'm off for the weekend."

"How come? Where you going?"

"Rendezvous. Remember the guy that used to own—"

"Cut the comedy. Where you going?"

"I'm telling you. I got a rendezvous with this gorgeous man I—"

"Look here," he cut in, "I'd invited Laney up to spend the weekend. That was before me and Vera got together again. I was wondering if you'd bail me out, maybe hang out with Laney till I can—"

"Heywood, you deaf? I just now told you I'm off to spend the—"

"Seriously?"

Made me so mad, I just hung up. Hung up and called me a fast cab.

III

Laney, Gayle, and me turn into Austin and run smack into a bunch of ghosts. Skeletons, pirates, and little devils with great flapping shopping bags set up a whirlwind around us. Laney spins around like in a speeded-up movie, holding Mary's dinner plate away from her dress and moaning,

comically. Comically at first. But then our bird friend in
the woods starts shrieking and Laney moaning for real.
Gayle empties her bag into one of the opened sacks, then
leans in to retrieve her wallet, though I can't see why. All I
got for the kids is a short roll of crumbly Lifesavers, hair
with tobacco and lint from my trench coat lining. Screaming and wooo-wooooing, they jack-rabbit on down Austin.
Then we heading past the fish truck, my mind on some
gumbo, when suddenly Gayle stops. She heard it soon's I
did. Laney still walking on till I guess some remark didn't
get a uh-hunh and she turns around to see us way behind,
Gayle's head cocked to the side.

"What it is?" Laney looking up and down the street for
a clue. Other than the brother dumping the last of the ice
from the fish truck and a few cats hysterical at the curb,
too self-absorbed to launch a concerted attack on the
truck, there ain't much to keep the eyes alive. "What?"
Laney whispers.

From back of the houses we hear some mother calling her son, the voice edgy on the last syllable, getting
frantic. Probably Miz Baker, whose six-foot twelve-year-
old got a way of scooting up and down that resembles too
much the actions of a runaway bandit to the pigs around
here. Mainly, he got the outlaw hue, and running too?
Shit, Miz Baker stay frantic. The boy answers from the
woods, which starts the bird up again, screeching, rip-
ping through the trees, like she trying to find a way out of
them woods and heaven help us if she do, cause she dangerous with rage.

"That him?" Gayle asks, knowing I'm on silence this
time of night.

"Who?" Laney don't even bother looking at me, cause
she knows I got a whole night of singing and running off
at the mouth to get through once Mary lets me out from
under the dryer and I get to the club. "Witchbird?"
Laney takes a couple steps closer to us. "Yawl better tell
me what's up," she says, "cause this here gettin spooo-
keeee!"

It's mostly getting dark and Laney don't wanna have to

take the shortcut through the woods. Witchbird gotta way
of screaming on you sudden, scare the shit outta you.
Laney trying to balance that plate of dinner and not lose
the juice. She is worried you can tell, and not just about
Mary's mouth over cold supper. Laney's face easy to read,
everything surfaces to the skin. Dug that the day Heywood brought her by. She knew she was being cut loose,
steered safely to cove, the boat shoving off and bye, baby,
bye. Sad crinkling round the eyes, purples under the chin,
throat pulsating. Gayle harder to read, a Scorpio, she
plays it close to the chest unless she can play it for
drama.

"Tell me, Gayle. What it is?"

"Heywood back in town."

"Ohhh, girl, don't tell me that." Laney takes a coupla
sideways steps, juggling the plate onto one hand so she
can tug down the jersey she barmaids in. "You better
come on."

"You know one thing," Gayle crooning it, composing a
monologue, sound like. "There was a time when that
laugh could turn me clear around in the street and make
me forget just where I thought I was going." On cue,
Heywood laughs one of his laughs and Gayle's head tips,
locating his whereabouts. She hands me her suede bag
heavy with the pic comb and the schoolbooks. It's clear
she fixin to take off. "I really loved that dude," she saying,
theatrics gone. Laney moves on, cause she don't want to
hear nuthin about Heywood and especially from Gayle.
"He gets his thing off," Laney had said to Gayle the night
she was dumped, "behind the idea of his harem sprawled
all over Honey's house gassing about him. I refuse," she
had said and stuck to it.

"I really, really did," Gayle saying, something leaking
in her voice.

Laney hears it and steps back. It's spilling on her shoes,
her dress, soaking into her skin. She moves back again
cause Gayle's zone is spreading. Gayle so filling up and
brimming over, she gotta take over more and more room
to accommodate the swell. Her leaking splashes up

against me too—Heywood taking a solo, teeth biting out a
rhythm on the back of his lower lip, Heywood at the
wheel leaning over for a kiss fore he cranks up, Heywood
wound up in rumpled sheets with his cap pulled down,
sweat beading on his nose, waiting on breakfast, Heywood
doing the dance of the hot hands and Gayle scrambling
for a potholder to catch the coffeepot he'd reached for
with his fool self, Heywood falling off the porch and
Gayle's daddy right on him. Gayle's waves wash right up
on me and I don't want no parts of it. Let it all wash right
through me, can't use it, am to the brim with my own
stuff waiting to be transformed. Washes through me so
fast the pictures blur and all I feel is heat and sparks. And
then I hear the laugh again.

"Oh, shit," Laney says, watching the hem of Gayle's
dress turning into the alley. "That girl is craaaaa-zeee, ya
heah?" Her legs jiggling to put her in the alley in more
ways than one, but that plate leaking pot likker and demanding its due.

Bright's strung up lights in the alley and you can make
him out clear, hunched over the bathtub swishing barbeque sauce with a sheet-wrapped broom. Cora visible too,
doing a shonuff flower arrangement on the crushed ice
with the watermelon slices. And there's Heywood, ole
lanky Heywood in his cap he says Babs Gonzales stole
from Kenny Clarke and he in turn swiped from Babs. One
arm lazy draped around Gayle's shoulders, the other
crooked in the fence he lounges against, sipping some of
Bright's bad brandy brew, speakeasy style. Other folks
around the card table sipping from jelly jars or tin cups.
But Heywood would have one of Cora's fine china numbers. He's looking good.

"What's goin on?" Laney asks in spite of herself, but refuses to move where she can see into the yard. All she got
to do is listen, cause Heywood is the baritone lead of the
eight-part card game opus.

"Ho!"

"Nigger, just play the card."

"Gonna. Gonna do that direckly. Right on yawl's ass."

"Do it to em, Porter."

"Don't tell him nuthin. He don't wanna know nuthin. He ain't never been nuthin but a fool."

Porter spits on the card and slaps it on his forehead.

"Got the bitch right here"—he's pointing—"the bitch that's gonna set ya."

"Nigger, you nasty, you know that? You a nasty-ass nigger and that's why don't nobody never wanna play with yo nasty-ass self."

"Just play the card, Porter."

"Ho!" He bangs the card down with a pop and the table too.

"Iz you crazy?"

"If Porter had any sense, he'd be dangerous."

"Sense enough to send these blowhards right out the back door. Ho!"

"You broke the table and the ashtray, fool."

"And that was my last cigarette too. Gimme a dollar."

"Dollar! I look like a fool? If you paying Bright a dollar for cigarettes, you the fool."

"I want the dollar for some barbeque."

"What! What!" Porter sputtering and dancing round the yard. "How come I gotta replace one cigarette with a meal?"

"Okay then, buy some watermelon and some of the fire juice."

"You don't logic, man. You sheer don't logic. All I owe you is a cigarette."

"What about the table?"

"It ain't your table, nigger."

Laney is click-clicking up the street, giving wide berth to the path that leads through the woods. "Why Gayle want to put herself through them changes all over again," she is mumbling, grinding her heels in the broken pavement, squashing the dandelions. "I wouldn't put myself through none of that mess again for all the money." She picking up speed and I gotta trot to catch up. "I don't know how you can stay friends with a man like that, Honey."

"He don't do me no harm," I say, then mad to break my silence.

"Oh, no?" She trying to provoke me into debating it, so she says it again, "Oh, no?"

I don't want to get into this, all I want is to get into Mary's shampoo chair, to laze under Mary's hands and have her massage all the hurt up out of my body, tension emulsified in the coconut-oil suds, all fight sprayed away. My body been so long on chronic red alert messin with them theater folks, messing with stock types, real types, messing with me, I need release, not hassles.

"You think it's no harm the way he uses you, Honey? What are you, his mother, his dumping grounds? Why you put up with it? Why you put up with us, with me? Oh, Honey, I—"

I walk right along, just like she ain't talking to me. I can't take in another thing.

IV

"Well, all right! Here she come, Broadway star," someone bellows at me as the bell over the door jangles.

"Come on out from under that death, Honey," Mary says soon's we get halfway in the door. "Look like you sportin a whole new look in cosmetics. Clown white, ain't it? Or is it Griffin All White applied with a putty knife?" Mary leaves her customer in the chair to come rip the wig off my head. "And got some dead white woman on your head too. Why you wanna do this to yourself, Honey? You auditioning for some zombie movie?"

"Protective covering," Bertha says, slinging the magazine she'd been reading onto the pile. "You know how Honey likes to put herself out of circulation, Mary. Honey, you look like one of them creatures Nanna Mae raised from the dead. What they do to you in New York, girl? We thought you'd come back tired, but not embalmed."

"Heard tell a duppy busted up some posh do on the hill last Saturday," Mary's customer saying. "Lotta zombies round here."

"Some say it was the ghost of Willie Best come back to kill him somebody."

"Long's it's some white somebody, okay by me."

"Well, you know colored folks weren't exactly kind to the man when he was alive. Could be—"

"Heard Heywood's back on the scene," Bertha comes over to say to me. She lifts my hand off the armrest and checks my manicure and pats my hand to make up for, I guess, her not-so-warm greeting. "Be interesting to see just what kinda bundle he gonna deposit on your doorstep this time." Laney cuts her eye at Bertha, surrenders up the juiceless meal and splits. "Like you ain't got nuthin better to do with ya tits but wet-nurse his girls."

I shove Bertha's hand off mine and stretch out in my favorite chair. Mary's got a young sister now to do the scratchin and hot oil. She parts hair with her fingers, real gentle-like. Feels good. I'm whipped. I think on all I want to do with the new music and I'm feelin crowded, full up, rushed.

"No use you trying to ig me, Honey," Bertha says real loud. "Cause I'm Mary's last customer. We got all night."

"Saw Frieda coming out the drugstore," somebody is saying. "Package looked mighty interesting."

Everybody cracking up, Bertha too. I ease my head back and close my eyes under the comb scratching up dandruff.

"Obviously Ted is going on the road again and Frieda gonna pack one of her famous box snacks."

"Got the recipe for the oatmeal cookies richeah," someone saying. "One part rolled oats, one long drip of sorghum, fistful of raisins, and a laaaarge dose of salt-peter."

"Salt pete—er salt pete—er," somebody singing through the nose, outdoing Dizzy.

"Whatchu say!"

"Betcha there'll be plenty straaange mashed potatoes on the table tonight."

The young girl's rubbin is too hard in the part and the oil too hot. But she so busy cracking up, she don't notice my ouchin.

"Saltpetertaters, what better dish to serve a man going on the road for three days. Beats calling him every hour on the half-hour telling him to take a cold shower."

"Best serve him with a summons for being so downright ugly. Can't no woman be really serious about messin with Ted, he too ugly."

"Some that looks ugly . . ." Couldn't catch the rest of it, but followed the giggling well enough after what sounded like a second of silence.

"Mary"—someone was breathless with laughter—"when you and the sisters gonna give another one of them balls?"

"Giiirl," howls Bertha. "Wasn't that ball a natural ball?"

V

Bertha and Mary and me organized this Aquarian Ball. We so busy making out the lists, hooking people up, calling in some new dudes from the Islands just to jazz it up, hiring musicians and all, we clean forgot to get me an escort. I'd just made Marshall the trumpet player give me back my key cause all he ever wanted to do was bring by a passel of fish that needed cleaning and frying, and I was sick of being cook and confidante. I bet if I lost weight, people'd view me different. Other than Marshall, wasn't no man on the horizon, much less the scene. Mary, me and Bertha playing bid whist and I feel a Boston in my bones, so ain't paying too much attention to the fact that this no escort status of mine is serious business as far as Bertha's concerned.

"What about Heywood?" she says, scooping up the kitty.

Right on cue as always, in comes ole lanky Heywood with his cap yanked down around his brow and umpteen scarves around his mouth looking like Jesse James. He's got a folio of arrangements to deliver to me, but likes to make a big production first of saying hello to sisters. So while he's doing his rhyming couplets and waxing lyric and whatnot, I'm looking him over, trying to unravel my feelings about this man I've known, worked with, befriended for so long. Good manager, never booked me in no dumps. Always sees to it that the money ain't funny. A good looker and all, but always makes me feel more mother or older sister, though he four months to the day older than me. Naaw, I conclude, Heywood just my buddy. But I'm thinking too that I need a new buddy, cause he's got me bagged somehow. Put me in a bag when I wasn't looking. Folks be sneaky with their scenarios and secret casting.

"Say, handsome," Bertha say, jumping right on it, "ain't you taking Honey here to the ball?"

"Why somebody got to take her? I thought yawl was giving it."

"That ain't no answer. Can't have Honey waltzin in without—"

"Hold on," he saying, unwrapping the scarves cause we got the oven up high doing the meat patties.

"Never mind all that," says Mary. "Who you know can do it? Someone nice now."

"Well, I'll tell you," he says, stretching his arm around me. "I don't know no men good enough for the queen here."

"You a drag and a half," says Bertha.

"And I don't want to block traffic either," he says. "I mean if Honey comes in with my fine self on her arm, no man there is—"

"Never mind that," says Mary, slapping down an ace. "What about your friends, I'm askin you?"

"Like I said, I don't know anybody suitable."

"What you mean is, you only knows the ladies," says Bertha, disgusted. "You the type dude that would proba-

bly come up with a basket case for escort anyway. Club
foot, hunchback, palsied moron or something. Just to
make sure Honey is still available for you to mammify."

"Now wait a minute," he says, rising from the chair and
pushing palms against the air like he fending us off. "How
I get involved in yawl's arrangements?"

"You a friend, ain't ya? You a drag, that's for sure."
Bertha lays down her hand, we thought to hit Heywood,
come to find she trump tight.

Heywood puts the folio in my lap and rewraps the
scarves for take-off, and we spend the afternoon being sullen, and damn near burnt up the meat patties.

"I'm getting tired of men like that," grumbles Bertha
after while. "Either it's 'Hey, Mama, hold my head,' or
'Hey, Sister,' at three in the morning. When it get to be
'Sugar Darling'? I'm tired of it. And you, Honey, should
be the tiredest of all."

"So I just took my buns right to her house, cause she
my friend and what else a friend for?" one of the women
is saying. Mary's easing my head back on the shampoo
tray, so I can't see who's talking.

"So did you tell her?"

"I surely did. I held her by the shoulders and said,
'Helen, you do know that Amos is on the dope now, don't
you?' And she kinda went limp in my arms like she was
gonna just crumble and not deal with it."

"A myth all that stuff about our strength and strength
and then some," Bertha saying.

"'If Amos blow his mind now, who gonna take care of
you in old age, Helen?' I try to tell her."

"So what she say?"

"She don't say nuthin. She just cry."

"It's a hellafyin thing. No jobs, nary a fit house in sight,
famine on the way, but the dope just keep comin and
comin."

I don't know Helen or Amos. Can't tell whether Amos is
the son or the husband. Ain't that a bitch. But I feel bad
inside. I crumple up too hearing it. Picturing a Helen see-

ing her Amos in a heap by the bathtub, gagging, shivering, defeated, not like he should be. Getting the blankets to wrap him up, holding him round, hugging him tight, rocking, rocking, rocking.

"You need a towel?" Mary whispers, bending under the dryer. No amount of towel's gonna stop the flood, I'm thinking. I don't even try to stop. Let it pour, let it get on out so I can travel light. I'm thinking maybe I'll do Billie's number tonight. Biting my lip and trying to think on the order of songs I'm going to get through this evening and where I can slip Billie in.

"What's with you, Honey?"

"Mary got this damn dryer on KILL," I say, and know I am about to talk myself hoarse and won't be fit for singing.

In honor of free women

SHERLEY ANNE WILLIAMS

I think that what started me on the road to being a writer was searching for books about black people in the library of Edison Jr./Sr. High School in Fresno, California, in the '50's and being too embarrassed, too shamed to ask for help from the librarian. I don't remember precisely how old I was—I entered Edison as a twelve-year-old seventh-grader and graduated five years later in 1962 and much of that time is a blur—maybe thirteen, fourteen, or fifteen. I do know I was having a lot of trouble—with my mother, the one sister who remained at home, my friends, myself. I felt abandoned by my two older sisters, who had married and seldom returned for visits, out of touch with my teachers, even those who befriended me. What did they know about being black, being on welfare, being solicited for sex by older black men in the neighborhood and the old white ones who cruised our streets on the weekends? And though I know now that need must have been written all over me, I would have died before exposing my family life or my longing to them.

Much as I loved Louisa May Alcott and Frank Yerby, they no longer transported me as they once had done. So, on infrequent class trips to the library (I never went unless forced to by class requirements, for I was set off enough from my classmates by my grades and my middle-class aspirations in my obviously underclass body), I roamed the room, surreptitiously studying the shelves, hoping to spot a title that would identify the books as Black. I read Black Boy, an obvious title, but worse than useless for me: it wasn't just that I didn't have to cope with that kind of overt racism in Fresno, California, the heart of the farm-rich San Joaquin Valley. I could identify only in part with Wright's conflicts with his family. I would have given a lot for just such signs of caring as his family's attempts to force him even into the Tom role. Rather than prizing my differences, I despised them and sought during this time to conform, only to discover that even my attempts at conformity set me apart.

I was led, almost inevitably, I think, to the autobiographies of women entertainers—Eartha Kitt, Katherine Dunham, Ethel Waters. The material circumstances of their childhood were so much worse than mine; they too had had to cope with early and forced sex and sexuality, with mothers who could not express love in the terms that they desperately needed. Yet they had risen above this, turned their difference into something that was respected in the world beyond their homes. I, in the free North, could do no less than endure.

And I did, helped immensely, immeasurably by my sister, Ruby, who returned home after the break-up of her marriage; she was eighteen, her daughter almost three. It is almost twenty years since this happened, yet I have never ceased to admire her and be amazed at the change "Ruise" wrought in my life. She worked as a maid/cook for a white family five days a week (and got twenty-five dollars, an amount that was later doubled when she moved to a new job with a new family), attended night school four nights a week to earn the high school diploma that pregnancy and marriage had forced her to abandon, partied at least two nights a week, took care of her daughter and counseled and guided me through the shoals of adolescence that had almost wrecked her own life. She paid for this schedule with ill-health which eventually forced her to quit work and go on welfare—but not before she had that high school diploma.

After my mother's death—I was then sixteen going on seventeen—I was placed in Ruise's custody and the money she received for my care—plus what we got from occasional field work—picking cotton, cutting grapes, holiday work as a stock clerk in a downtown store, the prize money from a story accepted by Scholastic Magazine— meant that we survived my last year in high school near the subsistence level. Ruise and her friends, young women much like herself, provided me with a community, with models, both real-life and literary. I was by that last year in high school more sophisticated in searching out black literature. But nowhere did I find stories of these heroic young women who despite all they had to do and endure laughed and loved, hoped and encouraged, supported each other with gifts of food and money and fought the country that was quite literally, we were convinced, trying to kill us. My first published story, "Tell Martha Not to Moan" (Mass. Review, 1967?, anthologized in The Black Woman and elsewhere), had its genesis in those years. Martha and her life are a composite of the women who made up that circle. Their courage and humor helped each other and me thru some very difficult years.

The years between then and now are not easily capsulized. Those women pushed me out into a world where I could no longer use their lives as guidelines. And much of that time has been spent in wandering from coast to coast, Nashville, Fresno, San Francisco, D.C., Birmingham, back to Fresno, L.A., back to Fresno, Providence, R.I., Fresno, and finally San Diego. I have moved Ruise to San Diego and plan to go back to collect Learn; my oldest sister is dead. The Peacock Poems (1975, Wesleyan University Press) contains something of that early, early life when my father and mother were alive and we followed the crops; "Someone Sweet Angel Chile," the unpublished and unfinished second collection of poems, will contain more because I think that our migrations are an archetype of those of the dispossessed and I want somehow to tell the story of how the dispossessed become possessed of their own history without losing sight, without forgetting the meaning or the nature of their journey.

I am not a very political person in the sense of joining organizations or espousing political philosophies—my disenchantment with the exponents of Black Power began in 1967 while a graduate student at Howard University when a friend and Black Power advocate disparaged my writing because I wasn't writing Richard Wright. I remain, more firmly now than then, a proponent of Black consciousness, of the "The Black Aesthetic," and so I am a political writer. I try to elucidate those elements in our lives on which constructive political changes, those that do more than blackwash or femalize the same old power structure, can be built.

Graduate school was necessary for my current livelihood—college teacher of Afro-American literature—though even there I drew the line finally at certain kinds of disciplines as extraneous to my real pursuit, which I have accepted as writing. I might have survived in the academic world with more ease had I a Ph.D., but my decision not to continue in the doctoral program at Brown was based on the understanding that I didn't want to spend the rest of my life poring over other people's work and trying to explain the world thru their eyes. Rather, what I gain from books and it is often a great deal—no book affected my life so much as reading Langston Hughes' Montage on a Dream Deferred, for here was my life and my language coming at me—must be melded with, refracted through my experiences and what I know of my contemporaries, my ancestors, my hopes for my descendants (and the "my" is used in the collective sense, implying we, implying our).

I was a "man" in Give Birth to Brightness (Dial Press, 1972), and a sexual voice in "The Blues Roots of Contemporary Afro-American Poetry" (Mass. Review, 1977), both critical works—and each of those disguises has helped me to come into my own voice, clarified my own vision. I am the women I speak of in my stories, my poems. The fact that I am a single mother sometimes makes it hard to bring this forth to embody it in the world, but it is precisely because I am the single mother of an only son that I try so hard to do this. Women must leave a record for their men; otherwise how will they know us?

I think it is significant that a number of white male editors took personal exception to Sherley Anne Williams' story "Meditations on History," most probably because of the unflattering portrait of white males in that story. Much of the story's meaning is conveyed—unwittingly— through the writer-interviewer, a white male historian—ultimately betrayed by his own presumptions of superiority to the slave woman, Odessa. As a technique it is important that the white writer tell Odessa's story because it is the white world with access to the lives of the slaves and in control of the printed media. His attitudes do not prevail, however, because what we learn of Odessa's true story is what he reveals inadvertently and unintentionally.

What holds the story together at its deepest level is the total sense of an underground slave community, inaccessible to the slaveholder, existing physically and psychologically to subvert the slave system. The slaves singing about "the soul's gon ride that heavenly train" are speaking to one another in a code of deliverance, but the white writer hears only a plaintive harmonic hymn.

In "Meditations" the black slave dialect and slave idiom are poetic and powerful, projecting a collective experience and the sensibility of an enslaved people. Odessa tells her interlocutor, "I kill that white man cause the same reason Mas kill Kaine. Cause I can." Always Odessa speaks with an integrity her examiner is entirely unequipped to handle. When he tries to get her to betray the others in the insurrection, she answers with double-edged meaning: "Onlest mind I be knowin' is mines."

Sherley Anne Williams has published two collections of poetry, *The Peacock Poems,* a 1976 National Book Award nominee, and *Someone Sweet Angel Chile,* a critical study of black literature, *Give Birth to Brightness* (Dial, 1972), and numerous articles on black poetry and black music. Along with her attempts to reconstruct the public and private history of black people, the trademark of Williams' work, as stated in her own words, is "the re-creation of a new tradition built on a synthesis of black oral traditions and Western literate forms."[1]

1 "The Blues Roots of Contemporary Afro-American Poetry," in *Massachusetts Review, XVII* (Autumn 1977), 554.

Meditations on History

BY SHERLEY ANNE WILLIAMS

The myth [of the black matriarchy and the castrating black female] must be consciously repudiated as myth and the black woman in her true historical contours must be resurrected. We, the black women of today, must accept the full weight of a legacy wrought in blood by our mothers in chains . . . as heirs to a tradition of supreme perseverance and heroic resistance, we must hasten to take our place wherever our people are forging on towards freedom.

from "Reflections on the Black Woman's Role in the Community of Slaves" by Angela Davis, to whom this story is respectfully, affectionately dedicated.

"Sho was hot out there today."

"Yeah, look like it fixin to be a hot, hot summer."

"Hope it don't git too hot."

"Naw, dry up the crop, it do."

The desultory conversation eddied around her but she took no part in it. The day's heat still hung in the air even though the sun was only a few minutes from setting. The sweaty dust that clung to her skin was reminder—and omen—enough of how hot it could get in the fields. It was enough to feel it; she didn't have to talk about it, too. Even the ones talking, Petey and Brady and them, didn't seem very interested in what they were saying. She smiled. Talkin bout "the weather" and "the crop"—knowin they jes puttin on fo Ta'va.

"I see ol crazy Monroe been ova Mas Jeff'son place agin."

She listened more carefully now. Monroe had been trying for the longest time to get Master's permission to be
with some girl over at the Jefferson plantation. But Young
Mistress had said all the girl was good for was housework
and they didn't need another wench up to the House. And
that should have been that, but Monroe kept sneaking
over to see her every chance he got—which was no more
than saying he made chances. As much as Boss Smith
worked people in the fields, there was no way any of them
were just going to *find* a chance to wander off and go
"visiting." All this was common knowledge among them,
though none of them ever said anything about when
Monroe left or when Monroe returned unless Boss Smith
learned on his own that Monroe had gone visiting before
the visit was over.

"What *did* they do him?" she asked when it seemed
that no one would answer—had it been Brud who asked
the first time? No matter; she knew they didn't want to
talk about Monroe in front of Tarver. But talk couldn't
hurt Monroe now and Harriet—that had been her talking—
shouldn't have brought it up if she didn't want to continue
with it. It was too hot to start thinking about something
and then have to stop just because Harriet didn't know
the difference between "talkin" and "talkin smart." "What
they do him?" she asked again.

"Mas jes chain him out to one-a the barns; say he gon
sell him," Santee, who walked a couple of feet ahead of
her, said over his shoulder.

"Lawd, why won't these chi'ren learn."

Sara was always making as if she were so old, so experienced in dealing with the world. She started to reply but
someone else spoke.

"Can't learn a nigga nothin."

The laugh Petey's quick answer brought took away
most of the evil Sara's statement and Harriet's reluctance
to answer had made her feel.

"Well," Brady said, breaking in on their laughter. "I
sho wished I knowed what that lil gal—what her name is?"

"Thank it Alberta," someone supplied.

"Yeah, that's it."

"Well, whatever it is, I sho wished I knowed what she got to make a nigga walk fifteen miles a night and jes be *da'in* a beatin when he get back."

"Don't know," Santee said loudly, "but it sho *gots* to be gooood."

"This one nigga won't never find out." Charlie was laughing with the others even as he said it.

"Now you talkin some sense." She hated it when Tarver broke in on their conversations. Since Boss Smith had made him driver, he thought he knew everything and was better than everybody else. She waited, her lips poked out, knowing whatever he said would make her angry. "Much give-away stuff as it is around here, ain't no way in the world I'd chance what Boss Smith put behind them licks jes to get some mo somewhere else."

Only way *you* get any, at all, is cause if a woman don't, you see Boss Smith or Mas hear bout it. But she didn't say it. Tarver wouldn't even have to run to Boss Smith or Master with that. He'd just slap her in the mouth and no one there would go against the skinny driver. That would mean that two—or however many more helped her—would get whipped instead of just one. But she couldn't resist cutting her eyes knowingly at the women who walked on either side of her. Polly looked as though she wasn't listening but Martha's lips were pushed forward in a taut line that flattened their fullness. Martha was the only lone woman Tarver never passed sly remarks with, and that was saying something. Since he had been made driver, Tarver wasn't even above trying to pat on women who already had men. But Tarver hadn't so much as looked at Martha for some time, now, and if he did say something to her it was only an order about what work she should do.

Martha put her hand on her hip, pulling the shapeless overblouse she wore tight against her heavy breasts, emphasizing the smallness of her waist, and she swung her hips in an exaggerated arc. Even dirty and with that old sweaty head rag on her hand, she looked good. "Yeah, I give it away—to some; othas got to take it."

There was a choked kind of laughter from the men and the other women hid their smiles behind their hands. Go on, girl, she thought and then, looking over at Tarver, she saw the muscle along his neck jump.

"Too bad you ain't gived Monroe none; if it all that good he might woulda stayed home," she laughed as she said it and pushed Martha lightly on the shoulder.

"Naw, Monroe was one that'd had to take it," Martha said with a sigh that caused even more laughter.

And she relaxed. Tarver was laughing, too.

"I jes meant, I don't want to *love* . . ." She liked to watch the older man shake his head like that when he talked; no matter what he said after he did his head like that, it was bound to be funny. "No, I'm a nigga," and again the shake of his head, "what can't *love* where he don't *live*."

"Listen to Charlie talk!"

She didn't join in their laughter this time. Someone was coming down the quarters. It was him. She knew that even before he raised his hand or opened his mouth—who else could still move like that at the end of the day, like he'd just started out fresh not two minutes ago; even without the banjo banging against his back, she would have known him—and she quickened her steps.

"Somebody sho is walkin fas all a sudden."

She heard the voice behind her as she pushed past the people in front of her but she paid no attention; already, and almost of their own will, her lips were stretched wide in a grin. She could see him clearly now though he was still some distance away, see the big head of nappy hair and the pants hiked up around his waist so that his dusty ankles showed. She stayed in front of the others, but now used the hoe like a cane, swinging it high in pretended nonchalance.

Hey, hey, sweet mamma

His voice, high and sweet and clear as running water in a

settled stream, always made her feel so good, so like dancing just for the joy of moving and all the moving would be
straight to him.

> *Say, hey now, hey now, sweet mamma*
> *Don't you hear me callin you?*

"Seem like they been wid each otha long nough now fo
them to stop all that foolishness."

Huh; you jes mad cause you ain't got nobody to be
foolish wid. But she didn't say it aloud. That had been
Jean Wee's voice and Jean Wee's man, Tucker, had been
sold to Charleston not three months ago. She simply
quickened her steps.

> *Hey, hey, sweet mamma, this Kaine Poppa*

His arms were outstretched and though she couldn't hear
them, she knew his fingers were snapping to the same
rhythm that moved his body.

> *Kaine Poppa calling his woman's name*

Behind her, they were laughing. Kaine could always give
you something to laugh about. He made jokes on the
banjo, came out with a song made up of old sayings and
words that had just popped into his head a second before
he opened his mouth, traded words with the men or
teased her and the other women. But she never more than
half heard the laughter he created. By then she'd thrown
the hoe aside and was running, running . . .

He caught her and lifted her off the ground and the
banjo banged against her hands as she threw her arms
around him. "What you doin down here so early?" She
was scared. After that first spurt of joy seeing him always
brought, she would get frightened. Lawd, if Boss Smith
saw him— And that no-good Ta'va was still behind them—
Why he want *do* crazy thangs like this.

"They thank I'm still up there at that ol piece-a green-
house tryin to make strawberries grow all year round."
This was said into her neck and as they turned to walk on.

Then he laughed aloud. "Why I jes got hungry fo my woman," he said with a glance back over his shoulder.

There was appreciative laughter from behind, but neither the laughter nor his words eased her fear. There must have been something for him to do back at the Big House. Either Childer could have found him a closet to turn out, some piece of furniture to move so the girls could clean behind it, or Aunt Lefonia might have had some spoons or some such to polish in the kitchen. And she knew Emmalina would have wanted him to help serve supper if there was nothing else he had to do. Master was always complaining about how they couldn't afford to have a nigger sitting around eating his head off while he waited for some flowers to grow. But Young Mistress would cry and say how the gardens at the House had always been the showplace of the county. Then, so Aunt Lefonia said—and Aunt Lefonia always knew—Old Mistress would get a pinched look around her mouth and her nose would turn up like she'd just smelled the assfidity bag Merry-Day wore around her neck when she had a cold in her chest, and start talking about how Master was forever trying to drag the Reeves down in the mud where he and the rest of the Vaunghams had come from. And Master would really get mad then and say the Reeves had finally arrived at their true place in life and since it was his money that kept the House a showplace, that nigger, meaning Kaine, better turn his hand to whatever needed doing. That would be the end of it until the next time Master got peeved about something and he would start again. Kaine wouldn't tell her about it, but Aunt Lefonia and Emmalina did and she was afraid that someday Master wouldn't care about Young Mistress' tears or Old Mistress throwing his family up in his face and would sell Kaine to Charleston or the next coffle that passed their way.

"You jes askin fo trouble, comin down here like this."

"Baby, I'm all *ready* in trouble."

The quarters were filling up now, people coming in from other parts of the plantation, the children who were too small to work coming back from Mamma Hattie's

cabin where she kept an eye on them during the day. A
few fires had already been lighted and she could smell
frying fat-back and wood smoke. Her breath caught at his
words.

"What you mean?"

"Mean a nigga ain't born to nothin *but* trouble." Lee
Tower, who headed the gang that worked the rice fields,
stopped as he spoke, "and if a nigga don't *cou't* pleasure,
he ain't likely to git none."

He was the best driver on the plantation, getting work
out of his people with as much kindness as he could show,
not with the whip like Luke, who headed the gang that
Master hired out to cut timber, or Tarver who drove the
group she worked with. But she couldn't return Lee
Tower's smile or laugh when Carrie Mae, who had come
up behind him carrying her baby on her hip, said, "Naw,
Mas done sent his butt down here to git it *out* o' trouble;
takin care that breedin bidness he been let slide."

"Now yo'all know I be tryin." Kaine was laughing too.
"But I got somethin here guaran*teed* to ease a troublin
mind." And he patted her shoulder and pinched her
lightly in her ribs.

Lee Tower and Carrie Mae laughed and passed on.

"Kaine—"

"Lefonia gived me—"

"Afta how much talkin?"

"Didn't take much."

The laugh was choked out of her; she had looked into
his eyes. They were alive, gleaming with dancing lights
(no matter what mamma-nem said; his eyes did sparkle)
that danced only for her. And when they danced, she
would love him so much that she had to touch him or
smile. She smiled and he grinned down at her. "Don't
neva take much—you got the right word, and you know
when it come to eatin beef, I *steal* the right word if it ain't
hidin somewheres round my own self tongue," he said as
he pulled her in their doorway. She laughed despite herself; he could talk and wheedle just about anything he

wanted. "And I pulled some new greens from out the patch and seasoned em wid jes a touch o' fat-back."

"A touch was all we had. Kaine, what—"

"Hmmmm mmmmm. But that ain't all I wants a touch of," he said holding her closer and pulling the dirty, sweaty rag from her head. "Touch ain't neva jes satisfied me."

She laughed and relaxed against him. They were inside, the rickety door shut against the gathering dusk. "Us greens gon get cold."

"But us ain't." He stood with one leg pressed lightly between her thighs, his lips nibbling the curve of her neck.

"I got to clean up a little." She said it more to tease, to prolong this little moment, than because she really felt the need to wash. Sometimes he got mad—not because she was dirty, but because the dirt reminded him that she worked the fields all day. She couldn't say why his being angry about this pleased her so, but it did. Or, sometimes, he would start a small tussle: she trying to get to the washbasin, he holding her back, saying she wasn't that dirty and even dirty she was better than most men got when their women were clean. And that response pleased her, too. She liked the little popping sound "men" made as it came from his mouth.

He ran the tip of his tongue down the side of her neck. "Ain no wine they got up to the House good as this." His fingers caught in her short kinky hair, his palms rested gently on her high cheekbones. "Ain't no way I'm eva gon let you get away from me, girl. Where else I gon find eyes like this?" He kissed her closed lids, his hands sliding down her neck to her shoulders and back, his fingers kneading the flesh under her tow sack dress, and she wanted him to touch all of her, trembled as she thought of his lips on her breasts, his hands on her stomach, or his legs between her own. "Mmmmmm mmmm." He pulled up her dress and his hands were inside her long drawers. "I sho like this be-hind." His hands cupped her buttocks. "Tell me all this goodness ain't mine," he dared her. "Whoa! and when it git to movin," and he moved, "and I

git to movin and we git to movin— Lawd, I knowed it was
gon be sweet but not this doggone *good!*"

This was love talk that made her feel almost as beautiful as the way he touched her. She shivered and pulled at
the coarse material of his shirt, not needing the anger or
the other words, now, because his hands and mouth made
her feel so loved. His skin was warm and dry under her
hands and even though she could barely wait to feel all of
him against all of her, she leaned a little away from him.
"Sho you want to be wid this ol dirty woman? Sho you
want—"

His lips were on hers, nibbling and pulling, and the
sentence ended in a groan. Her thighs spread for him, her
hips moved for him. Lawd, this man sho know how to
love . . .

It was gone as suddenly as it had come, the memory so
strong, so clear it was like being with him all over again.
Muscles contracted painfully deep inside her and she
could feel the warm moistness oozing between her thighs.
There was only the thin cotton coverlet that provided no
weight and little warmth, the noise the corn husk pallet
made each time she moved. It was moonlight that shined
in her eyes, not his eyes that had been the color of lemon-
tea and honey. She lay still but she could not conjure the
visions again, and finally she turned her back to the tiny
window where the moonlight entered, pulled the coverlet
up around her breasts and closed her eyes.

Hey, hey, sweet mamma

(She knew the words; it was his voice that had been the
music.)

> *Hey, sweet mamma, this Kaine Poppa*
> *Kaine Poppa callin his woman'name.*
> *He can pop his poppa so good*
> *Make his sweet woman take to a cane.*

Meditations on History

The Hughes Farm
Near Linden
Marengo County, Alabama.

June 9, 1829.

I must admit to a slight yearning for the comfort of the Linden House (comfort that is quite remarkable, considering Linden's out-of-the-way location), but Sheriff Hughes' generous offer of hospitality enables me to be close at hand for the questioning of the negress and this circumstance must outweigh the paucity of creature comforts which his gable room provides.

The negress is housed here in a little-used root cellar until such time as sentencing can be carried out. Hughes told me at dinner tonight the amusing story of how the negress came to be housed in his cellar. It seems that the town drunk, a rather harmless fellow who usually spends some portion of each week in housing provided at public expense, protested the idea of having to share quarters with the negress over an extended period of time. The other blacks involved in the uprising had, of course, been given a speedy trial and the sentences were carried out with equal dispatch, so the drunk—I cannot recall his name—had not been too inconvenienced. He drew the line, however, at protracted living with the wench in the close quarters which the smallness of the jail necessitates. In this he was supported by his wife, a papist from New Orleans but otherwise a good woman and normally a very meek one. She was convinced that the girl had the "evil eye" and was also possessed of a knowledge of the black arts—for how else, she asked at one point, could the negress have supplied the members of the coffle with the files which freed them when there were none to be had (a provocative question, but Hughes says that it was never proved that it was the negress who supplied the files). The woman demanded of Hughes, and later, when Hughes could give her no satisfaction, of the judge, the mayor and several of the large landowners in the vicinity, that the girl be moved or her husband be provided with separate quarters. She raised such a rumpus, invoking saints and all manner of idols, and pestered the gentlemen so repeatedly that Hughes in desperation offered his root cellar and, as his farm is also only a short distance from town, the village fathers jumped at his offer. Calmer reflection showed them the wisdom of this hasty decision: Jemina (a singularly inappropriate name for one of her size), the house servant here, is a noted midwife and excellent care is thus close at hand when the negress's time comes.

There is, however, some uncertainty about when that time will be. The Court, at Wilson's request, has postponed the hanging until after the birth of the child, which, according to Wilson's coffle manifest, should be two to three months hence. Hughes, however, says that it will be sooner. Jemina declares that the wench is eight months gone now and the entire district swears by the woman's prognostications. It is all in one to me, for, however far gone she proves to be, there is ample time for me to conclude my investigation of this incident before the law extracts the final punishment for her crimes. And the price will be paid. She will hang from the same gallows where her confederates forfeited their lives for the part they played in that perfidious and, fortunately, unsuccessful uprising.

It is late and the branches of the huge oak which commands the back yard brush softly at the shutters. It is a restful sound and the sense of urgency which had driven me since first I heard of this latest instance of negro savagery has finally eased. The retelling of this misadventure will make a splendid opening for the book and I am properly elated that I managed to reach Linden before the last of the culprits had come by their just deserts. It will be a curious, an interesting process to delve into the mind of one of the instigators of this dreadful plot. Is it merely the untamed, perhaps even *untamable* savagery of their natures which causes them to rise up so treacherously and repudiate the natural order of the universe which has already decreed their place, or is it something more amenable to human manipulation, the lack of some disciplinary measure or restraining word which brought Wilson and countless others to such tragic consequences? Useless to ponder now, for if I do not discover the answer with this one negress, I have every confidence that I shall find an answer in the other investigations I shall make.

June 10, 1829.

I have seen her: the virago, the she-devil who even now haunts the nightmares of Wilson. I had not thought it possible that one of his calling could be so womanish, for surely slave-trading is a more hazardous profession than that of doctor, lawyer or *writer*. Yet, this wench, scarcely more than a pickaninny—and the coffle manifest puts her age somewhere in the neighborhood of fifteen or sixteen—and one of such diminutive size at that is the self-same wench whom Wilson called a "raging nigger bitch." In recollecting the uprising, it is the thought of *this* darky which even now, weeks after the events, brings a sweat to his brow and a tremble to his hand. Why, her belly is bigger than she is and birthing the child she carries—a strong, lusty one if the size of her stomach is any indication—will no doubt kill her long before the hangman has a chance at her throat. Oh, she may be sullen and stubbornly silent. Although, in this initial visit, she appeared more like a wild and timorous animal finally brought to bay, for upon perceiving that Hughes was not alone she moved quickly if clumsily to the farthest reaches of the root cellar which her leg iron allows. Hughes attempted to coax her in a really remarkable approximation of what he says is her own speech, saying that I was not there to aggravate her with further questions as the other white men had done. She, however, would approach us no closer than just enough to ease the tension on her chains. Still, I can imagine the dangerously excitable state which Hughes confirms characterized her actions upon first being apprehended. According to Hughes, she was like a cat at that time, spitting, biting, scratching, apparently unconcerned about the harm her actions might bring to her child. The prosecutor was naturally relentless in his questioning and it is only since being removed to this farm that she has achieved a state of relative calm. Yet, to see in this one common negress the she-devil of Wilson's delirium is the grossest piece of nonsense. Hughes agrees with me, saying privately that he always believed that Wilson's loud harshness toward the blacks in his coffles hid a cowardly nature. Hughes, of course, has had more opportunity to judge of this than I, for Wilson has been bringing his coffles through Marengo County for well onto seven years. And this also confirms my own opinion of him. Even in that one brief visit I had with him in Selma, I detected the tone, the attitude of the braggart and bully.

I shall speak with Hughes about making other provisions for a meeting place. Even had I been of a mind to talk with the negress, the stench of the root cellar—composed almost equally I suspect of stale negro and whatever else has been stored there through the years—would have driven me away within the minute. And that would be a pity for there is no doubt that the negress was one of the leaders in that bloody proceeding. Her own testimony supports the findings of the Court. Now, she will be brought to re-create that event and all that led up to it for me. Ah, the work, *The Work* has at last begun.

June 13, 1829.

Each day I become more convinced of the necessity, the righteousness even of the work I have embarked upon. Think, I say to myself as I sit looking into the negress's face, think how it might have been had there been a work such as I envision after the Prosser uprising of 1800. Would the Vesey conspiracy and all the numerous uprisings which took place in between these two infamous events, would they have occurred? Would this wretched wench even now be huddled before me? No, I say. No, for the evil seeds which blossomed forth in her and her companions would never have been planted. I feel more urgency about the completion of *The Roots of Rebellion and the Means of Eradicating Them* (I have settled upon this as a compelling short title) than ever I did about writing *The Complete Guide for Competent Masters in Dealing with Slaves and Other Dependents*. I am honest enough to agree with those of my detractors who claim that *The Guide* is no more than a compendium of sound, commonsense practices gathered together in book form (they forget, however, that it is I who first hit upon the idea of compiling such a book and the credit of being first must always be mine). *The Guide* was, in some sense, a mere business venture. But *Roots*—even though the first word has yet to be written—looms already in my mind as a *magnum opus*.

Yet, being closeted with the negress within the small confines of the root cellar is an unsettling experience. Thus far, I have not been able to prevail upon Hughes to allow us the freedom of the yard for our meetings. Despite his bluff firmness in dealing with her, he is loath to allow the negress beyond the door of the root cellar. It is preposterous to suppose that anything untoward could happen. He vouches for the loyalty of his own darkies and has strictly forbidden them to have any intercourse whatsoever with her unless a white person is also present. The negress would, of course, be chained and perhaps under the open sky, I can free myself from the oppressive sense of her eyes casting a spell, not so much upon me (I know that should it ever come to a contest, God will prove stronger than the black devils she no doubt worships). No, not upon me is the spell cast, but upon the whole of the atmosphere from which I must draw breath. This last I

know is fanciful; I laugh even as I write it, and it is not
the reason for my long silence. She refused on two occasions to speak with me. I forebore carrying this tale to
Hughes. He is a crude, vulgar, even brutal man who
would doubtless feel that the best solution to the negress's
stubbornness is a judicious application of the whip. In another situation I might be inclined to agree with him—the
whip is most often the medicine to cure a recalcitrant
slave. In this instance, however, I feel that the information
I require must, if it is to be creditable, be freely given. I
trust that I have not placed too much dependence upon
her intelligence and sensitivity. Or, more likely, upon that
innate stubbornness and intractableness for which I believe blacks from certain parts of the dark continent are
well known. I think not, for upon the first occasion she appeared unmoved when I reminded her that although the
child she carries may save her yet a while from a hanging,
it was certainly not proof against a whipping. She cannot
be said to roll her eyes (a most lamentable characteristic
of her race), rather she *flicks* them across one—much in
the same manner a horse uses his tail to flick a bothersome
fly. It is a most offensive gesture. It was thus that she
greeted this statement. I was so angered that I struck her
in the face, soiling my hand and bloodying her nose, and
called to Hughes to open the door. I was almost immediately sorry for my impetuous action. Hughes thinks of me
as an expert negro tamer and although he has not, as he
told me, read *The Guide,* he has heard from respectable
sources that it has a "right good bit o' learnin and common sense" in it. I, therefore, do not want it ever to appear, for even a moment, that I have been or will ever be
defeated by a negress. As I take pains to point out in *The
Guide,* it is seldom necessary to strike a darky with one's
hand and to do so, except in the most unusual circumstances, is to lower one's self almost to the same level of
random violence which characterizes the action of the
blacks among themselves. It is always a lowering, even
repellent reflection to know that one has forgotten the
sense of one's own teachings. It was Willis, I believe, on

the plantation of Mr. Charles Haskin's near Valadosta in Lowndes County, Georgia, who carried a riding whip in order to correct just such subtle signs of insolence as the negress has tried my patience with. But the violence of my reaction has perhaps made any such response unnecessary in the future.

My latest attempt to have speech with her was this morning and I find it difficult to interpret her attitude. We heard upon approaching the cellar a humming or moaning. It is impossible to precisely define it as one or the other. I was alarmed, but Hughes merely laughed it off as some sort of "nigger business." He was perhaps right, for upon opening the door and climbing down the steps into the cellar proper, we found her with her arms crossed in front of her chest, her hands grasping her shoulders. She was seated in the stream of light which comes through the one window—an odd instance in itself for always before she had crouched away from the light so that her eyes gleamed forth from the darkness like those of a beast surprised in its lair. She rocked to and fro and at first I thought the sounds which came from her some kind of dirge or lamentation. But when I ventured to suggest this to Hughes, he merely laughed, asking how else could a nigger in her condition keep happy save through singing and loud noise, adding that a loud nigger was a happy one; it is the silent ones who bear watching. I asked tartly if he made no distinction between moaning and singing. Why should I, he replied with a hearty laugh, the niggers don't. I am obliged to rely upon Hughes' judgment in this matter; as slaveholder and sheriff he has had far greater contact with various types of darkies than I should ever wish for myself. And this last piece of information tallies with what I heard again and again while doing the research for *The Guide*.

Hughes left at this point and I was alone with the wench. I admit to being at a loss as to how to begin, but just as I was about to order her to cease her noise, she lurched to her feet and her voice rose to a climactic pitch. She uttered the words, "I bes. I bes." Just those two words on a loud, yes, I would say, even exultant note. Her arms were now at her side and she stood thus a moment in the light. Her face seemed to seek it and her voice was like nothing I had ever heard before. "I bes. I. And he in air on my tongue the sun on my face. The heat in my blood. I bes he; he me. He me. And it can't end in this place, not this time. Not this time. Not this. But if it do, if it do, it was and I bes. I bes."

I did not exist for her. And I knew then that to talk to her while she remained in such a state would be to talk to the air she now seems to claim to be. We will try what a little pressure can accomplish with her reluctant tongue. Perhaps a day spent on nothing but salt water will make her realize how lightly we have thus far held the reins.

I am somewhat surprised that she feels so little inclined toward boasting of her deeds, dark though they are. I do not make the mistake of putting her silence down to modesty or even fear but the above-mentioned stubbornness. She will find, however, that there are as many ways to wear stubbornness thin as there are to wear away patience.

June 17, 1829.

I have spent the last few days at the courthouse, going through the trial records of this appalling incident, hoping to get a better understanding of what transpired and some insight into the motivation of the darkies. It is a measure of Judge Hoffer's confidence in me and the work upon which I am engaged that I was allowed access to the records. While I do not envision a narrative such as was made of the trial records of the Denmark Vesey case (which was later destroyed because of the inflammatory material it contained), I shudder to think of the uses to which the information contained in these records might be put should they fall into the wrong hands. The trials were conducted in closed sessions so that, while the records themselves contain little more than what Wilson and

Hughes have already told me, none of this information is for public consumption.

The bare outline is this: Wilson picked up a consignment of slaves in Charleston at the end of March. While in the area, he attended a private sale where he heard of a wench, just entered upon childbearing age, and already increasing, that was being offered for sale on the plantation of Mr. Terrell Vaungham. He inquired at the plantation and was told that the wench was being sold because she had assaulted Vaungham. There is always a ready market for females of childbearing age with proven breeding capacity, so, despite the disquieting circumstances, Wilson chose to inspect the wench. There were still signs of punishment, raw welts and burns across the wench's buttocks and the inside of her thighs. Being in places which would only be inspected by the most careful buyer, such marks were not likely to impair her value. Thus satisfied, Wilson paid three hundred eighty-five dollars species for her: she would fetch at least twice that much in New Orleans. The wench gave every appearance of being completely cowed at the time of purchase and throughout the rest of the journey; thus no special guard was placed upon her. Also purchased at this time, through regular channels, were two bucks who were later whipped and branded as runaways because of their parts in the uprising. These purchases brought the number of slaves in the coffle to eighty: fifty males and thirty females ranging in age from about eleven to thirty (but then, no slave dealer will ever admit that any slave he wants to sell is older than thirty or younger than ten). Wilson will not take pickaninnies on these overland trips, feeling that they are more trouble than the price which they are like to fetch on the block warrants. Wilson and his partner, Darkmon, had with them six other men who acted as guards and drivers. It is generally agreed that this one-to-ten ratio is a proper one on a trip of this nature.

On the morning of March 30, 1829, they set out on the journey which would eventually end in New Orleans around the middle of June—had all gone well. There were no untoward events during the first portions of the journey, in fact, the coffle moved so smoothly that the regular security measures may have been somewhat relaxed (and Wilson's adamant denial of this does not convince me in the least. Men of his stripe are always more than willing to lay the blame for their own ineptness and laxity at someone else's door). As usual, Wilson continued to sell off and buy up slaves at each stop along the way. This practice, according to Wilson, serves to prevent trouble during the journey. The number of slaves on the coffle remains constant; there is, however, a continuous turnover of bodies. Thus, there is little chance for the blacks to become too intimate with one another. However, in checking the manifest (a copy of which was admitted as evidence) against the list of those apprehended, killed or convicted, I discovered a fact which had evidently escaped notice: a small group of twelve slaves had been with the coffle since Charleston. Of these, ten were directly involved in the uprising. It is also significant that two of the other blacks who were named as ringleaders had been with the coffle for some time. One must therefore conclude that a rapid and regular turnover of slaves does much to prevent the spread of discontent among them (perhaps this axiom can be modified and extended to include slaves on plantations and small farms).

Wilson had lately taken to chaining the blacks in groups of four and five to trees or other natural projections when no housing was available at night. He found that this method allowed them a more comfortable repose at night which in turn meant they were able to travel faster during the day and were also in better condition when they arrived at the market. He had saved considerable sums because the slaves no longer required expensive conditioning and grooming before being put up for sale. The darkies were strung together in the familiar single file when the coffle was ready to move. It is my firm belief that had Wilson used the tried and true method all along, he could have saved himself subsequent grief. A group of darkies had only to break away from the central chain which bound them to a projection in order to be free. This is precisely what happened.

In the early morning hours of April 29, the wench and the four bucks in her chain group managed to free themselves (whether with a file—which seems most likely—or because the locks were not properly secured—a terrifying oversight in a coffle of that size—was not revealed, even under the most intensive and painful methods of questioning. And the chains were never found). Two of these went to subdue the guards and drivers while the other three attacked Wilson and Darkmon, searching for the keys which would free the rest of the coffle. The negress attacked Darkmon and it was his death screams which awakened Wilson. He was immediately fighting for his own life, of course, and just as he managed to climb atop the darky and had raised his arm to strike him with the very rock with which he himself had been attacked, the negress fell upon him. She wielded a pick made from a stone sharpened to a stiletto point (the same one which she later used in attacking members of the posse). Evidently, her screams and "gleaming eyes" struck terror in Wilson's heart, for he is unable to recount what happened after this. Apparently, though, after Darkmon had been so foully murdered and while the negress went to the aid of the buck who had attacked Wilson, the other black used Darkmon's keys to free the others in the coffle. These quickly dispatched the drivers and guards who had not been subdued in the first onslaught. The darkies then took the horses and pack animals, some provisions and all the firearms and other weapons, and left Wilson and two of the drivers for dead. These lone survivors were found the next day on the trail to Linden, weak from loss of blood and babbling deliriously. A posse was quickly formed and set out in pursuit. They soon came upon the horses and other animals which the darkies had loosed, the better to cover their trail. The posse also found, throughout the course of their pursuit, a number of darkies who either could not keep up with the main body of renegades or who had repented of their impetuous action in following the malcontents and were eager to help in the capture. After three days of tracking the renegades back and forth in a northwesterly direction, the posse surprised them in a camp they had made some thirty-five miles north of Linden. After a fierce gun battle in which seven of the posse were wounded, two of whom did not recover from their wounds, the slaves were finally subdued in hand-to-hand combat at a cost to the posse of three dead and numerous minor injuries. A few renegades tried to slip away during the battle; they, too, were recaptured. However, three, seeing that the battle was lost, fled, and have thus far eluded capture. All told, there were some sixty-three blacks retaken, four having been killed in the initial skirmish with the drivers, eight, either outright or later as a result of their wounds, in the battle with the posse. The posse came up with the renegades on May 4; on the afternoon of the 6th, they arrived in Linden and the trials were held all day on the 8th. The slaves were tried in three groups: those who were thought to be ringleaders, those who were known to have been mostly directly involved in the attacks, either on the drivers or the posse (these groups often overlapped), and those who, perhaps, had been coerced into participation in these infamous proceedings. The sentences were carried out during the week of the 11th. The slaves were subjected to continual questioning from the time of their arrest until the time at which their sentences were carried out. I must commend the sheriff, the prosecutor and the judge on their ability to obtain so much information in such a short period of time.

Thirty-three blacks were tried (all adults above the age of fifteen): six were hanged and quartered as ringleaders, thirteen were hanged and quartered because of the ferocity with which they fought the posse (of these last two totals, six were females); three were whipped only; seven were branded only and three were whipped and branded (these last punishments infuriated Wilson when he learned of them. Branding makes the slave almost worthless, for no one in his right mind would buy a slave with such an extensive history of running away and rebelliousness as branding signifies. Wilson had preferred that they be hanged along with the others and thus save himself the cost of housing and feeding them). The negress still awaits her fate. The three bucks who eluded the posse were Big Nathan, a major plotter who had been chained with the negress the night of the uprising; Harker, who had been purchased in Atlanta; and Proud's Cully, who had been purchased in Jeffersonville just across the line in Georgia. According to the testimony of the slaves, it was this wench, the men in her chain group and five blacks from another group who were the sole plotters. The others had neither a part in the planning nor in the execution of these plans until all had been set free. This seems rather farfetched to me. Wilson, in his written statement to the Court, said that he changed the chain groupings at regular intervals. This would have made it easy for any plot to spread rapidly through the coffle. But as all maintained this posture, the Court accepted the statement of the blacks as true. In fact, one plotter, Elijah (charged by two of the others with being a "root-man," a dealer in black magic; but as there was no further substantiation of this charge, he was not tried on this count), was even rather contemptuous of the idea of telling any of the other slaves about the rebellion plot. They were, he said, white men's niggers who would have betrayed the plans at the first opportunity and who would accept freedom only if it were shoved down their throats. Big Nathan, Mungo and Elijah, who were hanged and quartered, and Black David, who was killed in the battle with the posse, were to lead them all to freedom, but none could specify where this place of freedom was. Elijah said that God would reveal the direction of and route to the free place at the proper time, that the means of escape had likewise been delivered into their hands by God and he would not question the will of God. This was all the "information" which the Court could obtain from any of them—save that the negress, when asked why she, rather than one of the males, had been chosen for so dangerous a task as securing the keys, would say only that it was best that way. (Questioning of her was not as severe as with the others. Wilson has developed an almost fanatical resolve to see in chains the child she carries and the doctor feared that, should she lose the baby before this had been accomplished, it might overset Wilson's reason. The Court took this medical opinion into account when deciding to delay the consummation of the wench's sentence.) It is my own belief that she was chosen because of her very unlikeliness. Who would think a female so far gone in the breeding process capable of such treacherous conduct?

That, in bare outline, is what happened; my chore now is to fill in that outline, to discover and analyze the motivating factors which culminated in this outrage against the public safety. I feel that I have been richly rewarded for these past few days of work. In retelling this outline, I am filled again with a sense of my mission. I look forward to dealing with the negress again on Monday.

June 19, 1829.

"Was I white, I might woulda fainted when Emmalina told me that Mas had done gon up-side Kaine head, nelly bout kilt him iff'n he wa'n't dead already. Fainted and not come to myself til it was ova, least ways all of it that could eva get ova. I guess when you faints you be out the world, that how Kaine say it be. Say that how Mist's act up at the House when Mas or jes any lil thang don't be goin to suit her. Faint, else cry and have em all, Aunt Lefonia, Feddy and the rest, comin, runnin and fannin and carin on, askin what wrong, who did it. Kaine hear em from the garden and he say he be laughin fit to split his side and diggin, diggin and laughin to hear how one lil sickly white woman turn a house that big upside down. I neva rightly believe it could be that way. But wa'n't no way fo me to know fo sho—I work the fields and neva goes round the House neitha House niggas, cept only Aunt Lefonia. Kaine, when me and him first be close and see us want be closer, he try to get me up to the House, ask

Aunt Lefonia if she see what she can do, talk to Mist's maybe. But Aunt Lefonia say I too light for Mist's and not light nough fo Mas. Mist's ascared Mas gon be likin the high colored gals same as he was fo they was married so she don't low nothin but dark uns up to the House else ones too old for Mas to be beddin. So I stays in the fields like I been. Kaine don't like it when Aunt Lefonia tell him that and he even ask Mist's please could I change, but Mist's see me and say no. Kaine mad but he finally jes laugh, say, what kin a nigga do? But I see Mist's that time close-up and I can't rightly believe all what Kaine say. Maybe he jes make it mo'n it bes so when he tell it I laugh. But I neva do know fo sho. Kaine mus know though. He been round the Houses, most a House nigga hisself, though a House nigga neva say a nigga what tend flovas any betta'n one what tend corn. He jes laugh when Childer try to come the big nigga ova him, tell him, say, Childer, jes cause you open do's for the white folks don't make you white. And Childer puff all up cause he not like it, you don't be treatin him some big and he was raised up with the old Mas, too? Humph. So he say to Kaine, say, steadda Kaine talkin back at the ones what betta'n him, Kaine betta be seein at findin him a mo likely gal'n me."

She paused, her head lifted, her eyes closed as though listening. "He chosed me." I could not read the expression on her face; the cellar was too dark. Something, however, seemed to have crept into her voice and I waited, hoping she would continue. "He chosed me. Mas ain't had nothing to do wid that. It Kaine what pick me out and say I be his woman. Mas say you lay down wid this'n or that un and that be the one you lay wid. He tell Carrie Mae she lay wid that studdin nigga and that who she got to be wid. And we all be knowin that it ain't fo nothin but to breed and time the chi'ren be up in age, they be sold off to notha 'tation, maybe deep south. And she jes a lil bitty thang then and how she gon be holdin a big nigga like that, carryin that big nigga child. And all what mamma say, what Aunt Lefonia and Mamma Hattie say don't make Mas no ne'mind. 'Luke known fo makin big babies

on lil gals,' Mas say and laugh. Laugh so hard, he don't be
hearin Mamma Hattie say how Luke studdin days be ova
'fo' he eva touch Carrie. Mas, he don't neva know it, but
Luke, he know it. But he don't tell cause the roots stop his
mouth from talkin to Mas same as they stop his seed from
touchin Carrie. Mas jes wonder and wonder and finally he
say Luke ain't good fo nothin no mo cept fo to drive otha
niggas inna field and fo to beat the ones what try fo to be
bad. Carrie bedded wid David then and Mas gots three
mo niggas fo to be studs, so he ain't too much carin. And
Carrie gots a baby comin. Baby comin . . . baby
comin. . . . But Kaine chosed me. He chosed me and
when Emmalina meet me that day, tell me Kaine don took
a hoe at Mas and Mas don laid into him wid a shovel,
bout bus' in his head, I jes run and when the hoe gits in
my way, I let it fall, the dress git in my way and I holds
that up. Kaine jes layin there on usses pallet, head seepin
blood, one eye closed, one bout gone. Mamma Hattie sittin side him wipin at the blood. 'He be dead o' sold. Dead
o' sold.' I guess that what she say then. She say it so many
times afta that I guess she say it then, too. 'Dead o' sold.'
Kaine jes groan when I call his name. I say all the names I
know, eva heard bout, thought bout, Lawd, Legba,
Shango, Jesus. Anybody, jes so's Kaine could speak.
'Nigga,' Kaine say. Nigga and my name. He say em ova
and ova and I hold his hand cause I know that can't be all
he wanna say. Nigga and my name, my name and nigga.
'Nigga,' he say. 'Nigga can do.' And he don't say no mo."

And that has what to do with you and the other slaves
rising up and killing the trader and the drivers, I asked
sharply, for it seemed as though she would not continue.

She opened her eyes and looked at me. Wide and black
they are. She had had them closed or only half open as
she talked, her head moving now and then, from side to
side, in and out of the light coming in through the tiny
unshuttered window. She opened her eyes and her head
was silhouetted in the light. I understood then what Wilson meant when he talked in his delirium about "devil
eyes," a "devil's stare." Long, black and the whites are un-

stained by red or even the rheumy color which characterizes the eyes of so many darkies whether of pure or
mixed blood, and she does not often blink them. "I kill
that white man," she said, and in the same voice in which
she talked about being allowed to work in the big house,
in which she had talked about the young darky's dying.
They were all the same to her. "I kill that white man
cause the same reason Mas kill Kaine. Cause I can." And
she turned her head to the dark and would not speak with
me anymore.

I have read again this first day's conversation with the
negress. It is all here—even that silly folderol about
"roots"—as much in her own words as I could make out. It
would seem that one must be acquainted with darkies
from one's birth in order to fully understand what passes
for speech amongst them. It is obvious that I must speak
with her again, perhaps several times more, for she answers questions in a random manner, a loquacious, round-
about fashion—if, indeed, she can be brought to answer
them at all. This, to one of my habits, is exasperating to
the point of fury. I must constantly remind myself that she
is but a darky and a female at that. Copious notes seem to
be the order of the day and I will cull what information I
can from them. And, despite the rambling nature of today's discourse, the fact that she did talk remains something of a triumph for *The Guide*. Light punishment followed by swift relaxation of the punitive measure is a
trick I learned of in Maryland, where they have long since
realized that the whippings which the abolitionists deplore
are not the only way to bring a rebellious darky to heel.

June 22, 1829.

She has talked again, perhaps the influence of the open air
or perhaps there was one thing in the long string of questions I asked which touched her thought more than another. I have asked the same basic questions at each meeting. Today, I grew more than a little impatient with the

response—or lack thereof—which I have thus far elicited, and would have despaired of completing my project, if completion depends upon this one negress—which, thank God! it does not. But it is not in my nature to admit defeat so readily and so, thinking to return to the one thing about which she had previously talked, I asked, How did it happen that this darky of whom you spoke attacked Mr. Vaungham? I had phrased this question in various ways and been met with silence. I had even nudged her slightly with the tip of my boot to assure myself that she had not fallen into a doze (they fall asleep, I am told, much as a cow will in the midst of a satisfying chew, though I, myself, have not observed this), but aside from that offensive flicking of the eye, she would not respond. I contained my irritation and my impatience and went on with my questioning. Was he crazed, drunk? Where did he get the liquor? She was seated on the ground at my feet, her back against the tree trunk. The chain which attached to her ankle was wound once around the tree and fastened to a rung of the chair in which I sat. The chair was placed to one side and a little behind so that she would have to look up at me. She would not. Sometimes she closed her eyes or looked out into space. At these times she would hum, an absurd, monotonous little tune in a minor key, the melody of which she repeated over and over. Each morning, we are awakened by the singing of the darkies and they often startle one by breaking into song at odd times during the day. Hughes, of course, finds this comforting. But thus far I have heard nothing but moaning from this wench. How did it happen that this darky attacked Mr. Vaungham? and I raised my voice so as to be heard over her humming.

She stopped humming for a second and when she resumed, she put words to the melody:

> "Lawd, gimme wings like Noah's dove
> Lawd, gimme wings like Noah's dove
> I'd fly cross these fields to the one I loves
> Say, hello darlin; say, how you be.

Mamma Hattie say that playin wid God, puttin yo self on
the same level's His peoples is on. But Kaine jes laugh and
say she ain't knowed no mo bout God and the Bible than
what the white folk tell her and that can't be too much
cause Mas say he don't be likin religion in his slaves. So
Kaine jes go on singin his songs to me in the e'nin afta I
gets out the fields. I be layin up on usses pallet and he be
leanin ginst the wall. He play sweet-soft cause he say that
what I needs, soft sweetin put me to sleep afta I done
work so all day. He really feel bad bout that, me inna
field and him in the garden. He even ask Boss Smith
could I come work at the House o' he come work the field.
I scared when he do that. Nobody ask Boss Smith fo
nothin cause that make him note you and the onliest way
Boss Smith know to note you is wid that whip. But Boss
Smith jes laugh and tell him he a crazy nigga. But Kaine
not crazy. He the sweetest nigga as eva walk this earth.
He play that banger, he play it so sweet til Mist's even
have him up to the House to play and she talk bout havin
a gang o' niggas to play real music fo when they be par-
ties and such like at the House. Ole Mist's used to would
talk like that, so Aunt Lefonia say, cause that was how
they done in Ole Mist's home. But it don't nothin comma
it then, not now neitha. Side, Kaine say the music he
know to play be real nough fo him. Say that that his
banger. He make it his'n so it play jes what he want play.
And he play it. Not jes strum strum wid all his fingers, but
so you hear each strang when he touch it and each strang
gots a diff'ent thang to say. And they neva talks bout bein
sad, bein lonesome cause Kaine say I hep him put all that
behind him. Even when us be workin and he be up to the
House and I be out inna field, it not bad, cause he be
knowin, when the bell rang, I be comin fix that lil bit ra-
tion and we lay up on usses pallet. 'Niggas,' he tell me,
'niggas jes only belongs to white folks and that bes all.
They don't be belongin to they mammas and daddys, they
sista, they brotha.' Kaine Mamma be sold when he lil bit
and he not even know her face. And sometime he thank
maybe his first Mas o' the driva o' maybe jes some white

man passin through be his daddy. Then he say mus been
some fine, big, black man muscled up like strong tree what
got sold cause he go fo bad. And he be wishin he took
looks afta his daddy, be big and strong like him, be *bad*,
steadda the way he do look, nappy head and light eyes.
Have a black man fo a daddy well as a white man, he say,
but he can't neva know, not fo sho, no way. He be sold hisself lotta time fo he come to Mas 'tation. So he don't know
bout stayin wid Mamma Hattie til you be big nough to
work the fields, o' bein woked up by mamma and eatin dry
cornbread and 'lasses fo day in the mornin wid evabody
and hearin Jeeter tease the slow pokes and havin mamma
fetch you a slap so Boss Smith won't fetch his whip at you
fo tarryin so. Onlest folks he eva belongs to is the white
folks and that not really like belongin to a body. He say
first time he hear anybody play a banger, he have to stop,
have to listen cause it seem like it talkin right at him. And
the man what play it, he a Af'ca black, not a reg'la nigga
like what you see eva day. And this Af'ca man say that
the music he play be from his home, and his home be his;
it don't be belongs to no white folks. Nobody there belongs to white folks, jes onlest theyselves and each otha.
He tell Kaine lotta thang what Kaine don't member cause
he lil bit then and this the first time he be sold. That in
Charleston and I know that close to where I'm is and I
wonder how it be if Mas had buyed Kaine then, steadda
when Kaine be grown. But, it happen how it happen and
that time in Charleston Kaine not know all what the Af'ca
man say, cept bout the home and bout the banger, how to
make it, how to play it. And he know that cause he know
if he have it, home be his and the banger be his. Cept he
ain't got no home, so he jes onlest have the banger.

"He make that banger hisself. Make it outen good
parchment and seasoned wood he get hisself and when
Mas break it seem like he break Kaine. Might well as had
cause it not right wid him afta tha. And I can't make it
right wid him. I tell him he can make notha one. I pick up
wood fo him from Jim Boys at the carp'ter shed, get
horsehair from Emmalina Joe Big down to the stables. But

Kaine jes look at it. 'Mas can make notha one,' he say, 'Nigga can't do shit. Mas can step on a nigga hand, nigga heart, nigga life, and what can a nigga do? Nigga can't do shit.

> *What can a nigga do when Mas house on fire?*
> *What can a nigga do when Mas house on fire?*
> *Bet NOT do mo'n yell, Fire, Fire!*
> *Let some'un else brang the wata*
> *Cause a nigga can't do shit!*

He sing that and laugh. And one day Emmalina meet me when I come in outten the field and tell me Mas don shoved in the side of Kaine head."

She looked up at the sun and blinked her eyes rapidly several times. I did not question her anymore.

This is still a far cry from just how five slaves managed to free themselves and loose the rest of the coffle, how, having achieved this, they managed to murder the drivers and one trader and dangerously injure another (and I begin to think, too, that she must have some inkling of where the three darkies that the posse couldn't find have gotten to), but I begin to perceive how I may get to this point. We shall see tomorrow. Enough for tonight. I sat late with Hughes over a very smooth Kentucky whiskey (I must admit to having misjudged Hughes. I had not thought from either the appointments of his house or the fare at his table that he was capable of such fine taste. Perhaps it is only from want of proper exercise that his discriminating faculties are not more in evidence. What I had thought dead may only be dormant. As for means—in the case of the whiskey, I would say that being sheriff must not be without its advantages). It is curious, though, how the negress, well, how she looks in the sun. For a moment today as I watched her I could almost imagine how Vaungham allowed her to get close enough to stick a knife between his ribs.

June 23, 1829.

She demanded a bath this morning, which Hughes
foolishly allowed her, and in the creek. Being without a
bathing dress, she must perforce bathe in her clothes and
dry in them also. A chill was the natural outcome, whose
severity we have yet to determine. And were that not bad
enough, she cut her foot, a deep slash across the instep
and ball, while climbing up the bank. Hughes thinks it a
reasonably clean cut but she bathed near the place where
the livestock come to water so there is no way of knowing.
He claims that he was so nonplussed, "flustered" as he
phrases it, at such a novel request coming from a nigger
and a wench ready to be brought to light, too, that he had
granted the request before he had time to think properly
of the possible outcome. Since she was shackled during
the whole business he thought no harm could be done, as
though darkies are not subject to the same chills and
sweats which overtake the veriest pack animals. It seems
that I am never to be spared the consequences of dealing
with stupid people. Pray God the wench doesn't die before I get my book.

June 27, 1829.

A curious session we had of it today. I know not what,
even now, to make of it. She spoke of her own accord
today, spoke to me, rather than the hot windless air, as
has been her custom. The air, even now, is oppressive,
hot, still, strangely dry, and it was obvious, even as
Hughes brought her up from the cellar, that the negress
also felt it. Her movements, always slow, were even
slower, her walk, not stumbling but heavy as though her
feet were weighted. She eased her bulk onto the ground
beneath the tree and leaned back against its trunk. Her
dark wooly hair—which fits upon her head almost like a
nubby cap—seemed to merge into the deeper shadows cast
by the thick low hanging branches of the tree. I sat in my

habitual place just behind her, stripped to my shirt sleeves and feeling that even this was not enough to lessen the sun's onslaught. The sharp, bright sunlight was too painful to gaze at from the depth of that shadow and I must look down at the pages of my notebook, blank save for the day's date, or at her. We were silent for some moments after she was seated, I thinking how limited my vision had become and she engaged in God knows what cogitations.

"That writin what you put on that paper?" I was somewhat startled by the question and did not immediately answer. "You be writin down what I say?" She was on her knees, turned to me now to see what was in the notebook. Instinctively, I held it away from her eyes and told her that although I had written nothing that day—we had said nothing so far—(I fear that this little pleasantry escaped her) I did indeed write down much of what she said. On a happy impulse, I flipped back through the pages and showed her the notes I had made on some of our previous sessions. "What that there . . . and there . . . and that, too?" I told her and even read a little to her, an innocuous line or two. She was entranced. "I relly say that?" And when I nodded she sat back on her haunches. "What you gon do wid it?" I told her cautiously that I would use it in a book I hoped to write. I was totally unsure of whether she would comprehend the meaning of that. "Cause why?" She was thoroughly aroused by this time and seemed, despite the chain which bound her, about to flee.

Girl, I said to her, for at that moment, I could not for the life of me remember her name, Girl, what I put in this book cannot hurt you now. You've already been tried and judged. She seemed somewhat calmed by this utterance, perhaps as much by the tone of my voice, which I purposely made gentle, as by the statement itself.

"Then for what you wanna do it?"

I told her that I wrote what I did in the hope of helping others to be happy in the life that has been sent them to live, a response with which I am rather pleased. Certainly, it succeeded in its purpose of setting her mind at ease about the possible repercussions to herself in talking freely with me, for she seemed much struck by the statement, looking intently into my face for a long moment before she again settled down into her habitual pose. I allowed her to reflect upon this for a moment. She was silent for so long that I began to suspect her of dozing and leaned forward the better to see her. Her eyes were open (she seemed not to have the same problem as I with the harsh sunlight), her hands cupped beneath the roundness of her stomach. Your baby seems to have dropped; according to the old wives' tale, you'll be brought to bed soon. It was merely an attempt at conversation, of course; I know no more about that sort of business than I know about animal husbandry or the cultivation of cotton. She, of course, did not treat my words as the conversational gambit they were; she jumped as though stung. I cursed my stupidity, knowing what this unthinking comment must have brought to her mind, even as I realized that this was the first time I had seen her hands anywhere near her stomach. After the initial start, she straightened her back and scooted nearer to the tree, but said nothing. I waited, somewhat anxiously, for the blank sullen look to return. It did not, however, and, emboldened, I ventured quietly, Girl, where did the others get the file? even as she said:

"Kaine not want this baby. He want and don't want it. Babies ain't easy fo niggas, but still, I knows this Kaine's and I wants it cause that. And . . . and, when he ask me to go to Aunt Lefonia . . . I, I nelly bout died. I know what Aunt Lefonia be doin, though she don't be doin it too much cause Mas know it gotta be some nigga chi'ren comin in this world. And was anybody but, but Kaine, I do it, too. First time, a anyway. But, but this Kaine and it be like killin parta him, parta me. So I talk wid him; beg him. I say, this us baby, usses. We make it. How you can say, kill it. It mine and it yo's. He jes look at me. 'Same way Lefonia sons be hers when Mas decide that bay geldin he want worth mo to him than they is to her. Dessa,' and I know he don't want hurt me when he call my name, but it so sweet til it do hurt. Dessa, jes soft like that. 'Dess, where yo brotha, Jeeter, at now?' I'm cryin already, can't cry no mo, not fo Jeeter. He be gon, sold, south, somewhere; we neva do know. And finally I say 'run' and he laugh. He laugh and say, 'Run, Dessa (Lawd. Ain't no body neva say my name so sweet. Even when he mad like that, Dessa. Dessa I always know the way he call my name). Dessa, run where?' 'No'th,' I whisper. I whisper cause I don't rightly thank I eva heard no nigga say that out loud like when anybody, even yo own self's shadow could hear you, less'n it right up on you. 'No'th? And how we gon get there?' 'You know, Kaine.' And he know. I know he know. He know if he wanna know. 'And what we gon do when we gets there?' I jes look at him. Cause he know. 'Dessa.' Say my name agin. 'You know what is no'th? Huh? What is no'th? Mo whites. Jes like here. You don't see Aunt Lefonia, I see her fo you.' But I don't go, not then. I waits and one night Kaine talk to me. I don't *know*, not then, bout all what he says, but I try to learn most o' it by heart so I can thank bout it and thank bout it til I does know. He tell me then how he been sold way from some massas, runned way from othas. He run, he say, tryin to find no'th and he lil then and not even know no'th a di-rection and mo places than he eva be able to count. He jes thank he be free o' whippins, free to belongs to somebody what belongs to him jes so long as he be no'th. Last time he runned way, he most get there and he thank, now he know which way free land is, what is a free town, next time he get there. But neva is no next time cause same time's patterrollers takes him back, they takes back a man what been no'th, lived there and what know what free no'th is. 'Now,' Kaine say, 'now this man free, bo'n free, but still, any white man what say he a slave be believed cause a nigga can't talk fo the laws, not ginst no white man, not even fo his own self. So this man gots to get a notha white man fo to say he is free and he couldn't find one quick nough so then the Georgia Man, that be what the no'th man call the patterrollers, they takes him back fo to be slave. That's right. But even fo the patter-rollers catched him, white man hit, he not lowed to hit back. He carpt'na but if the white mens on the job say

they don't want work wid him, he don't work and sucha
thangs as that. He say it hard bein a free man o' color, he
don't say nigga, say free man o' color, but it betta'n bein a
slave and if he get the chance he gon runned way.' But,
Kaine say, he ask hisself, 'That free? How that gon be
free? It still be two lists, one say "White Man Can," otha
say "Nigga Can't" and white man still be the onliest one
what can write on em.' So he don't run no mo. 'Run fo
what,' he say. 'Get caught be jes that much worser off.
Maybe is a place wid out no white, nigga can be free.' But
he don't know where that is. He find it, he say we have us
chi'ren then. That why he say go see Aunt Lefonia, but I
don't go. I jes can't. I know Kaine be knowin mo'n me. I
know that. He— He told me lotta thang I not eva thank
bout fo I wid him. But I does know us. I does. Me'n him.
I knows that. And I knows this usses baby. And I thank
bout what he say and I thank bout what I knows and I
know they all bes the same thang. How they gon be
diff'ent? I tell Kaine find it, least *try* fo you say see Aunt
Lefonia. I don't be cryin now and he don't be mad. Jes,
jes touch my face and say me name, Lawd, say my name.
Say my name and his body be so hard, so hard and stiff
ginst mine and I feel how he want me. 'I try, Dessa. I try
what I can do.' No matter though," she said looking up at
me. "Mas kill him fo it get time fo us to go."

We were both quiet for some time. I searched around
in my mind for some way to bring her train of thought
back to the immediate concern.

"You thank," she asked looking up at me, "you thank
what I say now gon hep peoples be happy in the life they
sent? If that be true," she said as I opened my mouth to
answer, "Why I not be happy when I live it? I don't
wanna talk no mo." And she did not.

It is only now that I become aware of my failure to em-
ploy the strategy I have devised. Yet, she now suffers from
no more than a small case of the sniffles and the gash,
while painful, perhaps, causes her no more than a slight
limp. Monday will thus do as well as today, for I feel that

we have achieved a significant level in our relationship. Today was a turning point and I am most optimistic for the future.

June 28, 1829.

As has been my custom in the past, I held no formal session with the negress this Sunday. But, in order to further cultivate the tentative rapport achieved in yesterday's session, I read and interpreted for her selected Bible verses. We were in our habitual place under the oak tree and I must admit that the laziness of the hot Sunday afternoon threatened at times to overcome me (as Hughes had warned me it would). As a consequence, he was reluctant to give me the keys to the cellar. He felt my vigilance would be impaired by the heat. I replied that in as much as the negress would remain chained as usual, there was no danger involved in such a venture—unless, of course, he feared that his own darkies would rise up and free her. He was somewhat stung by my retort, but he did surrender the keys. I shall make it my business to obtain another key to the cellar and to the chains with which she is bound to the tree—these are the only ones which in her quieted state she now wears. It is not to my liking to be required to *request* permission each time I wish to talk with the woman.

My drowsiness was compounded, I finally realized, by the monotonous melody which she hummed. I have grown, it appears, so accustomed to them that they seem like a natural part of the setting like the clucking of the hens or the lowing of the cattle. Thinking to trap her into an admission of inattention, I asked her to repeat the lessons I had just imparted to her. She did so and I was very pleased to find her so responsive. However, the humming became so annoying that I was forced to ask her to cease. She looked up at me briefly and though I had not threatened her, I believe she was mindful of previous punishments and of the fact that it is only through my influence that she is able to escape from her dark hole for these brief periods.

"Oh, this ain't no good-timmin song. It say bout the righteousness and heaven, same as what you say."

I asked her to sing it and I set it down here as I remember and understand it:

Gonna march away in the gold band in the army bye'n bye.
Gonna march away in the gold band in the army bye'n bye.
Sinner, what you gon do that day?
Sinner, what you gon do that day?
When the fire arollin behind you in the army bye'n bye?

It is, of course, only a quaint piece of doggerel which the darkies cunningly adapt from the scraps of scripture they are taught. Nevertheless, the tune was quite charming when sung; the words seemed to put new life into an otherwise annoying melody and I was quite pleased that she had shared it with me. We were both quiet for several moments after she had done. The heat was, by this time, an enervating influence upon me. She, too, seemed to be spent by that brief spurt of animation. After a few more moments of silence, I closed the Bible, prayed briefly for the deliverance of her soul, then returned her to the cellar.

June 29, 1829.

I asked how to pronounce the name of the young darky with whom she had lived (I am puzzled in my own mind about how to refer to him. Certainly, they were not married and she never speaks of having gone through even the slave ceremony of jumping over the broom). Did Kaine—is that how you pronounce—how you *say* his name? I asked her.

"You say it the same way you . . . you . . . spell? Spell it!"

Did Kaine talk much about freedom? This is part of my strategy, to frame all the questions in such a way that

Kaine can be referred to in some manner. Her attachment to this Kaine appears quite sincere and while it is probably rooted in the basest of physical attractions, I cannot summon up the same sense of contempt with which I first viewed this liaison. I must confess also that I feel some slight twinge— Not of guilt, rather of *compassion* in using her attachment to the young darky as a means of eliciting information from her. But the fact is that my stratagems— while not perhaps of the most noble *type*—are used in the service of a greater good and this consideration must sweep all else before it. And I fear that in concentrating upon obtaining this greater good, I had finished asking the first question before I realized that she had made a slight jest. Looking at her in some surprise, I told her that it was quite a good joke, both in what she had said and in my own rather slow and dull reaction to her pleasantry. She in turn smiled, revealing for the first time in my memory the even white teeth behind the long thick lips of her mouth. Kaine did speak, then, a great deal about freedom?

She sat back. "Don't no niggas be talkin too much bout freedom, cause they be knowing what good fo em."

I did not believe her, but I chose, for the time being at least, to allow her to think that I did. Then what was your idea in trying to escape from the coffle?

She picked up a twig and began to mark in the dirt and to hum—not the same tune as the previous days, but one equally monotonous. She looked up at me, finally, and widened her eyes. "Was you black, you wanna be sold deep south? I neva been deep south, but Boss Smith, he always threats lazy niggas wid that and they don't be too lazy no mo."

And the others, I asked, was this what was in their mind?

She shrugged her shoulders. "Onlest mind I be knowin is mines. Why fo you didn't ask them first?" I believe this was not insolence, rather it seems more simple curiosity, and I allowed it to pass, explaining that I had not heard of the incident until too late to speak with the others who had been charged as leaders. "You thank there be a place

wid out no whites?" I looked at her in some surprise and
she continued to herself, in a deeper dialect than she had
heretofore used, really almost a mumble, something about
Emmalina's Joe Big (I have yet to determine if this is the
name of Emmalina's son or her "husband." Because the
father is seldom, if ever, of any consequence after conception, the children of these unions take their surnames from
their owners and are distinguished from others of the
same given names by prefacing their names with a posses-
sive form of the mother's. This form of address, however,
is also used in referring to spouses. The question of Joe
Big's relationship to Emmalina, while of passing interest,
is certainly extraneous to the present discussion, so I did
not interrupt her ramblings) telling Kaine something and
going, but where I could not make out. "They caught Bi—
They caught the others what run?"

I asked quickly, perhaps too quickly, if she knew where
they were and the blank sullen look immediately returned
to her face. The humming started again. She moved as
though uncomfortable and touched, almost as if frightened, the big mound which rises beneath her dress. When
she spoke it was in the voice of the first day. "This all I
gotta Kaine. Right here, in my belly. Mist's slap my face
when I tell her that, say, don't lie, say, it must be Terrell,
that how she call Mas, Terrell, say it mus be hissen, why
else Mas want kill Kaine, best gard'er they eva has, what
cost a pretty penny. She say, well, Terrell live, he live
knowin his woman and his brat south in worser slavery
than they eva thought of and Aunt Lefonia stop me fo I
kills her, too."

It was almost like listening to the first day's recital and
I knew when she turned her head from me that for this
day, anyway, I had gotten all from her that I could. This,
together with the oppressive heat (the air has now become laden with moisture—a relief from the furnace-like
dryness of the last few days—and the whole atmosphere is
pregnant with the storm which must break soon), made
me close my notebook for the day. But I now know that
the thick-lipped mouth, so savage in its sullen repose, can

smile and even utter small jests, that lurking behind her all too often blank gaze is something more than the cunning stubbornness which, alone, I first perceived, even noted that her skin, which appeared an ashen black in the light of the root cellar, is the color of strong tea and that even in the shade it is tinged with gold (surely this is a sign of good health in her. The baby should fetch Wilson a handsome price to repay him in some measure for what he has had to suffer through her agency). So, this lapse does not unduly discourage me. I know that she does not understand the project—it would be a wretched piece of business if she did—but she begins to have less distrust of me. She was not overly free in her speech but I begin to believe that she inclines towards this more than in the past. I fancy that I am not overly optimistic in predicting that one, perhaps two more sessions and I will have learned all I need from her. I shall have to think of a provocative title for the section in which I deal with the general principles apparent in her participation in this bloody business. "The Female of the Species," something along those lines, perhaps.

Later

Hughes says there is talk of a "maroon" settlement, an encampment of runaway slaves, somewhere nearby. There have been signs of marauding about some of the farms and plantations farther out from town. In the latest incident, several blacks (the wife of the farmer could not give an accurate count) stole into a small farm about twenty miles east of here and took provisions and the farm animals and murdered the farmer when he tried to protect his property. Fortunately, the wife was hidden during the raid and thus escaped injury. Hughes was inclined to treat this as an isolated incident—claiming that the other cases had happened so long ago that they had become greatly exaggerated in the telling—and thus dismiss the maroon theory as merely a fearful figment in the imagination of the larger slaveholders. He put down the missing provi-

240

sions and the occasional loss of livestock to the thieving of
the planters' own darkies. I am aware, as I told him, that
an unsupervised darky will steal anything which is not
nailed down, yet, in light of Odessa's talk of a place without whites and her concern about the three renegades
who escaped capture by the posse—talk which I repeated
—I cannot dismiss the theory of an encampment of some
sort so easily. It is, of course, pure conjecture, but not, I
believe, groundless to say, as I did to Hughes, that perhaps these three had joined the maroons—which would
certainly be one place without whites. And, despite the
babbling of the fanatic Elijah, it is obvious that the darkies from the coffle had been making for *someplace* when
they were apprehended. Hughes was much impressed
with my theorizing and invited me to join the posse which
leaves at dawn tomorrow in search of the renegades. I
readily accepted, for, even knowing the imaginative flights
to which the darky's mind is prone, I put much faith in
this information precisely because it was given inadvertently. What information Hughes and the prosecutor
were able to obtain from the others and from Odessa herself regarding the uprising is as nothing compared to this
plum.

*On the Trail
North and West of Linden*

June 30, 1829.

We set out early this morning, picking up the trail of the
renegades at the farm where they were last seen. It led us
in a northerly direction for most of the day and then, just
before we stopped for the night, it turned to the west.
Most of the posse feel this is a good sign, for had the trail
continued north we should have soon found ourselves in
Indian territory and, with two enemies to contend with,
the chances of being surprised in ambush would have
greatly increased. The trackers expect to raise some
fresher sign of them tomorrow, for they are laden with

supplies and we are not (a fact to which my stomach can well attest. Dried beef and half-cooked, half-warmed beans are *not* my idea of appetizing fare). And, I am told, if the weather holds humid as it has been and does not rain, their scent will hold fresh for quite a while and the dogs will be able to follow wherever it leads.

I did see Odessa this morning before we departed. I heard singing and, at first, taking it to be the usual morning serenade of Hughes' darkies, I took no notice of it. My attention was caught, however, by the plaintive note of this song, a peculiar circumstance, for Hughes frowns upon the singing of any but the most lively airs. I listened and finally managed to catch the words:

Tell me, sista tell me, brotha how long will it be?
Tell me, brotha tell me, sista how long will it be
That a poor sinner got to suffer, suffer here?
Tell me, sista tell me, brotha when my soul be free?
Tell me, oh, please tell me, when I be free
And the Lawd calla me home?

I had no sooner figured out these words—and recognized Odessa's voice—when another voice, this one lower and more mellow, took up the melody, singing at a somewhat faster tempo while Odessa maintained her original pace.

Oh, it won't be long. Say, it won't be long
Poor sinner got to suffer here.
Soul's goin to heav'n, soul's gon ride that heav'nly train.
Cause the Lawd have called us home.

It gave the effect of close harmonic part singing and was rather interesting and pleasing to the ear, especially when other voices joined in, as they presently did.

I hoped that Odessa's singing betokened a reflective mood and I went round to the cellar window, thinking that I might induce her to talk. I called to her and she broke off her singing in mid-phrase. "Who dat?" She spoke barely above a whisper and I could catch no

glimpse of her, hidden as she was in the dark recesses of
the cellar. I stooped down by the window, the better to
see her. "Who dat?" she called again. The appearance of
her face at the window startled me, for I had heard no
warning sound of her approach. Her eyes gleamed once
briefly in her face and then she closed them or perhaps
only turned her head. I could not tell which, for the early
morning light was still uncertain. I told her that I would
be leaving in a few minutes and I do not think I imagined
her quickened interest. "You don't be comin back?" I then
assured her that I would indeed return in a few days and
we would resume our conversations at that time. Hoping
in this way to elicit some further information from her, I
told her that we were going in search of a nearby maroon
settlement. She clutched the bars of the window and
peered at me through them. "Maroon?" I explained this
term to her, telling her that it is rumored that there is one
in the vicinity. I thought I had perhaps imparted too much
information, but what can such news avail her in that cellar? And she merely responded with a dumb stare. I am
not even sure that she had understood what I said, for she
asked, "You a *real* white man, fo true? You don't be talkin
like one. Sometime I don't even be knowin what you be
sayin. You don't be talkin like Mas and he a real uppity
up white man, but not like trash neitha. Kaine says it bes
white man what don't talk white man talk. You one like
that, huh?" I had been angered, and, yes, I admit, a trifle
offended by her question, and her emendations to the
question only slightly mollified my emotions. I answered,
somewhat haughtily, that I and others like me taught her
master and his kind how to speak. My hauteur was, of
course, lost on her, for she exclaimed happily that I was a
"teacher man." It seemed unnecessarily heartless to destroy her felicitous mood by further probing so I held my
peace, which proved to be a fortuitous choice. She continued, "Was a teacher man on the coffle. He teached hisself
to read from the Bible, then he preach. But course, that
only be to the niggas and he be all right til he want teach

otha niggas fo to read the Good Word. That be what he call it, 'The Good Word,' and when his Mas find out what he be doin he be sold south same's if he be teachin a bad word or be a bad nigga or a prime field hand." I seized upon this, feeling that perhaps I had discovered the key to the insurrection, for no one of this description—except perhaps Elijah—had been implicated in the plot. Is he the one who obtained the file, I asked, and she laughed. She laughed. "Onlest freedom he be knowin is what he say the 'righteous freedom,' that what the Lawd be givin him or what the Mas be givin him and he was the firstest one the patterrollers kills." She moved back into the darkness of the cellar still laughing softly and when I called to her she would not respond. Finally she moved back so that I could see the outline of her form. "Whatcho want?" she called. "Whatcho want?" I could feel my anger rising at the insolence of her tone, but just then Hughes called that we were ready to start. I rose and brushed the dirt from the knees of my trousers. I did not want to leave then, for I felt that some barrier had risen between us which must be breached. I realize now, however, that it was a fortuitous circumstance that Hughes called at just that moment. Otherwise I might have been betrayed into some impetuous action that might have permanently harmed this project. You will learn what I require when I return, I flung at her, and went to join Hughes. I could hear her voice raised, joining with the others in the new song which the other darkies had commenced during my conversation with her:

Good news, Lawd, Lawd, good news.
My brotha got a seat and I so glad.
I hearda from heav'n today.
Good news, Lawdy, Lawd, Lawd. Good news.
I don't mind what Satan say
Cause I heard, yes I heard, well I heard from heav'n today.

Pray God that nothing happens to upset the mood evinced

by her singing. We have much to talk about, Odessa and I, when we resume our conversations.

Somewhere West of Linden

July 3, 1829.

A wild-goose chase and a sorry time we have had of it. There is doubt in my mind that such an encampment, as I first conceived of, exists, at least in this vicinity, for we have searched a large area and come up with nothing conclusive. Several times, we sighted what might have been members of such a band, but the dogs could not tree them and it was more than we ourselves could do to catch more than what we *hope* were fleeting glimpses of black bodies. Whether they took, indeed, to the trees, as some in the posse maintain, or vanished into the air, I have no way of knowing. If they exist, they are as elusive as Indians, nay, as elusive as *smoke* and I feel it beyond the ability of so large a posse as ours to move warily enough to take them unawares. To compound matters, the storm which has been threatening for days finally broke this morning, putting an end to our search and drenching us in the process. We have stopped to rest the horses, for Hughes estimates that if we push hard, we should reach Linden by nightfall. A bed will be most welcome after having spent so many days upon the back of this wretched horse, and I look forward to resuming my conversations with Odessa. She has a subtle presence, almost an influence which I have only become aware of in its absence. Perhaps—but that is useless speculation and must wait upon the certainty of Wilson's return. Hughes has given the call to mount and so we are off.

July 4, 1829.
Early Morning.

I put the date in wearied surprise. We have been out most of the night scouring the countryside for signs of Odessa, but there were none that we found and the rain has by now washed away what we must have missed. It is as though the niggers who crept in and stole away with her were not human blood, human flesh, but sorcerers who whisked her away by magic to the accursed den they inhabit. Hughes maintained that the devil merely claimed his own and gave up the search around midnight. But reason tells me that the niggers were not supernatural, not spirits or "haints." They are flesh and bone and so must leave some trace of their coming and going. The smallest clue would have sufficed me, for I should have followed it to its ultimate end. Now the rain has come up and even that small chance is gone, vanished like Odessa.

And we did not even know that she was gone, had, in fact, sat down to eat the supper left warming at the back of the stove against the chance that we would return, to talk of the futile venture of the last few days, to conjecture on God knows what. Unsuspecting we were, until the darky that sleeps with Jemina came asking for her. Hughes went to inquire of his wife—who had not arisen upon our return, merely called down to us that she was unwell and that food had been left for us. I was immediately alarmed, prescience I now know, upon learning that the woman had not seen Jemina since the wench had taken supper to Odessa earlier in the evening. And Hughes' assurances that Jemina was a good girl, having been with the wife since childhood, did nothing to calm my fears. Such a slight indisposition as his wife evidently had was no reason to entrust the keeping of so valuable a prisoner to another negress who is no doubt only slightly less sly than Odessa herself. I protested thus to Hughes, too strongly I now see, for he replied heatedly that if I did not keep my tongue from his wife—I marvel, even now in my exhaustion, at the quaintness of his phrasing—my slight stature would not keep me from a beating. I am firm in my belief that these impetuous words of mine were a strong factor in his early abandonment of the search and I regret them accordingly. There are stronger words in my mind now, but I forbore, at that time, carrying the discussion farther. I knew, even then, without really knowing why, that time was of the essence. But he shall find on the morrow that even one of my *slight stature* has the means of prosecuting him for criminal neglect. To think of leaving Odessa in the care of another nigger!

The root cellar when we reached it was locked, but the relief I felt was short-lived. It was Jemina inside and the wench set up such a racket, then, when it could not possibly serve any useful purpose, that one would have thought the hounds of hell pursued her. Even had I not recognized that such a cacophony could never issue from Odessa's throat, Hughes' startled exclamation was enough to alert me. The wench was, of course, incoherent—when was a nigger in excitement ever anything else?—but we finally pieced together, between the wench's throwing her apron over her head and howling, "oh, Mas, it terr'ble; they was terr'ble fierce," and pointing to her muddied gown to prove it, what must have happened. Three niggers (she said three the first time and the number has increased with each successive telling; perhaps there were only one or two, but I settle upon three as the most likely number, for they were obviously the niggers with whom Odessa was in league in the uprising on the coffle. I could scream to think that even as we were out chasing shadows, the cunning devils were even then lying in wait to spirit her away. And to think that she—*she* was so deep as to give never an indication that they were then lurking about. Both Jemina and that woman of Hughes swear that except for a natural melancholy—which in itself was not unusual—*I* have been the only one to succeed in coaxing her into animated spirits—there was nothing out of the ordinary in Odessa's demeanor these last days. And knowing now the cupidity of which she is capable, I must believe them). The three bucks overpowered the wench just as she opened the door to the cellar to hand down the evening meal to Odessa. At this point, Hughes ejaculated something to the effect that it was a good thing "my

Betty" was not present, at which the negress began what must have been, had I not intervened, a long digression on the "Mist's" symptoms and how she might, at long last, be increasing. But I could *feel* those niggers getting farther away with Odessa and so could not bear the interruption. The niggers forced Jemina into the cellar, bound her, took up Odessa and escaped into the night. The wench swears she heard no names called, that except for one exclamation from Odessa, of surprise or dismay, she could not tell which, they fled in silence, swears also that she could not see well enough to describe either of the niggers, save to state that they were big and black and terrible as though that would help to distinguish them from any of the hundreds, *thousands* of niggers in this world who are equally as big and as black and as terrible. The wench could not even tell whether they went on horseback or afoot, nor explain how a woman almost nine months gone could move so quickly and so quietly as to give no clue to the direction they took, nor less explain how it came about that she herself did not cry out, for surely if she had someone must have heard. This last question was again the occasion for that banshee-like wail about how "terr'ble fierce" the niggers were.

Hughes numbers among his four slaves one he termed an expert tracker, skilled in the ways of the Indians in hunting and trapping, but we did not need his help in finding the place where they had lain in wait for someone to open the cellar door. The earlier rain had made their sign quite plain. We found, also, with heartening ease the place where they had tied their animals. It was muddied and much trampled so we could not tell what kind of animals they were—whether horses or mules—nor even how many. Hughes' jocular, and inappropriately so, prediction that we should find Odessa and her newborn brat—for what female as far gone as she could stand the strain of a quick flight without giving birth to something—lying beside the trail within a mile or so proved incorrect, for the tracks disappeared into the deep underbrush a short distance from the place where the animals had been tied. Both the nigger and the one bloodhound Hughes keeps were alike worthless in the quest. And then the rain came up, driven by a furious wind, lashing the needle-like drops into our faces; washing away all trace of Odessa. Hughes, in giving up the hunt, charged that I acted like one possessed. He could not say by what and I know that this was merely his own excuse for failing in his lawful duty. For myself, I have searched, hunted, called and am now exhausted. She is gone. Even the smallest clue—but there was nothing, no broken twig to point a direction, no scent which the hound could hold for more than a short distance. Gone. And I not even aware, not even suspecting, just—just gone.

"i am not movin"

---

comin to terms

BY NTOZAKE SHANGE

they hadnt slept together for months/ the nite she pulled
the two thinnest blankets from on top of him & gathered
one pillow under her arm to march to the extra room/
now 'her' room/ had been jammed with minor but telling
incidents/ at dinner she had asked him to make sure the
asparagus didnt burn so he kept adding water & they, of
course/ water-logged/ a friend of hers stopped over & he
got jealous of her having so many friends/ so he sulked cuz
no one came to visit him/ then she gotta call that she made
the second round of interviews for the venceremos brigade/
he said he didnt see why that waz so important/ & with
that she went to bed/ moments later this very masculine
leg threw itself over her thighs/ she moved over/ then a
long muscled arm wrapped round her chest/ she sat up/
he waz smiling/ the smile that said 'i wanna do it now.'

mandy's shoulders dropped/ her mouth wanted to pout
or frown/ her fist waz lodged between her legs as a barrier
or an alternative/ a cooing brown hand settled on her back-
side/ 'listen, mandy, i just wanna little'/ mandy looked
down on the other side of the bed/ maybe the floor cd
talk to him/ the hand roamed her back & bosom/ she
started to make faces & blink a lot/ ezra waznt talkin any-
more/ a wet mouth waz sittin on mandy's neck/ & teeth
beginnin to nibble the curly hairs near her ears/ she started
to shake her head/ & covered her mouth with her hand
sayin/ 'i waz dreamin bout cuba & you wanna fuck'/ 'no,
mandy, i dont wanna fuck/ i wanna make love to . . . love
to you'/ & the hand became quite aggressive with mandy's
titties/ 'i'm dreamin abt goin to cuba/ which isnt impor-

tant/ i'm hungry cuz you ruined dinner/ i'm lonely cuz
you embarrassed my friend: & you wanna fuck'/ 'i dont
wanna fuck/ i told you that i wanna make love'/ 'well you
got it/ you hear/ you got it to yr self/ cuz i'm goin to dream
abt goin to cuba'/ & with that she climbed offa the hand
pummelin her ass/ & pulled the two thinnest blankets &
one pillow to the extra room.

the extra room waz really mandy's anyway/ that's where
she read & crocheted & thot/ she cd watch the neighbors'
children & hear miz nancy singin gospel/ & hear miz nancy
give her sometimey lover who owned the steepin tavern/
a piece of her mind/ so the extra room/ felt full/ not
as she had feared/ empty & knowin absence. in a corner
under the window/ mandy settled every nite after the
cuba dreams/ & watched the streetlights play thru the lace
curtains to the wall/ she slept soundly the first few nites/
ezra didnt mention that she didnt sleep with him/ & they
ate the breakfast she fixed & he went off to the studio/
while she went off to school he came home to find his
dinner on the table & mandy in her room/ doing something
that pleased her. mandy was very polite & gracious/ asked
how his day waz/ did anything exciting happen/ but she
never asked him to do anything for her/ like lift things or
watch the stove/ or listen to her dreams/ she also never
went in the room where they usedta sleep together/ tho
she cleaned everywhere else as thoroughly as one of her
mother's great-aunts cleaned the old house on rose tree lane
in charleston/ but she never did any of this while ezra waz
in the house/ if ezra waz home/ you cd be sure mandy waz
out/ or in her room.

one nite just fore it's time to get up & the sky is lightening
up for sunrise/ mandy felt a chill & these wet things on her
neck/ she started slappin the air/ & without openin her
eyes/ cuz she cd/ feel now what waz goin on/ ezra pushed
his hard dick up on her thigh/ his breath covered her face/
he waz movin her covers off/ mandy kept slappin him & he
kept bumpin up & down on her legs & her ass/ 'what are

you doin ezra'/ he just kept movin. mandy screamed/ 'ezra what in hell are you doin.' & pushed him off her. he fell on the floor/ cuz mandy's little bed waz right on the floor/ & she slept usually near the edge of her mattress/ ezra stood & his dick waz aimed at mandy's face/ at her right eye/ she looked away/ & ezra/ jumped up & down/ in the air this time/ 'what are you talkin abt what am i doin/ i'm doin what we always do/ i'm gettin ready to fuck/ awright so you were mad/ but this cant go on forever/ i'm goin crazy/ i cant live in a house with you & not fu . . . / not make love. i mean.' mandy still lookin at the pulsing penis/ jumpin around as ezra jumped around/ mandy sighed 'ezra let's not let this get ugly/ please, just go to sleep/ in yr bed & we'll talk abt this tomorrow.' 'what do you mean tomorrow i'm goin crazy' . . . mandy looked into ezra's scrotum/ & spoke softly 'you'll haveta be crazy then' & turned over to go back to sleep. ezra waz still for a moment/ then he pulled the covers off mandy & jerked her around some/ talkin bout 'we live together & we're gonna fuck now'/ mandy treated him as cruelly as she wd any stranger/ kicked & bit & slugged & finally ran to the kitchen/ leavin ezra holdin her torn nitegown in his hands.

'how cd you want me/ if i dont want you/ i dont want you niggah/ i dont want you' & she worked herself into a sobbin frigidaire-beatin frenzy . . . ezra looked thru the doorway mumblin. 'i didnt wanna upset you, mandy. but you gotta understand. i'm a man & i just cant stay here like this with you . . . not bein able to touch you or feel you'/ mandy screamed back 'or fuck me/ go on, say it niggah/ fuck.' ezra threw her gown on the floor & stamped off to his bed. we dont know what he did in there.

mandy put her gown in the sink & scrubbed & scrubbed til she cd get his hands off her. she changed the sheets & took a long bath & a douche. she went back to bed & didnt go to school all day she lay in her bed. thinkin of what ezra had done. i cd tell him to leave/ she thot/ but that's half the rent/ i cd leave/ but i like it here/ i cd getta dog

to guard me at nite/ but ezra wd make friends with it/ i cd
let him fuck me & not move/ that wd make him mad & i like
to fuck ezra/ he's good/ but that's not the point/ that's not
the point/ & she came up with the idea that if they were
really friends like they always said/ they shd be able to
enjoy each other without fucking without having to sleep
in the same room/ mandy had grown to cherish waking
up a solitary figure in her world/ she liked the quiet of her
own noises in the night & the sound of her own voice soothin
herself/ she liked to wake up in the middle of the nite &
turn the lights on & read or write letters/ she even liked the
grain advisory show on tv at 5:30 in the mornin/ she hadda
lotta secret nurturin she had created for herself/ that ezra
& his heavy gait/ ezra & his snorin/ ezra & his goin-crazy
hard-on wd/ do violence to . . . so she suggested to ezra
that they continue to live together as friends/ & see other
people if they wanted to have a more sexual relationship
than the one she waz offering . . . ezra laughed. he thot
she waz a little off/ til she shouted 'you cant imagine me
without a wet pussy/ you cant imagine me without yr god-
damed dick stickin up in yr pants/ well yr gonna learn/ i
dont start comin to life cuz you feel like fuckin/ yr gonna
learn i'm alive/ ya hear' . . . ezra waz usually a gentle sorta
man/ but he slapped mandy this time & walked off . . . he
came home two days later covered with hickeys & quite
satisfied with himself. mandy fixed his dinner/ nothin spe-
cial/ & left the door of her room open so he cd see her givin
herself pleasure/ from then on/ ezra always asked if he
cd come visit her/ waz she in need of some company/ did
she want a lil lovin/ or wd she like to come visit him in his
room/ there are no more assumptions in the house.

Medley

BY TONI CADE BAMBARA

I could tell the minute I got in the door and dropped my
bag, I wasn't staying. Dishes piled sky-high in the sink
looking like some circus act. Glasses all ghosty on the
counter. Busted tea bags, curling cantaloupe rinds, white
cartoons from the Chinamen, green sacks from the deli,
and that damn dog creeping up on me for me to wrassle
his head or kick him in the ribs one. No, I definitely
wasn't staying. Couldn't even figure why I'd come. But
picked my way to the hallway anyway till the laundry-
stuffed pillowcases stopped me. Larry's bass blocking the
view to the bedroom.

"That you, Sweet Pea?"

"No, man, ain't me at all," I say, working my way back
to the suitcase and shoving that damn dog out the way.
"See ya round," I holler, the door slamming behind me,
cutting off the words abrupt.

     *   *   *

Quite naturally sitting cross-legged at the club, I em-
broider a little on the homecoming tale, what with an audience of two crazy women and a fresh bottle of Jack
Daniels. Got so I could actually see shonuff toadstools
growing in the sink. Cantaloupe seeds sprouting in the
muck. A goddamn compost heap breeding near the stove,
garbage gardens on the grill.

"Sweet Pea, you oughta hush, cause you can't possibly
keep on lying so," Pot Limit's screaming, tears popping
from her eyes. "Lawd hold my legs, cause this liar bout to
kill me off."

"Never mind about Larry's housekeeping, girl," Sylvia's soothing me, sloshing perfectly good bourbon all over the table. "You can come and stay with me till your house comes through. It'll be like old times at Aunt Merriam's."

I ease back into the booth to wait for the next set. The drummer's fooling with the equipment, tapping the mikes, hoping he's watched, so I watch him. But feeling worried in my mind about Larry, cause I've been through days like that myself. Cold cream caked on my face from the day before, hair matted, bathrobe funky, not a clean pair of drawers to my name. Even the emergency ones, the draggy cotton numbers stuffed way in the back of the drawer under the scented paper gone. And no clean silverware in the box and the last of the paper cups gone too. Icebox empty cept for a rock of cheese and the lone water jug that ain't even half full that's how anyhow the thing's gone on. And not a clue as to the next step. But then Pot Limit'll come bamming on the door to say So-and-so's in town and can she have the card table for a game. Or Sylvia'll send a funny card inviting herself to dinner and even giving me the menu. Then I zoom through that house like a manic work brigade till me and the place ready for white-glove inspection. But what if somebody or other don't intervene for Larry, I'm thinking.

The drummer's messin round on the cymbals, head cocked to the side, rings sparkling. The other dudes are stepping out from behind the curtain. The piano man playing with the wah-wah doing splashy, breathy science fiction stuff. Sylvia checking me out to make sure I ain't too blue. Blue got hold to me, but I lean forward out of the shadows and babble something about how off the bourbon tastes these days. Hate worryin Sylvia, who is the kind of friend who bleeds at the eyes with your pain. I drain my glass and hum along with the opening riff of the guitar and I keep my eyes strictly off the bass player, whoever he is.

Larry Landers looked more like a bass player than ole Mingus himself. Got these long arms that drape down

over the bass like they were grown special for that purpose. Fine, strong hands with long fingers and muscular
knuckles, the dimples deep black at the joints. His calluses
so other-colored and hard, looked like Larry had swiped
his grandmother's tarnished thimbles to play with. He'd
move in on that bass like he was going to hump it or
something, slide up behind it as he lifted it from the rug,
all slinky. He'd become one with the wood. Head dipped
down sideways bobbing out the rhythm, feet tapping, legs
jiggling, he'd look good. Thing about it, though, ole Larry
couldn't play for shit. Couldn't never find the right place-
ment for the notes. Never plucking with enough strength,
despite the perfectly capable hands. Either you didn't
hear him at all or what you heard was off. The man
couldn't play for nuthin is what I'm saying. But Larry
Landers was baad in the shower, though.

He'd soap me up and down with them great, fine
hands, doing a deep bass walking in the back of his
mouth. And I'd just have to sing, though I can't sing to
save my life. But we'd have one hellafyin musical time in
the shower, lemme tell you. "Green Dolphin Street" never
sounded like nuthin till Larry bopped out them changes
and actually made me sound good. On "My Funny Valen-
tine" he'd do a whizzing sounding bow thing that made
his throat vibrate real sexy and I'd cutesy up the introduction, which is, come to think of it, my favorite part.
But the main number when the hot water started running
out was "I Feel Like Making Love." That was usually the
wind up of our repertoire cause you can imagine what
that song can do to you in the shower and all.

Got so we spent a helluva lotta time in the shower. Just
as well, cause didn't nobody call Larry for gigs. He a nice
man, considerate, generous, baad in the shower, and good
taste in music. But he just wasn't nobody's bass player.
Knew all the stances, though, the postures, the facial ex-
pressions, had the choreography down. And right in the
middle of supper he'd get some Ron Carter thing going in
his head and hop up from the table to go get the bass.

Haul that sucker right in the kitchen and do a number in
dumb show, all the playing in his throat, the acting with
his hands. But that ain't nuthin. I mean that can't get it. I
can impersonate Betty Carter if it comes to that. The arms
crooked just so, the fingers popping, the body working,
the cap and all, the teeth, authentic. But I got sense
enough to know I ain't nobody's singer. Actually, I am a
mother, though I'm only just now getting it together. And
too, I'm an A-1 manicurist.

Me and my cousin Sinbad come North working our
show in cathouses at first. Set up a salon right smack in
the middle of Miz Maybry's Saturday traffic. But that
wasn't no kind of life to be bringing my daughter into. So
I parked her at a boarding school till I could make some
other kind of life. Wasn't no kind of life for Sinbad either,
so we quit.

Our first shop was a three-chair affair on Austin. Had a
student barber who could do anything—blow-outs, do's,
corn rows, weird cuts, afros, press and curl, whatever you
wanted. Plus he din't gab you to death. And he always
brought his sides and didn't blast em neither. He went on
to New York and opened his own shop. Was a bootblack
too then, an old dude named James Noughton, had a
crooked back and worked at the post office at night, and
knew everything about everything, read all the time.

"Whatcha want to know about Marcus Garvey, Sweet
Pea?"

If it wasn't Garvey, it was the rackets or the trucking
industry or the flora and fauna of Greenland or the
planets or how the special effects in the disaster movies
were done. One Saturday I asked him to tell me about the
war, cause my nephew'd been drafted and it all seemed
so wrong to me, our men over there in Nam fighting folks
who fighting for the same things we are, to get that blood-
sucker off our backs.

Well, what I say that for. Old dude gave us a deep
knee bend, straight up eight-credit dissertation on World

Wars I and II—the archduke getting offed, Africa cut up like so much cake, Churchill and his cigars, Gabriel Heatter on the radio, Hitler at the Olympics igging Owens, Red Cross doing Bloods dirty refusing donuts and bandages, A. Philip Randolph scaring the white folks to death, Mary McLeod Bethune at the White House, Liberty Bond drives, the Russian front, frostbite of the feet, the Jew stiffs, the gypsies no one mourned . . . the whole johnson. Talked straight through the day, Miz Mary's fish dinner growing cold on the radiator, his one and only customer walking off with one dull shoe. Fell out exhausted, his shoe rag limp in his lap, one arm draped over the left foot platform, the other clutching his heart. Took Sinbad and our cousin Pepper to get the old man home. I stayed with him all night with the ice pack and a fifth of Old Crow. He liked to die.

After while trade picked up and with a better class of folk too. Then me and Sinbad moved to North and Gaylord and called the shop Chez Sinbad. No more winos stumbling in or deadbeats wasting my time talking raunchy shit. The paperboy, the numbers man, the dudes with classier hot stuff coming in on Tuesday mornings only. We did up the place nice. Light globes from a New Orleans whorehouse, Sinbad likes to lie. Brown-and-black-and-silver-striped wallpaper. Lots of mirrors and hanging plants. Them old barber chairs spruced up and called antiques and damn if someone didn't buy one off us for eight hundred, cracked me up.

I cut my schedule down to ten hours in the shop so I could do private sessions with the gamblers and other business men and women who don't like sitting around the shop even though it's comfy, specially my part. Got me a cigar showcase with a marble top for serving coffee in clear glass mugs with heatproof handles too. My ten hours in the shop are spent leisurely. And my twenty hours out are making me a mint. Takes dust to be a mother, don't you know.

It was a perfect schedule once Larry Landers came into

my life. He part-timed at a record shop and bartended at
Topp's on the days and nights I worked at the shops. That
gave us most of Monday and Wednesdays to listen to
sides and hit the clubs. Gave me Fridays all to myself to
study in the library and wade through them college bulle-
tins and get to the museum and generally chart out a routine for when Debbie and me are a team. Sundays I always drive to Delaware to see her, and Larry detours to
D.C. to see his sons. My bankbook started telling me I
was soon going to be a full-time mama again and a college
girl to boot, if I can ever talk myself into doing a school
thing again, old as I am.

Life with Larry was cool. Not just cause he wouldn't
hear about me going halves on the bills. But cause he was
an easy man to be easy with. He liked talking softly and
listening to music. And he liked having folks over for dinner and cards. Larry a real nice man and I liked him a lot.
And I liked his friend Hector, who lived in the back of the
apartment. Ole moon-face Hector went to school with
Larry years ago and is some kind of kin. And they once
failed in the funeral business together and I guess those
stories of them times kinda keep them friends.

The time they had to put Larry's brother away is their
best story, Hector's story really, since Larry got to play a
little grief music round the edges. They decided to pass
up a church service, since Bam was such a treacherous
desperado wouldn't nobody want to preach over his body
and wouldn't nobody want to come to hear no lies about
the dearly departed untimely ripped or cut down or whatever. So Hector and Larry set up some kind of pop stand
awning right at the gravesite, expecting close blood only.
But seems the whole town turned out to make sure ole
evil, hell-raising Bam was truly dead. Dudes straight from
the barber chair, the striped ponchos blowing like wings,
fuzz and foam on they face and all, lumbering up the hill
to the hole taking bets and talking shit, relating how Ole
Crazy Bam had shot up the town, shot up the jail, shot up

the hospital pursuing some bootlegger who'd come up one keg short of the order. Women from all around come to demand the lid be lifted so they could check for themselves and be sure that Bam was stone cold. No matter how I tried I couldn't think of nobody bad enough to think on when they told the story of the man I'd never met.

Larry and Hector so bent over laughing bout the funeral, I couldn't hardly put the events in proper sequence. But I could surely picture some neighbor lady calling on Larry and Bam's mama reporting how the whole town had turned out for the burying. And the mama snatching up the first black thing she could find to wrap around herself and make an appearance. No use passing up a scene like that. And Larry prancing round the kitchen being his mama. And I'm too stunned to laugh, not at somebody's mama, and somebody's brother dead. But him and Hector laughing to beat the band and I can't help myself.

Thing about it, though, the funeral business stories are Hector's stories and he's not what you'd call a good storyteller. He never gives you the names, so you got all these he's and she's floating around. And he don't believe in giving details, so you got to scramble to paint your own pictures. Toward the end of that particular tale of Bam, all I could picture was the townspeople driving a stake through the dead man's heart, then hurling that coffin into the hole right quick. There was also something in that story about the civil rights workers wanting to make a case cause a white cop had cut Bam down. But looked like Hector didn't have a hold to that part of the story, so I just don't know.

Stories are not Hector's long suit. But he is an absolute artist on windows. Ole Moon-Face can wash some windows and make you cry about it too. Makes these smooth little turns out there on that little bitty sill just like he wasn't four stories up without a belt. I'd park myself at the breakfast counter and thread the new curtains on the rods while Hector mixed up the vinegar solution real chef-like. Wring out the rags just so, scrunch up the news-papers into soft wads that make you think of cat's paws. Hector was a cat himself out there on the sill, making these marvelous circles in the glass, rubbing the hardhead spots with a strip of steel wool he had pinned to his over-alls.

Hector offered to do my car once. But I put a stop to that after that first time. My windshield so clear and spar-kling felt like I was in an accident and heading over the hood, no glass there. But it was a pleasure to have coffee and watch Hector. After while, though, Larry started hint-ing that the apartment wasn't big enough for four. I agreed, thinking he meant Earl had to go. Come to find Larry meant Hector, which was a real drag. I love to be around people who do whatever it is they do with style and care.

Larry's dog's named Earl P. Jessup Bowers, if you can get ready for that. And I should mention straightaway that I do not like dogs one bit, which is why I was glad when Larry said somebody had to go. Cats are bad enough. Horses are a total drag. By the age of nine I was fed up with all that noble horse this and noble horse that. They got good PR, horses. But I really can't use em. Was a fire once when I was little and some dumb horse almost burnt my daddy up messin around, twisting, snorting, broncing, rearing up, doing everything but comin on out the barn like even the chickens had sense enough to do. I told my daddy to let that horse's ass burn. Horses be as dumb as cows. Cows just don't have good press agents is all.

I used to like cows when I was real little and needed to hug me something bigger than a goldfish. But don't let it rain, the dumbbells'll fall right in a ditch and you break a plow and shout yourself hoarse trying to get them fools to come up out the ditch. Chipmunks I don't mind when I'm at the breakfast counter with my tea and they're on their side of the glass doing Disney things in the yard. Blue jays are law-and-order birds, thoroughly despicable.

And there's one prize fool in my Aunt Merriam's yard I will one day surely kill. He tries to "whip whip whippoorwill" like the Indians do in the Fort This or That movies when they're signaling to each other closing in on George Montgomery but don't never get around to wiping that sucker out. But dogs are one of my favorite hatreds. All the time woofing, bolting down their food, slopping water on the newly waxed linoleum, messin with you when you trying to read, chewin on the slippers.

Earl P. Jessup Bowers was an especial drag. But I could put up with Earl when Hector was around. Once Hector was gone and them windows got cloudy and gritty, I was through. Kicked that dog every chance I got. And after thinking what it meant, how the deal went down, place too small for four and it was Hector not Earl—I started moving up my calendar so I could get out of there. I ain't the kind of lady to press no ultimatum on no man. Like "Choose, me or the dog." That's unattractive. Kicking Hector out was too. An insult to me, once I got to thinking on it. Especially since I had carefully explained from jump street to Larry that I got one item on my agenda, making a home for me and my kid. So if anybody should've been given walking papers, should've been me.

Anyway. One day Moody comes waltzing into Chez Sinbad's and tips his hat. He glances at his nails and glances at me. And I figure here is my house in a green corduroy suit. Pot Limit had just read my cards and the jack of diamonds kept coming up on my resource side. Sylvia and me put our heads together and figure it got to be some gambler or hustler who wants his nails done. What other jacks do I know to make my fortune? I'm so positive about Moody, I whip out a postcard from the drawer where I keep the emeries and write my daughter to start packing.

"How much you make a day, Miss Lady?"

"Thursdays are always good for fifty," I lie.

He hands me fifty and glances over at Sinbad, who

nods that it's cool. "I'd like my nails done at four-thirty. My place."

"Got a customer at that time, Mr. Moody, and I like to stay reliable. How bout five-twenty?"

He smiles a slow smile and glances at Sinbad, who nods again, everything's cool. "Fine," he says. "And do you think you can manage a shave without cutting a person's throat?"

"Mr. Moody, I don't know you well enough to have just cause. And none of your friends have gotten to me yet with that particular proposition. Can't say what I'm prepared to do in the future, but for now I can surely shave you real careful-like."

Moody smiles again, then turns to Sinbad, who says it's cool and he'll give me the address. This look-nod dialogue burns my ass. That's like when you take a dude to lunch and pay the check and the waiter's standing there with *your* money in his paws asking *the dude* was everything all right and later for *you*. Shit. But I take down Moody's address and let the rest roll off me like so much steaming lava. I start packing up my little alligator case—buffer, batteries, clippers, emeries, massager, sifter, arrowroot and cornstarch, clear sealer, magnifying glass, and my own mixture of green and purple pigments.

"Five-twenty ain't five-twenty-one, is it, Miss Lady?"

"Not in my book," I say, swinging my appointment book around so he can see how full it is and how neatly the times are printed in. Course I always fill in phony names case some creep starts pressing me for a session.

For six Thursdays running and two Monday nights, I'm at Moody's bending over them nails with a miner's light strapped to my forehead, the magnifying glass in its stand, nicking just enough of the nails at the sides, tinting just enough with the color so he can mark them cards as he shuffles. Takes an hour to do it proper. Then I sift my talc concoction and brush his hands till they're smooth. Them cards move around so fast in his hands, he can actually tell me he's about to deal from the bottom in the next three moves and I miss it and I'm not new to this. I been a gambler's manicurist for more years than I care to mention. Ten times he'll cut and each time the same fifteen cards in the top cut and each time in exactly the same order. Incredible.

Now, I've known hands. My first husband, for instance. To see them hands work their show in the grandstands, at a circus, in a parade, the pari-mutuels—artistry in action. We met on the train. As a matter of fact, he was trying to burgle my bag. Some story to tell the grandchildren, hunh? I had to get him straight about robbing from folks. I don't play that. Ya gonna steal, hell, steal back some of them millions we got in escrow is my opinion. We spent three good years on the circuit. Then credit cards moved in. Then choke-and-grab muggers killed the whole tradition. He was reduced to a mere shell of his former self, as they say, and took to putting them hands on me. I try not to think on when things went sour. Try not to think about them big slapping hands, only of them working hands. Moody's working hands were something like that, but even better. So I'm impressed and he's impressed. And he pays me fifty and tips me fifty and shuts up when I shave him and keeps his hands off my lovely person.

I'm so excited counting up my bread, moving up the calendar, making impulsive calls to Delaware and the two of us squealing over the wire like a coupla fools, that what Larry got to say about all these goings-on just rolls off my back like so much molten lead.

"Well, who be up there while he got his head in your lap and you squeezing his goddamn blackheads?"

"I don't squeeze his goddamn blackheads, Larry, on account of he don't have no goddamn blackheads. I give him a shave, a steam, and an egg-white face mask. And when I'm through, his face is as smooth as his hands."

"I'll bet," Larry says. That makes me mad cause I expect some kind of respect for my work, which is better than just good.

"And he doesn't have his head in my lap. He's got a whole barbershop set up on his solarium."

"His what?" Larry squinting at me, raising the wooden spoon he stirring the spaghetti with, and I raise the knife I'm chopping the onions with. Thing about it, though, he don't laugh. It's funny as hell to me, but Larry got no sense of humor sometimes, which is too bad cause he's a lotta fun when he's laughing and joking.

"It's not a bedroom. He's got this screened-in sun porch where he raises African violets and—"

"Please, Sweet Pea. Why don't you quit? You think I'm dumb?"

"I'm serious. I'm serious and I'm mad cause I ain't got no reason to lie to you whatever was going on, Larry." He turns back to the pot and I continue working on the sauce and I'm pissed off cause this is silly. "He sits in the barber chair and I shave him and give him a manicure."

"What else you be giving him? A man don't be paying a good-looking woman to come to his house and all and don't—"

"Larry, if you had the dough and felt like it, wouldn't you pay Pot Limit to come read your cards? And couldn't you keep your hands to yourself and she a good-looking woman? And couldn't you see yourself paying Sylvia to come and cook for you and no funny stuff, and she's one of the best-looking women in town?"

Larry cooled out fast. My next shot was to bring up the fact that he was insulting my work. Do I go around saying the women who pass up Bill the bartender and come to him are after his joint? No, cause I respect the fact that Larry Landers mixes the best piña coladas this side of Barbados. And he's flashy with the blender and the glasses and the whole show. He's good and I respect that. But he cooled out so fast I didn't have to bring it up. I don't believe in overkill, besides I like to keep some things in reserve. He cooled out so fast I realized he wasn't really jealous. He was just going through one of them obligatory male numbers, all symbolic, no depth.

Like the time this dude came into the shop to talk some trash and Sinbad got his ass on his shoulders, talking about the dude showed no respect for him cause for all he knew I could be Sinbad's woman. And me arguing that since that ain't the case, what's the deal? I mean why get hot over what if if what if ain't. Men are crazy. Now there is Sinbad, my blood cousin who grew up right in the same house like a brother damn near, putting me through simple-ass changes like that. Who's got time for grand opera and comic strips, I'm trying to make a life for me and my kid. But men are like that. Gorillas, if you know what I mean.

Like at Topp's sometimes. I'll drop in to have a drink with Larry when he's on the bar and then I leave. And maybe some dude'll take it in his head to walk me to the car. That's cool. I lay it out right quick that me and Larry are a we and then we take it from there, just two people gassing in the summer breeze and that's just fine. But don't let some other dude holler over something like "Hey, man, can you handle all that? Why don't you step aside, junior, and let a man . . ." and blah-de-da-de-dah. They can be the best of friends or total strangers just kidding around, but right away they two gorillas pounding on their chest, pounding on their chest and talking over my head, yelling over the tops of cars just like I'm not a person with some say-so in the matter. It's a man-to-man ritual that ain't got nothing to do with me. So I just get in my car and take off and leave them to get it on if they've a mind to. They got it.

But if one of the gorillas is a relative, or a friend of mine, or a nice kinda man I got in mind for one of my friends, I will stick around long enough to shout em down and point out that they are some ugly gorillas and are showing no respect for me and therefore owe me an apology. But if they don't fit into one of them categories, I figure it ain't my place to try to develop them so they can make the leap from gorilla to human. If their own mamas and daddies didn't care whether they turned out to be amoebas or catfish or whatever, it ain't my weight. I got my own weight. I'm a mother. So they got it.

Like I use to tell my daughter's daddy, the key to getting along and living with other folks is to keep clear whose weight is whose. His drinking, for instance, was not my weight. And him waking me up in the night for them long, rambling, ninety-proof monologues bout how the whole world's made up of victims, rescuers, and executioners and I'm the dirty bitch cause I ain't rescuing him fast enough to suit him. Then got so I was the executioner, to hear him tell it. I don't say nuthin cause my philosophy of life and death is this—I'll go when the wagon comes, but I ain't going out behind somebody else's shit. I arranged my priorities long ago when I jumped into my woman stride. Some things I'll go off on. Some things I'll hold my silence and wait it out. Some things I just bump off, cause the best solution to some problems is to just abandon them.

But I struggled with Mac, Debbie's daddy. Talked to his family, his church, AA, hid the bottles, threatened the liquor man, left a good job to play nurse, mistress, kitten, buddy. But then he stopped calling me Dahlin and started calling me Mama. I don't play that. I'm my daughter's mama. So I split. Did my best to sweeten them last few months, but I'd been leaving for a long time.

The silliest thing about all of Larry's grumblings back then was Moody had no eyes for me and vice versa. I just like the money. And I like watching him mess around with the cards. He's exquisite, dazzling, stunning shuffling, cutting, marking, dealing from the bottom, the middle, the near top. I ain't never seen nothing like it, and I seen a whole lot. The thing that made me mad, though, and made me know Larry Landers wasn't ready to deal with no woman full grown was the way he kept bringing it up, always talking about what he figured was on Moody's mind, like what's on my mind don't count. So I finally did have to use up my reserves and point out to Larry that he was insulting my work and that I would never dream of accusing him of not being a good bartender, of just being another pretty face, like they say.

"You can't tell me he don't have eyes," he kept saying.

"What about my eyes? Don't my eyes count?" I gave it
up after a coupla tries. All I know is, Moody wasn't even
thinking about me. I was impressed with his work and
needed the trade and vice versa.

One time, for instance, I was doing his hands on the solarium and thought I saw a glint of metal up under his
jacket. I rearranged myself in the chair so I could work
my elbow in there to see if he was carrying heat. I
thought I was being cool about it.

"How bout keeping your tits on your side of the table,
Miss Lady."

I would rather he think anything but that. I would
rather he think I was clumsy in my work even. "Wasn't
about tits, Moody. I was just trying to see if you had a
holster on and was too lazy to ask."

"Would have expected you too. You a straight-up, direct
kind of person." He opened his jacket away with the heel
of his hand, being careful with his nails. I liked that.

"It's not about you," he said quietly, jerking his chin
in the direction of the revolver. "Had to transport some
money today and forgot to take it off. Sorry."

I gave myself two demerits. One for the tits, the other
for setting up a situation where he wound up telling me
something about his comings and goings. I'm too old to be
making mistakes like that. So I apologized. Then gave myself two stars. He had a good opinion of me and my work.
I did an extra-fine job on his hands that day.

Then the house happened. I had been reading the
rental ads and For Sale columns for months and looking
at some awful, tacky places. Then one Monday me and
Sylvia lucked up on this cute little white-brick job up on a
hill away from the street. Lots of light and enough room
and not too much yard to kill me off. I paid my money
down and rushed them papers through. Got back to

Larry's place all excited and found him with his mouth all poked out.

Half grumbling, half proposing, he hinted around that we all should live at his place like a family. Only he didn't quite lay it out plain in case of rejection. And I'll tell you something, I wouldn't want to be no man. Must be hard on the heart always having to get out there, setting yourself up to be possibly shot down, approaching the lady, calling, the invitation, the rap. I don't think I could handle it myself unless everybody was just straight up at all times from day one till the end. I didn't answer Larry's nonproposed proposal cause it didn't come clear to me till after dinner. So I just let my silence carry whatever meaning it will. Ain't nuthin too much changed from the first day he came to get me from my Aunt Merriam's place. My agenda is still to make a home for my girl. Marriage just ain't one of the things on my mind no more, not after two. Got no regrets or bad feelings about them husbands neither. Like the poem says, when you're handed a lemon, make lemonade, honey, make lemonade. That's Gwen Brook's motto, that's mine too. You get a lemon, well, just make lemonade.

"Going on the road next week," Moody announces one day through the steam towel. "Like you to travel with me, keep my hands in shape. Keep the women off my neck. Check the dudes at my back. Ain't asking you to carry heat or money or put yourself in no danger. But I could use your help." He pauses and I ease my buns into the chair, staring at the steam curling from the towel.

"Wicked schedule though—Mobile, Birmingham, Sarasota Springs, Jacksonville, then Puerto Rico and back. Can pay you two thousand and expenses. You're good, Miss Lady. You're good and you got good sense. And while I don't believe in nothing but my skill and chance, I gotta say you've brought me luck. You a lucky lady, Miss Lady."

He raises his hands and cracks his knuckles and it's like

the talking towel has eyes as well cause damn if he ain't checking his cuticles.

"I'll call you later, Moody," I manage to say, mind reeling. With two thousand I can get my stuff out of storage, and buy Debbie a real nice bedroom set, pay tuition at the college too and start my three-credit-at-a-time grind.

Course I never dreamed the week would be so unnerving, exhausting, constantly on my feet, serving drinks, woofing sisters, trying to distract dudes, keeping track of fifty-leven umpteen goings on. Did have to carry the heat on three occasions and had to do a helluva lotta driving. Plus was most of the time holed up in the hotel room close to the phone. I had pictured myself lazying on the beach in Florida dreaming up cruises around the world with two matching steamer trunks with the drawers and hangers and stuff. I'd pictured traipsing through the casinos in Puerto Rico ordering chicken salad and coffee liqueur and tipping the croupiers with blue chips. Shit no. Was work. And I sure as hell learned how Moody got his name. Got so we didn't even speak, but I kept those hands in shape and his face smooth and placid. And whether he won, lost, broke even, or got wiped out, I don't even know. He gave me my money and took off for New Orleans. That trip liked to kill me.

       *   *   *

"You never did say nothing interesting about Moody," Pot Limit says insinuatingly, swinging her legs in from the aisle cause ain't nobody there to snatch so she might as well sit comfortable.

"Yeah, she thought she'd put us off the trail with a riproaring tale about Larry's housekeeping."

They slapping five and hunching each other and making a whole lotta noise, spilling Jack Daniels on my turquoise T-straps from Puerto Rico.

"Come on, fess up, Sweet Pea," they crooning. "Did you give him some?"

"Ahhh, yawl bitches are tiresome, you know that?"

"Naaw, naaw," say Sylvia, grabbing my arm. "You can tell us. We wantta know all about the trip, specially the nights." She winks at Pot Limit.

"Tell us about this Moody man and his wonderful hands one more time, cept we want to hear how the hands feel on the flesh, honey." Pot Limit doing a bump and grind in the chair that almost makes me join in the fun, except I'm worried in my mind about Larry Landers.

Just then the piano player comes by and leans over Sylvia, blowing in her ear. And me and Pot Limit mimic the confectionary goings-on. And just as well, cause there's nothin to tell about Moody. It wasn't a movie after all. And in real life the good-looking gambler's got cards on his mind. Just like I got my child on my mind. Onliest thing to say about the trip is I'm five pounds lighter, not a shade darker, but two thousand closer toward my goal.

"Ease up," Sylvia says, interrupting the piano player to fuss over me. Then the drummer comes by and eases in on Pot Limit. And I ease back into the shadows of the booth to think Larry over.

I'm staring at the entrance half expecting Larry to come into Topp's, but it's not his night. Then too, the thing is ended if I'd only know it. Larry the kind of man you're either living with him or you're out. I for one would've liked us to continue, me and Debbie in our place, him and Earl at his. But he got so grumpy the time I said that, I sure wasn't gonna bring it up again. Got grumpy in the shower too, got so he didn't want to wash my back.

But that last night fore I left for Birmingham, we had us one crazy musical time in the shower. I kept trying to lure him into "Maiden Voyage," which I really can't do without back-up, cause I can't sing all them changes. After while he come out from behind his sulk and did a Jon Lucien combination on vocal and bass, alternating the sections, eight bars of singing words, eight bars of singing bass. It was baad. Then he insisted on doing "I Love You More Today Than Yesterday." And we like to break our arches, stomping out the beat against the shower mat.

The bathroom was all steamy and we had the curtains open so we could see the plants and watch the candles burning. I had bought us a big fat cake of sandalwood soap and it was matching them candles scent for scent. Must've been two o'clock in the morning and looked like the hot water would last forever and ever and ever. Larry finally let go of the love songs, which were making me feel kinda funny cause I thought it was understood that I was splitting, just like he'd always made it clear either I was there or nowhere.

Then we hit on a tune I don't even know the name of cept I like to scat and do my thing Larry calls Swahili wailing. He laid down the most intricate weaving, walking, bopping, strutting bottom to my singing I ever heard. It inspired me. Took that melody and went right on out that shower, them candles bout used up, the fatty soap long since abandoned in the dish, our bodies barely visible in the steamed-up mirrors walling his bathroom. Took that melody right on out the room and out of doors and somewhere out this world. Larry changing instruments fast as I'm changing moods, colors. Took an alto solo and gave me a rest, worked an intro up on the piano playing the chords across my back, drove me all up into the high register while he weaved in and out around my head on a flute sounding like them chilly pipes of the Andes. And I was Yma Sumac for one minute there, up there breathing some rare air and losing my mind, I was so high on just sheer music. Music and water, the healthiest things in the world. And that hot water pounding like it was part of the group with a union card and all. And I could tell that if that bass could've fit in the tub, Larry would've dragged that bad boy in there and played the hell out of them soggy strings once and for all.

I dipped way down and reached way back for snatches of Jelly Roll Morton's "Deep Creek Blues" and Larry so painful, so stinging on the bass, could make you cry. Then I'm racing fast through Bessie and all the other Smith singers, Mildred Bailey, Billie and imitators, Betty

Roche, Nat King Cole vintage 46, a little Joe Carroll, King Pleasure, some Babs. Found myself pulling lines out of songs I don't even like, but ransacked songs just for the meaningful lines or two cause I realized we were doing more than just making music together, and it had to be said just how things stood.

Then I was off again and lost Larry somewhere down there doing scales, sound like. And he went back to that first supporting line that had drove me up into the Andes. And he stayed there waiting for me to return and do some more Swahili wailing. But I was elsewhere and liked it out there and ignored the fact that he was aiming for a wind-up of "I Love You More Today Than Yesterday." I sang myself out till all I could ever have left in life was "Brown Baby" to sing to my little girl. Larry stayed on the ground with the same supporting line, and the hot water started getting funny and I knew my time was up. So I came crashing down, jarring the song out of shape, diving back into the melody line and somehow, not even knowing what song each other was doing, we finished up together just as the water turned cold.

Other new fiction from VIRAGO PRESS

SHADES OF GREY

Nicole Ward Jouve

Published to great acclaim in France, these stories – vivid, erotic, poetic – explore the power of female nature and the ambiguity of the female situation.

The women they describe are not at ease. Living lives 'neither black nor white, but only shades of grey', their interior worlds are stormy, passionate. Strange encounters are captured here, where inner and outer worlds conflict, sometimes at the edges of madness: a mother's joy at the birth of her child is crushed by a bullying matron; an Indian woman on a Greyhound bus reminds an inhibited white girl of the power of racial tension; a young woman with her leg in plaster is absurdly overwhelmed with lust. These remarkable stories unfold in language as subtly probing as the insights they reveal, marking the arrival of a significant new talent.

'A collection of astonishing quality' – *Guardian*

Available in hardback and paperback

TEA AND TRANQUILLISERS
The Diary of a Happy Housewife

Diane Harpwood

Jane starts her day the Valium way. We meet our heroine after ten years of marriage, with two children, surviving (only just) the strange mixture of drama and boredom, fulfilment and frustration, affection and baffled rage that is the life of a wife and mother.

Her diary records, wittily, remorselessly, the truth behind the detergent ads: washing baskets like bottomless pits, the malign magic of the sink that is never emptied, the refrigerator that never stays full, the never-ending meals – in short, the relentless daily round of the happy housewife.

The hours are long, the work hard. And the rewards? Dubious, she thinks; brief moments of harmony and bliss that don't last. She loves her husband – when he's not hiding behind the sports pages or down the pub playing darts. She loves her children, but dreams of the deep, peace of solitary confinement. And of course she has her friends, the other happy housewives, who tell her about *their* children, *their* pregnancies – and also about their affairs, the husbands who are leaving them. At least in this woman's world, *women* know how it is.

This is the black humour of everyday life as it is lived by millions, the inside story of every girl's dream. It's hilarious and heartbreaking, bitter and thought-provoking, and life at home will never seem the same again.

Available in hardback and paperback from October 1981

BENEFITS

Zoë Fairbairns

It is summer . . . a heat wave . . . tense, uneasy days in the city.
There are ominous signs of political turbulence in the dying
years of the twentieth century. Welfare benefits for women are
under attack from a government struggling for survival. But
women fight back. They begin to organise, using unorthodox
weapons . . . Feminism has become a threat to the social order.

Lynn Byers, trying to decide whether to have a baby, accepts
neither her friends' dreams of worldwide feminist revolution
nor the government's demand for a return to 'womanly duties'.
But as desperate politicians use increasingly savage methods of
control, she can no longer stand aside and watch.

With irony and compassion, this talented novelist has created
an all-too-possible future, ruled by the cold dictates of a
superbureaucracy. But there is hope too – for women, and,
through them, for humankind.

'Full of wonders . . . a female H. G. Wells. Not just an
achievement but a gift to the rest of us' – FAY WELDON

Available in hardback and paperback. Already published.

Virago

If you would like to know more about Virago books, write to us at
Ely House, 37 Dover Street, London W1X 4HS for a full catalogue.

Please send a stamped addressed envelope

Book Tokens

Give them
the pleasure of choosing
Book Tokens can be bought
and exchanged at most
bookshops